THE CRETE CONNECTION

A novel by
John Manuel

Copyright © 2020 John Manuel

First published in English worldwide by
Lulu Press, www.lulu.com

All rights reserved. Apart from any use permitted under copyright law, this publication may only be reproduced, stored, or transmitted, in any form, or by any means, with prior permission in writing of the publishers or of the author. It may not be otherwise circulated in any form of binding or cover other than that in which it is published and without a similar condition being imposed on the subsequent purchaser.

Typeset in 10pt Garamond

1st edition.

ISBN 978-0-244-26638-7

All characters in this book are entirely fictional. If, by any chance they resemble any real living or deceased person, this is entirely coincidental and no responsibility will be accepted for such coincidence.

Cover design by the author.

Also by John Manuel

The *"Ramblings from Rhodes"* series
of lighthearted Grecian travel memoirs:
Feta Compli!
Moussaka To My Ears
Tzatziki For You To Say
A Plethora Of Posts

The other memoir:
A Jay in the Jacaranda Tree

The Novels:
The View From Kleoboulos
A Brief Moment of Sunshine
Eve of Deconstruction
Sometimes You Just Can't Tell
Two in the Bush
Panayiota

All of the above available from Amazon worldwide in paperback or Kindle format, or directly from the publisher, ***www.lulu.com***

More information about the above titles can be found on John Manuel's blog:
https://honorarygreek.wordpress.com
and on his website:
http://johnphilipmanuel.wix.com/works

"Grief is like the ocean; it comes on waves ebbing and flowing. Sometimes the water is calm, and sometimes it is overwhelming. All we can do is learn to swim."

–Vicki Harrison

A note about the spelling of Greek words

The Greek language is much more complicated than English. In Greek, nouns are conjugated in what are called *'cases.'* In a nutshell, the end of the word changes, depending on whether it's the subject, the object or perhaps, in the case of a person, the one being spoken to.

Basically, if a noun is the subject of a sentence, as in the name Nikos, for example, then it is spoken and spelt with the letter 's' on the end. If, however, it's the object, or the name of the person being spoken to, then it's a different *'case'* (most commonly *'the accusative'*) and in that instance the letter 's' is left off the end.

To illustrate, then: Nikos got off the bus, which was when I caught sight of Niko.

See? You've already cottoned on! So now you'll understand when you read some names, including the names of places, that to the English speaker may look at first glance like 'typos,' when in fact I'm simply following the *'case'* rules.

John M.

The Crete Connection

1. Lyneham, Wiltshire, England. September 1997

The autumn of 1997 was one of the sunniest on record up until that time. Marsha, as was her usual habit, was walking her baby in the stroller along the pavement towards the post office, which was about fifteen minutes along the road from her home in Pound Close. It was a warm weekday morning and she felt happy, which was not something she felt all that often.

Oh, she loved Rebecca, of course, her child of around six months of age. But she was alone and still felt as though life had robbed her, when the baby's father had been killed in a freak road accident while she was still carrying their daughter. They were going to be married. It was all going to be put to rights. Richard was a good sort. Always slightly mad behind the wheel, but she could forgive him that because he'd promised to stand by her. Now, though, he was gone. His family didn't want to know and she didn't have a family to care anyway.

Marsha Travers was Wiltshire born and bred. Always ever-so-slightly the wild one during her school years, her good looks had served her ill more often than not. She was the one all the boys used to talk about, the one they'd so often boast about, often making up stories of their escapades with the best-looking girl in the year. Some girls would have taken exception to the claims she so often heard about herself. Marsha couldn't have cared less.

Once she met Richard, who'd been just that little bit older than her, she began to feel that she'd do OK in life. She wouldn't need to worry too much about providing for herself, because Richard was a guy with a well-paying job, albeit one that took him away from home a lot of the time. It hadn't taken long for her to fall pregnant, and he'd promised that they'd sort it all out, find a house to share, maybe in Wootton Bassett, just a little closer to Swindon, where the lorry depot was based, and he'd be happy for Marsha to stay at home and be a good mother cum-homemaker, while he'd bring home the bacon, as it were.

Yes, just nine months ago, everything had been hunky dory. Then he was involved in a pile-up on the M4, involving several large trucks and numerous cars. His was the only truck whose cab caught fire. He couldn't get out. She was left alone, bereft, pregnant, bitter.

Once she gave birth, though, that wondrous little face, those tiny little finger nails and those amazing little sounds that Rebecca made, soon softened Marsha's anger, though not completely. But she'd get through. She'd manage. Rebecca would have the best upbringing that her disadvantaged mother could manage, largely on state benefits, it had to be admitted, but she'd eventually try and find some way of earning some cash too. Up until now, when Rebecca was 6 months old, Marsha still couldn't countenance the idea of meeting another guy. Plus, he'd have to be something special to take on a girl with a 6 month-old, and there weren't too many of those about in a small country town in Wiltshire.

No, she'd have to make her own way. One thing was for certain, the child was all she had left of Richard. She was the whole world to Marsha. Without Rebecca, there would be no reason to go on.

So, when the child was gone, Marsha was so distraught as to almost lose her sanity.

Every week, on the same day each week, she'd walk the child to the post office, which also served as a paper shop. She'd draw her benefit and buy her favourite magazine, the one that gave her a few moments escape from the drear routine she was forced to follow. She could flick through that magazine and imagine herself living the high life of the gods and goddesses of the showbiz world that featured in full colour on every page. It was the one luxury she'd allow herself.

On this particular Thursday morning, she arrived outside the post office as usual. It was around 9.30am. It was very quiet everywhere. The filling station just a few metres away was devoid of vehicles and the girl inside the reinforced glass booth where people would go to pay for their fuel was busy tapping away on her mobile phone. It was a toss-up over which was the more interesting to her, the phone or her fingernails. So she was shifting her attention from one to the other and back again, but not looking up at all.

Marsha arrived at the post office door, kicked on the brake on the child's buggy and pushed with her back against the strong spring of the shop door. Often she'd manoeuvre the stroller in through the door but, today, as it was bright and warm, she decided that she could leave Rebecca outside just for the couple of minutes it would take to accomplish her mission within. The baby was sleeping soundly, and to wrestle her way through that door, with its strong return spring, would certainly have woken her up. It didn't seem worth it at the time.

She'd already glanced inside, through the local ads for window cleaners, chests of drawers for sale and home-hairdressers offering their services, and seen that the desk was devoid of customers. She'd only be minutes, literally. What danger could there possibly be? This was

Lyneham, after all, a sleepy little country town, whose only claim to fame was the military air base which had brought the place its prosperity for a few decades following the second world war. Nothing of any note happened here, apart perhaps from the occasional garden shed robbery, when some hapless retired gent would arise to find his lawnmower had been half-inched during the night.

Inside, Marsha greeted Sally, the rather portly woman who was always to be found behind the counter, whether it be at the sweets and cigarette kiosk end, or the toughened glass post office section, and pushed her benefit book across the counter. Sally knew the magazine that Marsha would want, and so handed her the cash, minus the cost of the periodical, which Marsha had already grabbed from the display. They exchanged a trite word of greeting and Marsha headed for the door.

Once outside, she kicked off the brake and began pushing the stroller. It only took her a second or two to feel the difference. The weight of her daughter gave pushing the stroller a completely different feel from when it was empty, and empty it now was, save for the blanket and a dummy (pacifier), which lay on the padded seat area where her daughter had been only minutes earlier.

Marsha didn't register right away. Her disbelief kicked in first and she bent down to look more closely. Her brain wasn't permitting her to accept what she was seeing. Her beloved Rebecca, her six-month-old, the very centre of her life, was not there. This could not be. This simply could not be.

Yet, the reality slowly began to seep through. Panic began to set in. Marsha stood erect and stared up and down the road. There was no one about. She ran back into the post office, startling her friend Sally out of a reverie over a cup of coffee and a page in the daily newspaper.

"What?" Asked Sally. "What's up? Did you forget something? I can't see your purse anywhere. You haven't lost it, have you?"

"What? NO, NO! It's Becca, my baby, my BABY! She's gone. She can't be. But, she's... she's..."

With that she ran back outside to the stroller, which had rolled a few feet into a depression where there was a drain cover, Marsha having not reapplied the brake. It had fallen over and the dummy had dropped through the grill.

Frantically, she looked in every direction, several times. There had to be someone, there HAD to be. Yet no. There wasn't a soul within shouting distance. Just along the pavement a few metres was the roundabout on the green. A few cars were negotiating their way around it, but there were no pedestrians, no one she could run after, no one she could grab. Sally emerged from the post office door.

"What do you mean Marsha, she's gone? Who's gone. Surely you don't mean..." She answered her own question on spotting the stroller on its side. Righting it for her friend she added:

"Maybe she's crawled off somewhere. Let's..."

"Where? WHERE? There IS nowhere she could have gone in such a short time. Someone's snatched her." At this point it all became too much for the poor girl, and she sank to the ground on the filling station forecourt, where the girl behind the glass didn't even raise her head to see what was going on. Her jaw continued to chew on her gum as she picked at one of her nails, chipping off the old varnish with great concentration.

Sally pulled out her mobile and quickly dialled the local police. Marsha, meanwhile, sat on the tarmac, and began to let out a wail, the like of which would turn anyone's blood cold. It was the wail of complete loss, of someone whose sole lynchpin to sanity had just been pulled. It was the wail of grief over her lost lover too, since she'd still not fully grieved when Richard had died, being so occupied as she had been with the final days of her pregnancy. Now, though, there was nothing. Marsha Travers was alone in the world and there was no one to either care for, or to be loved by.

Her utter desperation, as she looked first this way, then that, at the realisation that she didn't know even where to start, which direction to run in, flooded over her. Every second that passed, her baby would be further away, and she had not the vestige of a clue as to which direction the kidnapper had gone. All she could see was that empty stroller, and the picture in her mind's eye of her baby on someone else's car seat, or wrapped in someone else's arms, moving away from her at the speed of light.

2. Heraklion, Crete, Summer 2018

Jerome Pillinger thanked the cabin staff and stepped out on to the top of the stairway, which had been rolled up to the aircraft soon after it had come to a halt on the apron of Heraklion airport. He had just turned nineteen years old and was about to embark on his first great adventure in life. Later that year he'd be starting four years at university, but for the next few months he'd be ploughing his way through all the money he'd saved from part-time jobs over the last two years, not to mention quite a few Greek islands too, if he had anything to do with it.

He took a moment to breathe the aviation fuel-tinged air, to feel the hot Greek sun on his skin, and to reflect on the exciting fact that the pilot, not long before they had landed, had told his passengers that the temperature on the ground was around 34 degrees Celsius. That would do very nicely, thank you very much. Just a tad warmer that the 20 degrees it had been when they'd taken off from Gatwick around four hours earlier. He was soon brought back from his momentary reverie when the passengers behind him started to gently nudge him from behind. Time to get down those stairs and on to the waiting bus below, for the short hop to the terminal building.

Jerome had done a small amount of research and decided that northern Crete was as good a place as any from which to set out. There were a couple of ferry lines that came into Heraklion that he could use to get to Santorini, maybe Naxos, Mykonos, those kinds of places. Plus there was one that stopped off along the coast at Sitia on its way to Kassos, Karpathos and eventually Rhodes. Yup, he thought to himself, there was quite a lot to look forward to. He was travelling alone, which meant he could rough it wherever necessary, plus he would be able to change his plans on a whim. He'd already read up on facts like which countries were generally considered to be the safest for the young independent traveller, and Greece had come out very near the top for lack of security risks and general safety for the likes of him. Apart from the obvious one of Knossos, he had a few Greek locations marked down as 'essentials,' including Lindos, on Rhodes, those iconic windmills on Mykonos, as well as the Portara, on Naxos.

His anticipation was palpable as he marched past the baggage carousel. He'd only brought the one rucksack, no hold baggage, which had been the first way in which he'd saved himself the equivalent of his first taverna meal, maybe two, on Greek soil. He hadn't quite been ready for the queue at the passport desk, or the hard, rather suspicious kind of look that the man in the uniform had given him before handing his passport back and welcoming him to Greece in a manner that kind of suggested that he didn't want the likes of Jerome coming into the country anyway. He soon got over that, though, concluding that it was the job of such people to make potentially undesirable aliens think twice before starting anything and thinking that they might get away with it.

The only thing Jerome was hoping to start was a summer of hedonism. The list he was hoping to tick off included girls, beer, more girls, more beer and a good tan.

Before he even thought about hopping to some other islands, though, he was going to bum around some of the sites of the huge island that is Crete. He may have been out for a good time, but he was nevertheless, when all said and done, an intelligent young man. Not for nothing was he going to read history at uni, and thus he'd already earmarked the archeological site at Knossos as one of the first things he had to see.

Jerome was born and raised in Salisbury, on the edge of the majestic plain that bears the town's name, in deepest Wiltshire. He'd grown up cycling the length and breadth of the plain with his best mate from school, Paul Hopkins, and from this had grown his love of the outdoors. His parents were Gavin and Julie Pillinger, a fairly nondescript couple, who nevertheless had a good marriage and had given Jerome and his sister a fairly stable upbringing. Jerome's sister, Amanda, was just a little older than he, by around two years.

Leaving the airport and tracking down the bus depot, he was soon travelling into the town to find the small studio that he'd pre-booked on-line. He had all the required sat-nav gadgetry on his phone, so he'd never be lost.

It didn't take him long to make a few friends when he hit the bars of Heraklion late in the evenings, at that time of year when to wear anything more than some shorts and a t-shirt or vest, was to invite a dose of heat stroke. He soon learned too, that a mosquito repellent plugged into the socket in his room was a must, after he'd been bitten for the tenth time. After only three nights, and having ticked the awesome Knossos off his 'to do' list, he'd teamed up with two other guys and a girl, from Germany, Finland and The Netherlands, and they were setting off one morning for the island's south east coast, to a tiny resort called Makrigialos, around twenty-five kilometres east of the town of Ierapetra. They'd hired a small car between them and were in high spirits, singing Led Zeppelin and Queen songs at the top of their voices as they sped along with the windows all open.

They were going to Makrigialos because Lars, the Finnish guy, said he had been there before and knew a couple of tavernas where they'd probably be able to earn a little cash unofficially, or at the very least sleep in studios upstairs from the dining terrace and get their meals for free if they waited at tables a little or did the menial jobs in the kitchen. These days, since the financial crisis had kicked in and the Greek austerity era had begun, the government was making a concerted effort to stamp out unofficial labour. It was about time that all the due taxes were paid, after generations had successfully managed to get by with paying next to no tax whatsoever. To actually work there without a permit was an offence, and anyone running a business and employing unofficial workers could have their establishment closed down at a moment's notice if the inspectors turned up and discovered the irregularities. Still, Lars was sure that, in this quiet little backwater, they'd do OK.

Thus it was that Jerome Pillinger ended up living above a small taverna right on the sea front. When he'd first walked out on to his modest little balcony, he'd decided that, yes, he'd 'died and gone to heaven.'

Nikos, who ran the taverna, was very careful about how he did things. As a rule the unofficial workers, and he'd taken on two of the party, Jerome and Lars himself, were not allowed to serve customers. They could, however, clear tables and, if anyone started asking questions, they were to say that they were 'family' helping out. This was a ruse facilitated by the fact that his ex-wife had been British, but had returned to the UK when they'd split up after almost twelve years together. Their marriage had produced one daughter, Christina, who was fluent both in Greek and English, and had originally gone to the UK with her mother, since she was only eleven when the split occurred. After barely a year, though, her mother had reluctantly agreed for her to come back and live with her father, after her distress at having left the climate of southern Crete for the mid-west of England had begun to seriously affect her wellbeing. The girl was, after all, primarily Greek, having spent the first five or six years of her school life in a Greek school, with the other Greek children. The 'culture', such as it is in the UK nowadays, was simply soul-destroying to the girl.

It was his first sighting of Christina that kind of scuppered Jerome's plans to move on and start the island hopping phase of his adventure.

3. Lyneham, September 1997

A lot can happen in eight minutes. You can boil an egg, twice. You could listen to Bohemian Rhapsody by Queen (with more than two minutes to spare), Stairway to heaven by Led Zeppelin, or perhaps You Can't Always Get What You Want, by the Rolling Stones. Mind you, Stairway to Heaven would take you beyond the eight minutes by two whole seconds, and the Rolling Stones song would leave you around thirty seconds to twiddle your thumbs.

There are some quick dishes that you could knock up in the kitchen well within eight minutes (especially if you were to employ a microwave), and, if you were to drive at a mere thirty miles per hour (50kph), you'd cover a distance of four miles, or six and a half kilometres.

Eight minutes and seven seconds after Sally, the portly post office lady, had called the police, a patrol car arrived outside the store with its blue lights flashing importantly. In the mean time, Sally had tried to get Marsha back inside so that she could sit her down and put the kettle on, but to no avail. Instead, Marsha had continually paced back and forth, occasionally at a trot, looking first one way, then the other, desperately hoping that some miracle would occur and that she'd see her baby Rebecca sitting on the pavement, or maybe the grass verge, or coming back towards her, perhaps being carried by some well-meaning public-spirited helper.

She'd time and again looked forlornly inside the stroller, gazing intensely in complete disbelief, willing her child to reappear, and for the entire thing to have been a momentary bad dream. She kept saying things to herself like "This can't be," and, "No, no, no, no." She'd also gone into the garage forecourt shop and pleaded with the indifferent and unconcerned attendant to tell her what she'd seen. The young girl's response had been simply, "I never saw nothing. No one came past here," after which she'd assumed an expression that showed that she was willing the poor frantic woman to go away and leave her to her own devices. Had it not been the case that no one had passed, she'd never have known anyway, because in that brief few minutes there had been no vehicles pulling in to fuel up, and thus she'd had no reason to look up from either her phone or the urgent business she'd been occupied with of picking old nail varnish from her fingernails.

Eight minutes passed in which time stood still. Count them if you can. Eight minutes is an eternity when you want something either to happen, or not to have happened at all. Stand on a railway platform, or a bus stop, and see that eight minutes remain until your train or bus is due to arrive, and appreciate just how much of an age they can be. When your mind is occupied solely with the thought that your most treasured possession in the world, your six-month-old child, is travelling away from you, most likely in a vehicle, then you go some way as to understanding the desperation, the agony which Marsha Travers was suffering.

The police got out of the car, and Sally rushed out from the post office door to greet them. Marsha ran towards them from a few feet away and both began talking at once. Both of the police officers were male, and each turned to one or other of the women and tried to get them to become coherent. Marsha was very soon grabbing at the lapels of her officer and gesticulating wildly, frantically, whilst Sally was trying to start with an explanation of events.

The officers eventually persuaded the women that it would be better for all of them to go into the post office, perhaps through to a back room, where they could sit down and take the details of what had occurred in some kind of sensible order. This was extremely difficult for Marsha, because she was conscious of the fact that time was ticking by, and who knows how much further away her poor child was getting while all of this went on? One of the officers was eventually able to tell her:

"Listen, miss; in our experience, there's no substitute for going about these kinds of incidents in a logical and orderly manner. So let's see if we can calm down just a tad, and, in all probability, we'll soon be on the way to getting the situation resolved, all right?"

'All right' it most certainly was not for Marsha, but there wasn't much she could do about that. One of the officers was a sergeant, and he it was who took control of the conversation.

"Now, let's start from the beginning. Tell us exactly what happened, and try not to leave anything out. You never know what tiny details, which might seem insignificant at first, might turn out to be pivotal. I'm not going to pretend we understand how you're feeling miss, mrs..?"

"It's miss, Miss Travers, Marsha. I was going to be married to the baby's father, but he was killed in a motorway pile-up not long before Becca was born." Talking at this moment was anything but easy for Marsha, who inside was going frantic, but she was struggling hard to keep some kind of composure, so as to give the police the best chance of helping her.

"Was that the incident just east of Junction 16, last year? I remember that. Bad one that was. I was one of those who attended. It was your young man in the lorry that..?" He checked himself. He knew, and she knew, only too well what had happened. He continued, "I'm very sorry for your loss Miss Travers, truly I am." After giving her a second or two, he went on:

"So, tell us your every movement from when you approached the post office this morning."

As Marsha, and then Sally, told the officers all they could, another vehicle pulled up urgently outside and two more officers entered the post office. One was a plain clothes and the other a uniformed female, evidently detailed to offer support to the distressed mother.

The sergeant deferred to the plain clothes officer right away. "DCI Southern, this is the mother whose child apparently has been snatched." He extended a hand towards Marsha, and the Detective Chief Inspector turned toward Marsha.

"This fits the description of a critical incident, miss, and as such we shall immediately be putting a team on to it. All we can ask is for you to be patient, and Constable Drysdale here will do her utmost to keep you informed every step of the investigation. We can offer no assurances, but I have to say that, in my experience, such matters as these are more often than not resolved successfully.

"Now, can you think of anyone you know, or have come to know, in recent weeks who may for one reason or another want to harm you or the child?"

Marsha's brow furrowed, she thought for a while. The presence of these officers all around her, and the fact that Sally had now managed to shove a hot cup of sweet tea into her shaking hand, had the effect of pacifying her to some degree. She replied, "No, no one at all. I hardly see anyone. I don't lead much of a social life right now."

After a couple more questions, the DCI left Marsha to be comforted by Constable Helen Drysdale, while he and the other uniformed officers took a brief statement from Sally, then talked alone.

"So, I've already commissioned the team. You'll be the Polsa [*Police Search Advisor*] and Drysdale here is F-L-O [*Family Liaison Officer*] for this one. First thing now is to get as many officers as we can going house to house, starting in the road where she lives. You have that info already I assume?"

"Yes, of course, sir. She lives at Pound Close. Not more than..."

"I know it, Sergeant. OK, well, let's get this show on the road then."

The police team had ascertained that, strange as it seemed, there wasn't any evidence of anyone being around while Marsha had gone into the post office at around 9.30am. The junior of the two officers in the patrol car was sent to talk to the petrol station girl, but he soon discovered that she'd seen nothing, heard nothing, and wanted nothing to do with the whole thing anyway. The post office was a single-storey building set beside a parking area behind and to one side of the garage forecourt, just off the main Wootton Bassett road, not more than a few metres from the roundabout on the Green. To all intents and purposes, at first glance it seemed that baby Rebecca had simply disappeared into thin air.

A week passed and nothing had been turned up by the police investigation. A door to door search had been carried out in the entire village, and special note taken of every household where a baby of similar age to Rebecca was discovered. In each incidence, where such was the case, documents were requested by the police officers who'd knocked the door. They wanted to see birth certificates, maybe evidence of medical attention having been sought, those kinds of things. In every case, though, whatever was requested had been produced by the parents in question. The police team began to feel that it had to have been a vehicle job and that the child was perhaps stolen to order and spirited away quickly, towards the M4 motorway and to who-knew-where after that? The lack of any evidence of a car having been in the vicinity was perplexing, but not conclusive. Some of these professional gangs that specialise in such abductions have very sophisticated methods. They may have had a runner, who took the child and tore off on foot for a couple of hundred metres to a waiting vehicle, perhaps parked in a lay-by with the engine running. There could have been powerful motorcycles involved too. A small baby will fit into a motorcycle 'top-box', at least temporarily. All reports of stolen vehicles in the week leading up to the incident were re-checked to see if those that had been recovered could possibly have been in the vicinity of the crime at the time of the snatch.

Lyneham is in a predominantly rural area, so it would have been very easy to take off in a car and not to have been noticed by anyone. It was just after 9.30am on a weekday that the abduction had taken place, a good half an hour after the end of the local area's rush hour, such as it was.

DCI Southern and his team worked their socks off, with the limited manpower at their disposal, but couldn't make any headway.

Weeks turned into months, and Marsha sat at home, often spending hours sitting on a chair, gazing at her baby's cot and stroking a baby-grow, or fiddling with another of Rebecca's dummies, clutching one of her feeding bottles, fingering her baby blankets, but not wanting to move anything. One or two concerned neighbours brought her food a few times each week, went to the post office to draw her benefit, something which she hadn't been able to do ever since that day when it had happened. She couldn't go anywhere near the Green and the filling station or the post office any more. She became unkempt in her appearance, often going days without even getting undressed to go to bed, or to take a shower. Her home didn't become especially dishevelled, because she hardly moved. The winter set in and the long nights, the frigid cold of an English February came and went. PC Drysdale visited less and less often, feeling more embarrassed each time by the lack of anything new to report.

In fact, the young policewoman herself began to receive counsel because of her own distress over what had become of Marsha Travers.

Then, one morning in May 1998, Marsha got up from the chair, went into the kitchen and emptied out the earthenware biscuit barrel that she'd always used as a stash for cash. She'd hardly spent anything since last autumn, when Rebecca had disappeared and, despite her very limited income, had amassed a half-decent sum. She packed a small case in an almost obsessive manner, and then went out for the first time in weeks. She took a bus into Swindon and went into the first travel agent she came across. There she bought a reasonably-priced package holiday to a small studio on the south coast of Crete. She would be flying in a few weeks time.

She had decided that she had to get away. Had to go somewhere where nothing was familiar, where nothing could remind her of her absent child, her Becca. Maybe whilst out there she would top herself, or simply do a Shirley Valentine. It would have to be one or the other, but she was resolved that she wouldn't be coming back on the return flight that was booked with the package, not if she could help it.

Wednesday June 17th, 1998, Marsha walked out of the plane door at Heraklion Airport and down the steps. She boarded the transfer coach laid on by the tour operator and an hour and forty-five minutes later, put her case on the crisp, white sheets of the bed in a small studio on a hillside overlooking the bay in the tiny seaside resort of Makrigialos. Then she threw herself down beside it and wept.

4. Lyneham

This is either going to work, or it isn't. There's no middle ground. Either I go through with it or I admit defeat. It isn't fair. Life isn't fair. Why should it be me? I never hurt anyone. She was so beautiful, perfect in every detail.

I know her movements. After all I've had long enough to study her. She's definitely a creature of habit, which helps, helps a lot. She's so much like me too. We have so much in common, at least from where I'm standing we do.

It should be easy enough. I have all I need. No one will be any the wiser. Sometimes it's an advantage not having any family left. Here am I saying that, yet when I finally ended up alone, I felt that wasn't fair either. It wasn't. It wasn't fair, but you have to make the best of the hand you've been dealt. She's got more than I have, she has a better chance of getting her life back on track than I do. She's better looking. She won't have any trouble finding someone else, whereas I'm plain Jane. No one takes to me. No one will show me any kindness. No one cares if I live or die.

So it's only right that I do something for myself. No one else will, after all.

Everything's cleaned up and put away now. She's cold, so cold, but not hurting. She's not suffering. She's in a nice place, with a wonderful view. There was nothing else I could have done for her, after all, it wasn't my fault. She'll be left alone, I'm sure.

This week, maybe it's time. I'll do it this week. As long as she does what she usually does, it'll be a cinch. Piece of cake. It should go like clockwork. I have the route all worked out. And anyway, if anything unexpected happens, I'll abort. Leave it until another time. Nothing lost, just a temporary setback.

It almost makes me feel like a shock of electricity is running through my body, it's such a thrill. The danger of it makes it exciting, daring, but, mainly, it's surely for my good and hers. She doesn't deserve her, whereas I do. I never did anything, I didn't. It wasn't me.

I wasn't to blame.

I wasn't.

5. Jerome. Makrigialos, 2018

This is June, and I've got until late September before I have to go home. And what a place to start my adventure. This little studio couldn't be better really. Along the west end of the bay there are bars and just a little nightlife. Not too much, but that's OK, it looks like it'll suit me fine. I can walk everywhere here, too, another bonus. And look at that view. Right below my modest little balcony, which has a white plastic table and two matching chairs, is the equally-modest terrace of the taverna that Nikos owns and runs. He's a really nice bloke and, I have to hand it to Lars, he came up trumps. If it hadn't been for Lars, I'd in all probability never have ever come to Makrigialos. After all, it's all I can do to pronounce it, leave alone find it from as far away as Heraklion.

And running right up to the taverna terrace, immediately below me, is the beach, which is mainly sand, with a little shingle here and there. If I were to throw a stone from this very chair, it would easily drop into that amazingly blue sea. There are a few sunbeds and umbrellas here and there, but this is about as far away from a Spanish Costa as you could hope to be without maybe going long-haul and leaving Europe entirely. What's really cool too, is that the sea doesn't go anywhere. You know like, back in England, when we used to go to the seaside on summer days, dad would drive us down to Swanage, maybe Weymouth, occasionally Bournemouth, and there would be a tide. One minute the sea would be so close that the beach was a narrow strip, and the next it was half a mile away. We were always packing up all our stuff and moving it down the beach, or back up again. On more than one occasion I can remember when we left it too late, probably playing French cricket or something, and the sea beat us to it and all our stuff got soaked.

Here, the sea's in the same place all the time, plus it's a lot warmer, and a lot bluer. I can see myself taking a dip every morning when I get up, it's so close. I'll just run down to the water in my shorts, and I'll only need a towel, nothing else. Then get back up here for a spot of breakfast.

These Greeks are so lucky. They wake up every day to the same weather. The sun rises to my left, does its thing all day, and sets over there on the right, just behind the small cluster of buildings at that end of the bay that make up the village. The only white I can see in the sky is the occasional vapour trail from some airliner that's so far up you can't hear anything, you just see a glint of something shiny as it trawls across the sky.

Now, wait a minute. Who is THAT?

Now, there's a bonus if ever I saw one. Mr. Nikos has agreed that I can stay here, and eat here, if I wash up every night and help re-set the tables for the next day before knocking off and hitting one of the bars along the bay around midnight. He doesn't seem to have a wife around anywhere, but surely this vision I see below me, placing menus and small glass jars with a single flower in each on the tables, is his daughter. She's much too young to be his significant other. Unless he's a cradle-snatcher. No, can't be. She's either his daughter or a girl from the village. She isn't Romanian, or Ukrainian or anything, like the few I chatted up in Heraklion. Hair's too dark.

No, she's Greek, surely.

Yes! See? I was right. She's just looked up and, responding to some clattering noises coming from the kitchen out back, she called out "Papa!"

And now he's answering and they're having a conversation in Greek. I can see myself hanging around here a while, truly I can.

Oh, whoops, she's noticed me. What made her look up? Must have been her dad telling her about me.

"Hi! Good morning! I'm Christina, welcome to our humble establishment, Jerome! You want some bacon and eggs, maybe some fruit juice, for breakfast?"

She speaks perfect English. Not just English, but no-accent English. How could that be? Better answer her anyway.

"You bet! I'll be down now."

You know how sometimes you see a girl and she's so good-looking you find it hard to act normal? I think I've just arrived in such a situation. Not complaining, mind you.

So I amble downstairs and Christina greets me at the kitchen serve-over with a double-cheek kiss and a hug (my face must be a deep shade of beetroot, by now, surely).

"Sit over there if you like. Dad and I will join you. Time you received your briefing, eh?" She says this with such a beguiling smile that I'm now convinced that my face must be vermillion. Maybe I mean puce. No, vermillion probably. Either way, I hope I'm not letting on too much.

I obey, and before long she and her father are sitting with me. She's eating from a yogurt carton with honey poured into it and he's drinking coffee from one of those tiny cups. It looks more like syrup to me. Must have enough caffeine in that to keep a long-distance lorry driver awake for a week. My eggs and bacon are delicious. How come they never tasted like this at home?

We talk for half an hour. Nikos says I can go out on to the beach and collect the cash for people using the sun beds too. That's give me something to do in the middle of the day. If anyone wants a drink or something to eat, they get their sunbed money back. Sounds like a good deal to me. I'd be up for that. In the evenings I'll clear tables and wash dishes and glasses in the kitchen, maybe learn how to knock up a Greek salad. He says he can't pay me, but I won't have to worry about my meals, or my accommodation. That'll make my funds go on forever if all I have to worry about is drinks in the bar after midnight each day. I feel like my idea of spending a whole summer in Greece was one of the best I ever had.

What time is it? It's still only around 10.00am and Nikos stands up, drains his coffee and shakes my hand vigorously. He's off in his four-by-four to Ierapetra for some supplies. Christina will show me anything I need to see, where to find the stock of paper table cloths, serviettes, that kind of thing. Before I know it I'm alone with this very cute girl and burning to find out how come she speaks such amazing English. When they're together her dad and her gabble on in Greek and I don't get a single word of what they're saying. She turns to me and, when she talks to me, sounds like she could be from Salisbury.

She decides that we'll start then, by me familiarising myself with the sun loungers on the beach. They have around fifteen umbrellas, each with two beds, that's it. Just to the side of the building there are a few spare beds and a chest containing cushions for them, plus a cloth and a dustpan/brush set for cleaning off the beds when people leave. All seems pretty straightforward to me. They also have a ticket book for giving people a simple receipt when they pay for their beds. It's a really laid-back spot. There are no other sun loungers for at least a hundred metres in both directions along the beach. People can either turn up by strolling along the beach, or they can walk through from the modest beach road behind the building and emerge via the taverna/bar terrace.

"If they want to order a drink, or some food, you ask them for that receipt back and then what they paid for the beds is deducted from their drinks or food bill. Reckon you can handle that?"

"With my eyes closed." I reply. Although why I should want to close my eyes with Christina around I don't know. I'm burning with curiosity. So I venture a question.

"OK, then, so tell me how come you speak such amazing English. I mean, you're obviously Nikos' daughter, but you don't speak English like you learned it in school. Have you spent time in the UK or something?"

"I have, but I could speak English well before that." She pauses, obviously to build my anticipation. "My mother is English."

Mystery solved. But I haven't seen anyone around yet who may perhaps be Christina's mother. I'm just about to ask, when two girls of similar age to her come down the beach from the terrace. They're probably her local best friends or something. Her attention is soon diverted from me, she makes her excuses, asks me if I can hang around and just keep an eye in case any early sun worshippers turn up, and is soon sitting on a stool at the kitchen serve-over and talking in hushed tones with her friends. All three of them are also thumbing their mobile phones at the same time.

I decide to run upstairs for my iPod and swimming gear, and then I'll settle on that rather inviting looking sun lounger that's set under it's own tiny pergola a little way from the tourist umbrellas, the one that's provided for the likes of me, or whoever's on duty looking after the sun loungers.

I'm in Greece. I'm on a quiet beach in southern Crete, and I'm keeping watch over a few umbrellas. The weather's perfect, my landlord's got a gorgeous daughter.

Can I think of anything else I'd rather be doing? Anywhere else I'd rather be?

Nope. Think it's time I WhatsApp-ed some folks back home. Tell them how tough life is out here right now. I have a good feeling about this, I really do.

6. Marsha, Makrigialos, 1998

After a couple of hours, Marsha got up off the bed, pulled herself together and tried to resolve to start the rest of her life from here. That is, if her present miserable existence could still be called a life, she thought. She walked through the blue-painted wooden shutters of her room and out on to her tiny balcony and was struck by the beauty of the view. The apartment block was set on a hillside, just a couple of hundred metres up a concrete lane from the beach, at the far end of the gently curving bay from the main village of Makrigialos. Standing on her balcony, she took in the wonderful landscape. The balcony wasn't all that far above the lane that continued up the gentle slope beside the building. She counted, the whole place looked like it only had around ten small apartments, or studios, that was it. Not too small, but not so big as to be manic with screaming kids. There was, however, a modest swimming pool on its own private terrace, with around six umbrellas set around the perimeter, each set into the concrete, and each with a couple of sunbeds beneath it.

'There, you see?' She thought, 'I had to think about screaming kids, didn't I. I don't have any. Least, not any more.'

Even though it had been nine months since Rebecca was taken, all too often something would bring it all back. Marsha took herself in hand and tried to re-focus. She came out here to try and see if she could start afresh.

The police had tried, but they'd drawn blank after blank. It was as if her precious baby daughter had simply vanished, dematerialised. No clues, no witnesses. No one in the entire village had seen anything. The house-to-house enquiries had come across a few babies of Rebecca's age, one or two even in Marsha's road, but they were all well documented, with a birth certificate to prove who they were, who they belonged to. There had been no one who had aroused suspicion, no one who had seemed like they were hiding anything. The last communication she remembered having from Drysdale was that DCI Southern was now convinced that Becca had been stolen to order. It was like, perhaps there was a wealthy couple in eastern Europe, for example, who couldn't have children. For whatever reason, they didn't want to go through normal adoption channels, or maybe there just weren't any children available that appealed to them. So some slime ball from the underworld had brought in a professional gang who operated all over the world, and they'd sent out their spies to see what was about. Maybe they even had 'sleepers' out there waiting to be called upon, and with the understanding that, if they came up with anything, they'd be paid handsomely.

Someone had studied Marsha, decided that she was an easy target and then, boom. They struck. Becca could have been a hundred miles away by the end of the first day. Probably spirited across the channel on a fast speedboat under cover of darkness. A few bank notes change hands, and pretty soon a rich Russian couple have their new baby.

Of course, all of this was speculation, but it broke Marsha's heart when she thought about her own baby girl growing up speaking some other language, never even knowing what her true origins were. Despite her having resolved to try and do something to get herself out of the slough of despondency, Marsha struggled continually with her heartbreak, her devastation at losing her baby, the gnawing, gut-wrenching ache that simply wouldn't go away.

'Anyway,' she thought, 'I'm here, and I'd best see what I can do to occupy myself.'

As the evening drew on, with few hours of daylight still remaining, since it was June, Marsha showered, put on some glad rags and went for a walk along the sea front towards the village and the makeshift little harbour about a kilometre along the beach from the apartment.

As she passed along the small, quiet road that runs from her end of the bay to the village, she glanced into various properties along the way. There were a few bars, a car hire office or two, the occasional souvenir shop and some tavernas, often with a fifty metre gap or more between them, which afforded a glimpse of the beach and the gently lapping sea. She was about half-way along the bay when she stopped to stare at the menu outside one of these. It had an inviting-looking arched door (faux trad.) and offered a tantalising glimpse right through the building to the beach at the other end, where she could see some tables, each with a sole tea light or some such sitting in the middle, glowing in the gathering dusk. Above the tables she could see the boughs of a tamarisk tree, gently swaying this way and that, through which the glistening sea twinkled and above it the sky peeped, a little way beyond the terrace.

She found herself staring through to the terrace rather than at the menu, when a male voice spoke to her.

"We have specials too this evening. Would you like to see them? You can come and look in the kitchen if you like."

Looking slightly down, she could see no one. Then her eyes adjusted to the shade of the portico of the building, where a man was sitting on a chair, extending an arm into the building in invitation. He looked slightly older than her 27 years, maybe in his early thirties. He had classic Greek thick, dark hair, slightly dishevelled, but in an attractive kind of way, and a face Marsha thought was characterful, even slightly Timothy Dalton-esque. He wore a brilliantly white shirt with a button-down collar, and black trousers.

"Umm, I was..."

"No pressure." he continued. "But, if I say so myself, our food is the best in the village." Now he was smiling in a way that had Marsha wondering whether he was being comedic, or entirely sincere.

"Ah, but they'll all tell me that, won't they." She replied.

"They will. So, how are you going to find out who's telling the truth?" He gave her a second or two, but when no answer was forthcoming, got up and came to stand beside her. Pointing at a spot on the English section of menu, he went on, "Our lamb *kleftiko* is made to our own unique recipe. And, if you like *meze*, we do probably the largest selection in the area. Even our *fasolakia* is done in our own chef's way, so it has to be tasted to be believed. You'll sample our *dakos* for starters too, it's exquisite. May I ask what you like to eat?"

"I don't know anything about Greek food. It's my first time in the country, so I've no idea what you've been telling me about, sorry."

"Ah, well, Greek food is special, of course. But Cretan food is even more so. You know we Cretans are Cretan first, and Greek second. Allow me to offer you a few starters on the house, along with, of course, some of my very own retsina, made from grapes from my own vines. May I ask, are you dining alone, or do you have others in your party who have yet to arrive?"

Marsha was unconsciously already beginning to step towards the door, with her host's hand gently persuading her from the small of her back. "No, I'm all alone I'm afraid. And rather a killjoy too, you'll probably find."

"Not at all. But allow me, then, to hopefully lighten your mood this evening for just a few hours. Do we have a deal?"

They did. Marsha's answer was to walk a little faster as this charming Greek restaurateur led her to a table in the corner of the taverna's beachside terrace, with a stunning view back along the beach towards her accommodation. The moon was just rising over the dark horizon, throwing a million jewels across the calm surface of the Libyan Sea. The very inexperienced Greco-virgin was hooked. She found herself castigating herself from within for being such a pushover but, what the hell, nothing really mattered. She had no other plans and had never been here before. Marsha didn't even have any idea of the reputation of Greek men for beguiling women from overseas. It probably wouldn't have mattered if she did.

Once he'd pulled out her chair for her to sit down, he handed her a menu, and told her he'd be back in a trice. True to his word, he was back in seconds with a carafe of draught retsina and a small glass. While the condensation formed on the glass sides of the carafe, he poured her a glassful and placed the carafe down in the corner of her table.

"Now, I shall regale you with some of the best that our island has to offer. As I said, the starters are on the house, as is the wine. If you tell me at the end of the evening that you didn't like the food, then you won't pay me anything. How's that, Miss...?"

His sentence ended in such a way as to leave her in no doubt that he wanted to know her name.

"It's Marsha, Marsha Travers."

"And I am Nikos, and this is my restaurant. Welcome to Crete, *kyria* Marsha. You are about to fall in love!" And with that, he marched off toward the kitchen.

Quite what he meant by that last bit, she wasn't too sure. Did he mean that he expected her to fall head over heels for him and become a pushover in more ways than one? Or was he perhaps referring to her falling in love with his island and his country? She decided to give him the benefit of the doubt, and plumped for the latter.

Not much time elapsed before he'd placed a wooden basket of freshly-baked brown bread rolls on the table, then some *fasolakia, dakos, gigantes* and *saganaki*. Apart from the bread, Marsha gazed at these platters with very little idea as to what was in them, although with some careful study she soon identified the primary ingredients. For months on end she hadn't been hungry, had eaten like a sparrow. Somehow this evening, she was ravenous, and set about the food before her with enthusiasm and relish. Once she'd demolished the starters, she decided on her first night to have a fish done over the charcoal, which was cooked to perfection, and she watched as Nikos expertly extracted most of the bones from the flesh, before squirting a generous amount of lemon juice over the meat and wishing her for probably the fifth time, *kali orexi!* Accompanying the fish was some broccoli, a kind of sauce that Marsha found to be delicious and could only guess that it contained probably celery, onion, and one or two other ingredients, and some kind of rice concoction that had some different-coloured specs in it and tasted like no rice she'd ever eaten in her entire 27 years.

At some time around ten thirty, with the restaurant about half-full and the sky now completely dark, save for a cream-coloured moon that was now almost directly overhead and playing peekaboo through the boughs of the tamarisk tree, Marsha realised that she was actually feeling quite good. The gentle buzz of the other guests talking, punctuated by the occasional outburst of companionable laughter, coupled with the fact that she felt wonderfully warm in just a spaghetti-strap top, and warm on the inside from having consumed half a litre of this strange, but easy-to-get-used-to wine that they called retsina, all combined to bring on a kind of pleasant torpor that she realised was acting like an anaesthetic for her inner pain.

Having cleared away most of the debris from her meal, Nikos placed a small glass of golden liquid in front of her.

"Here, Kyria Marsha, you had better round off the evening with a Metaxa."

"A what?" Marsha asked, but not in any way that could be construed as offensive, but rather enquiring, yet again.

"It's Metaxa, the best brandy in the world, because, of course, it's Greek! And this, my friend, is the seven star version. Try it."

She didn't need much persuading. 'In for a penny,' she thought, and raised the glass to her lips. The first drop to make contact with her tongue made her think that it had caught fire, but she was rather surprised to find that the aftertaste was very much to her liking. It didn't take her long to get used to it, and Nikos wasn't slow in pouring her a second one.

Although Marsha was by now quite intoxicated, she wasn't drunk. The fact that she'd eaten more in one session that she had in months may have helped to some degree. Before long there were a couple of helpers clearing tables, and the sound of cutlery and crockery being sorted out for cleaning was to be heard drifting out from the kitchen. Marsha was surprised to find that she was enjoying the sound, because it meant that she didn't have to be concerned with any of it. When was the last time she'd gone out to eat? She couldn't even remember, and if she could have, it would have been some kind of budget pub meal anyway, not a restaurant where she was served at table for the duration.

As the evening reached that phase where everything became lethargic, the music, such as it was, was turned down a notch or two, and her host came again to stand beside her and asked,

"May I join you for a while? No agenda, please. Don't worry, but I have to say that I am intrigued by what it is that makes you seem so sad. If you don't want to talk about it, no problem. But I am happy to listen, if it would help. It bothers me that a young, and if I may say, beautiful, woman like yourself should be so down."

As he pulled the chair from under the table across from her, Marsha gave a wave of her hand as if to say, 'by all means.' As he made himself comfortable, poured himself an ouzo and placed the bottle on the table, then produced a tobacco pouch and some papers, she found herself studying him as he went about the ritual of rolling himself a cigarette.

He was evidently in no hurry. Was this how Greeks did things then? She'd heard all about the Spanish and their 'mañana' mentality, so why should it be any different here in Greece? It's the Mediterranean, after all. Must be the same, or very similar, climate, and hence way of life, right? Was he yet planning to come on to her? And if he did, would she be receptive? She found herself thinking, 'Do I care, either way?'

After some minutes, at the end of which he'd folded his tobacco pouch and placed it on the table in front of him, produced a small plastic lighter and lit his cigarette, then taken a sip of ouzo, he turned to her and smiled.

"So, you want to talk? You want to tell me what a young woman like you is doing here all alone? You don't look like someone who would have a problem finding a male companion. Surely things can't be that bad, can they?"

She didn't answer right away, but rather, by her look, indicated that she was now intrigued by yet another drink that she wasn't familiar with. The bottle's label clearly read 'Ouzo,' and even from where she was sitting she could smell aniseed. Nikos picked up on this and called one of his helpers to bring a small glass. Once it was placed on the table, he poured a couple of fingers into it from the bottle and, with a gesture of his hand, bade her give it a try.

She picked the glass up and took a sip. Once again, it seemed to Marsha that yet another new experience of Greek produce was a hit. Only maybe it was a little strong-tasting.

"Do you always drink this neat?" She asked, with a slight wince on her face.

Laughing, Nikos replied, "NO, of course not. You can have it with a little ice, water, or even Sprite, or Seven Up."

"OK, a little water, then, thank you."

There was already a half-empty bottle of mineral water on the table, so Nikos poured an inch into her ouzo, and repeated, "So, like I said, you want to tell me why you're alone and so sad? If you don't answer this time, I'll not ask you again. And I hope you'll forgive me for being too nosey."

Marsha suddenly found it was all flooding back. The last hour or two had been too good to be true. This man's questions made her think back, and her half-smile became a grimace, then her eyes moistened, and finally, she cried. She wanted to begin an explanation, but couldn't. The tears came thick and fast, and she felt an overwhelming sense of guilt at having stopped grieving over Rebecca for most of the evening. How could she have been so callous? Didn't her baby deserve better? Didn't she owe it to Becca to remain moribund and morose? What right did she have to lighten her mood when her baby was gone? Wasn't she to blame too? How many times over the months had she castigated herself for thinking that, even in a small country town like hers, such things couldn't happen. Had she bothered to negotiate that stroller through the post office door, which would only have taken her a minute or two, then she'd still have her baby with her now. She'd be changing nappies, soothing her as her first teeth began pushing through, sneezing from inhaling talcum powder and nestling her nose into Becca's tummy after a bath.

But now, here she was, trying in vain to shake off her depression. Thinking that she might have been able to go on with her life. What a fool she was. As she convulsed, her host began to worry that he'd pushed her too far and regretted his inquisitiveness. Yet he couldn't just sit there and let her cry like this. Oh, he didn't care about the other guests, who were dwindling fast by now anyway, but he found himself deeply concerned over just what it was that was making this woman this way. Nikos rose and came around the table. Bending over Marsha from above, he put a hand on her shoulder, grabbed a couple of paper napkins from the holder on the table with the other and offered them to her.

As she took them from him and blew her nose and wiped her eyes, he said:

"Look, I'm so very sorry, I don't know who I think I am, pushing you to talk about your problems. Please, don't feel you have to talk. Only I can't let you go off back to your room tonight until I know you're going to be OK. Could I perhaps..." She interrupted:

"No, NO. It's not your fault. I will tell you. I want to tell you. Perhaps it would be better for me to tell someone, and I've no one back home. My relatives, such as they are, are distant and we don't keep in touch. I've had no one to confide in for too long anyway. I had a baby. I had a baby and someone took her."

7. Gavin, January 1998

Gavin Pillinger was a Somerset lad. Born in February 1969, he was the son of a couple of budding West Country hippies, and couldn't have grown up more different from his parents in every way. Gavin was always good at maths and economics at school. He didn't go to university, but got a job on leaving the sixth form with a major branch of the HSBC bank and worked his way up. His parents continued to go to Glastonbury, where they'd taken him in a canvas sling when the festival was first held in the summer of 1970, and never failed to keep their hair long. Even when there was more of it down his back in a pony tail than there was on the crown of his head, Gavin's dad never gave in.

In January 1998 Gavin was a senior in the investment and financial advice section of the bank at its largest Swindon branch, and he was quite happy with how his life was going. He was almost twenty nine and punching well above his weight in the hierarchy at the bank. The only thing he needed was someone to share his life with. It was just over forty miles from Swindon to Bristol, but he'd occasionally make the trip there of an evening when he wanted to see some live music at the Colston Hall. After all, it was motorway all the way and he'd regularly get there in around fifty minutes, door to door.

It was on just such an evening that he met Julie. She'd gone to the same gig, but, like Gavin, had stayed in the bar when the main act came on stage, because she'd gone primarily to see the support band. She'd hitched a lift there with a couple of girl friends, whereas Gavin had driven from Swindon with his friend Dave from the bank. There weren't that many people left in the bar once the main act had got into full swing, so, amid the background rumble coming from the main auditorium, Gavin pounced.

Julie was at the bar paying for a couple of glasses of white wine, and Gavin made sure to stand beside her. He liked what he saw and so nudged her shoulder, trying to make it seem like an accident, and then started apologising profusely and offering to mop up the wine that had been spilt with his handkerchief. Of course, he couldn't believe his luck when the conversation continued and, in the end, having found out that she lived in Lyneham, he offered to take her home with he and Dave, since it wasn't far out of their way. Julie had soon sorted it out with her friends, since one of their party of four was also still in the bar with her, and they were fine with her not going back with them.

Dave, in the end, ducked out too. He had friends in Bristol and, since it was a Friday, texted one of them and arranged to stay over and go into town the next day. Thus it was that, after a fairly average Indian meal out somewhere off Park Street, Gavin was driving back along the M4 with his new girlfriend in the passenger seat. He couldn't believe his luck, and she kept telling herself that she hoped he wasn't a serial rapist or murderer, as he seemed such a nice chap.

"So, tell me about yourself. I want to hear your entire history." said Gavin, as he drove them up the M32 towards the M4 junction a few miles to the north.

"Oh, I don't know if you want to hear it all. It's not all that interesting." It was at this point that Julie began to worry. Since she'd had Amanda, she'd found it slightly more tricky hanging on to a new boyfriend. By and large they didn't want to know once they discovered that she came with baggage. Amanda had been born in February 1997, after a rather rash night out with a printer from Swindon. He didn't want to know once she told him she was pregnant, but she'd decided to keep the child and had showered it with all the love she could give. Her mum was a widow and didn't act in any way judgmentally about her daughter's predicament. Instead, she'd stepped in to look after the child in the beginning, while Julie was able to keep her job as a dental receptionist. Unfortunately, only a couple of months after the child's birth, Julie's mother had died suddenly and unexpectedly from a massive stroke.

Thus Julie lost the job and fell upon the state to look after her needs, such as they were. She was intelligent, not at all lacking in the intellect department, but, like so many girls of her generation, allowed herself to be lax for just one time too often, and now she was the single mother of an eleven-month-old. The pressure on the young of today to get physical in their relationships right off the bat is immense.

How to tell Gavin, that was her dilemma. She had a local girl who lived around the corner babysitting this particular night, a good girl in her mid-teens who doted on Amanda and was very happy to stay the whole night if required. Her parents knew Julie and so approved of the arrangement, since Julie would pay the girl well, even though her resources were limited. The fact was, she hardly went out socially anyway, so when she did, she thought it was worth it.

'Try me." Said Gavin.

So she did. She took a deep breath and, whilst the gantry lights over the carriageway sped by, she explained about her brief, very brief fling with Phil the printer, and the upshot of that, her young baby of eleven months, Amanda. When she got to the point where she explained that she had a young teenage babysitting neighbour waiting at home that very night, she shut up and waited for Gavin's inevitable, 'Ah, sorry, but...'

Instead, he took a full minute or so to respond, and when he did so, it was in a way that both shocked and excited Julie. He said, "Well, I'd better meet this young lady then, hadn't I?"

And saying this, he turned momentarily to look at his pretty young passenger, and gave her a genuine, warm smile that definitely included not only his lips, but his eyes also. Then and there Julie knew that he wasn't referring to the babysitter.

The weeks went by and it became evident to Julie that Gavin was comfortable with the fact that his new girlfriend already had a young baby. In fact, he was soon spending time at her modest little housing-association home cooing over Amanda and playing with her for hours, while Julie either got ready to go out with him, or fixed a meal, or did some household chores.

Gavin Pillinger even surprised himself at how he took to the child. He had a well-paying job and didn't really want to go through a succession of relationships with insincere women. It seemed to him that Julie had gone out of her way to try and facilitate his copping out, so as not to make him feel that she was in any way possessive, or even engaged in some kind of entrapment procedure to secure her financial stability. He'd spent most of his twenties climbing the hierarchical ladder in the bank, leaving little time for any half-decent social life. So it struck him as happy happenstance that he'd come across Julie in the way that he had. The more they got to know each other, the more they found that they had in common.

In the spring Gavin proposed and in September of that same year, 1998, they were married in a civil ceremony in Swindon, with Gavin's friend Dave and a few of his relatives in attendance. On Julie's side there was the family of her teenage babysitter, that was about it. Julie couldn't believe how things had turned out. She found herself living in Gavin's very acceptable detached house in Pewsey, not far south of Marlborough. Julie could already drive and, by the time their son Jerome was born, which was in June of 1999, Gavin had bought Julie a neat little sports hatch to run around in to replace the decrepit old mini-hatch that she'd had before, and they'd moved to the outskirts of Salisbury, since Gavin had transferred to the bank's main Salisbury branch.

Gavin couldn't have been happier. It suited him to have a model nuclear family. It certainly did his image no harm with one or two of the more senior members of staff at the bank, the old school types, too. He legally adopted Amanda and truly became a dad to her. By the time Jerome had come along, Amanda was two years and five months old and into everything.

Even Gavin's ageing hippy parents would turn up in their vintage VW camper van at his house now and then to dote on their new daughter-in-law and their two young grandchildren.

For Gavin Pillinger, life took on a rosy glow. He had everything he could have wished for and more. His relationship with Julie grew ever closer and they seldom argued. His friends all took to her, beguiled by her charms, and never once took Amanda to be anything other than Gavin's daughter.

8. Lyneham

This doesn't make sense. This can't be right. Why isn't she breathing? Why isn't she crying? I shake her to wake her up. She doesn't respond. I haven't done anything. I love her, she's the centre of my world.

Yet she lies there, still. I tap the mobile that hangs above her cot. It jingles and jangles, but she doesn't respond to that either. It's all wrong. This isn't meant to happen to me. No.

I rush out of the door, leaving her there, still, soundless, and I go the the local library. I find an appropriate book and look up cot death, or as the Americans call it, 'crib death.' Seems its proper name is '*Sudden Infant Death Syndrome*,' and there's no way of knowing when and where it's going to strike.

So why should it strike me? My baby? No, this is all wrong. All wrong.

I'll need to do something about this. I can't be left alone. Mummy left me. Daddy years before her. I had no siblings. She was my world, my sole reason to exist.

She hasn't gone. She can't have. She must be somewhere else. I just need to find her, that's all.

I never did anything, I didn't. It wasn't me.

I wasn't to blame.

I wasn't.

9. Jerome. Makrigialos, 2018

I can't stop thinking about Christina. She seems not to notice the effect she has on me. Not sure her dad Nikos hasn't noticed though, but he doesn't seem to mind too much if he has. He hasn't taken me aside and warned me, or asked why I look at her, gaze more like, in the way I do. Still, I'm a bit dubious about whether it would be OK to ask her out. I mean, yeah, she's a bit young, but she acts very grown-up. I think she's seventeen, which is plenty old enough in the UK.

I wonder if she's noticed anything about me. I get the feeling she may be interested, but she doesn't give too much away. She does tend to be very easy in my company, and likes to joke around when we're setting the tables in the mornings. She seems to want to eat breakfast at the same time as me too, so maybe that's a sign. The thing is, in a small place like this, I'm not sure quite what we'd do if we had a date anyway. There's no cinema, no cool hangouts, just a couple of good and slightly more lively bars along the west end of the bay. They stay open almost 'til dawn, and, now and then, people dance. I can hardly take her out for a meal when we both work in her dad's restaurant, now can I? And what would he say if I did take her to one of the bars and we didn't get back until four o'clock in the morning? Wonder if he's got a shotgun.

I haven't seen Lars for a couple of weeks, so he must have jacked this job in and gone off somewhere. Same applies to the others who came here with me. I can't complain if they've taken off without telling me. I was hardly one of the gang in the first place. There were no strings when we came down here. Everyone is free to do his or her own thing. If I ever bump into Lars again, I can hardly get mad when, if it hadn't been for him, I'd never have ended up with this easy job, if you can call it that, and this little Aphrodite to work along with. He didn't seem too keen on doing any graft in the first place, so maybe Nikos told him to sling his hook anyway.

Oh boy, hope I'm not blushing. Here she comes, barefoot and wearing shorts and a bikini top. Gulp.

"Hi Jerome, how's it going?" I'm stretched out on the sun bed under the beach shade, manning the umbrellas. It's around one in the afternoon. "You want a beer?" She asks me.

Now, come on! Is this the best job in the world or isn't it? OK, so I don't get paid, but already Nikos has thrown me a fifty note once or twice and told me it's a little bonus. I get to sleep with my shutters open and with the sea lapping just a few metres away, I get to eat anything I want and my boss' daughter comes and offers me a beer while I'm taking the money for the umbrellas and sun beds. This autumn I'm meant to be off to uni to read history. At this rate I might just jack it all in and stay here.

"Oh, all right. I suppose I'd better have one, since you ask." I reply.

She smiles at me and walks back up the beach to the drinks fridge on the taverna terrace. A minute later she's sneaked up from behind, and pressed a cold bottle of Amstel against my back. Do I jump, or what? I won't even mention what I say in response, but I spin around and grab her wrist, which spills a little of the beer, since she's already opened the bottle. I've never held her arm before. In fact, apart from the kiss on both cheeks and a polite and distant hug when I first met her, I haven't so much as touched her in the three weeks since I started here.

She looks at her hand, which is now covered in spilt beer. Without a word I draw it up to my lips and lick the beer from the back of her hand, keeping eye contact, to see how she reacts. She doesn't try to retract it. Good sign.

"Sorry Chrissy, won't do it again. Promise. That's if you won't either, of course." I say. Testing the waters. Isn't that what they call it?

"All bets are off, I'm afraid." She replies. What does she mean by that? Am I in or am I out? Clever kid, but she's smiling. Teasing, I'd say. I want this conversation to continue, so I say:

"You haven't told me yet about your mother, where she is, what happened between Nikos and her. Is it a secret, or can I know?"

"You can know, it's no big deal." She sits on the sun bed, her thigh millimetres from mine. She bends down and fingers the sand between her toes, and begins, staring out to sea as she does so.

"Mum came out here, ooh, must have been around 1998. She was a tortured soul. She came on her own and ended up having her first meal right here, in our place. Dad was still single. One thing led to another and, before you know it, they got married. Oh, she never became Greek Orthodox or anything like that, but they got round it. They went to Rhodes and had a wedding like the tourists do. My Greek family weren't well pleased, but there aren't many of them left, and even back then there weren't either. Yeah, OK, so most of the village is related in one way or another, but the more distant ones, the cousins and all that, they all work in the tourist line during the season, so they all know what happens. In fact there are one or two Russian, German and even Ukrainian girls living around here now who all started out as tourists and fell for the old Greek charm. It's hardly the most recent story on earth, eh?

"Anyway, I came along in October 2001 and, not long after that things started to go a bit pear-shaped. I wouldn't say they got mad at each other. There was no violence, or anything like that. It's just that, well, in essence, it was the culture clash I suppose. Mum began to get restless, couldn't hack the small Greek community life. It's OK in the summer, with the place overrun by tourists and the like. But in winter, when there are only a couple of hundred people here and everyone is into everyone else's business, and the nearest centre of civilisation, as you might call it, is more than twenty-five kilometres west of here in Ierapetra, well, she just got island fever I suppose. And, there was something else involved too."

I find myself staring at the side of her face. I could think of a lot of less attractive things to look at. Not many that are more beautiful, though. Hope she doesn't turn to look at me, because I may have to look away, for fear she thinks I'm staring too much. But she keeps looking from the patterns her finger is making in the sand to the sea and back again. I don't say anything, I know she'll go on when she's ready.

I swig my beer. She starts again. As her body relaxes just a tad, her thigh presses against mine. She doesn't seem to notice. Or does she and she decides it's OK? Hope it's the latter.

"See, it's complicated. Well before she came out here she had another child. A baby girl it was. She called her Rebecca. The father was a long distance lorry driver and he got killed in a motorway pile-up months before the baby was born. Mum came over here eventually to try and snap out of her depression over what happened. She never got over her guilt feelings. Only once in my life did she tell me all of the details, but I remember all of it. She told it with such intensity. Well, you would, wouldn't you? I mean a baby is as much a part of a mother as anything possibly can be, right?

"So, somewhere out there I have a half-sister. I often muse over it. I worked out that she would be around twenty one by now. What does she look like? What language does she speak? What country does she live in? Mum would often become depressed, tell me she was worthless, a bad mother. I would tell her to stop being stupid. She'd been a wonderful mother to me, still is. All the time she lived over here she'd kept her small flat going back in the UK. She had a second bedroom, Rebecca's room. She hadn't touched anything in there from the day the baby disappeared."

Just a little confused, I have to interject. "What are you saying? What happened then? Where did Rebecca go? From what you're saying you think she's still alive somewhere. How come she isn't with you, with your mum? I'm not getting something here. When you said she came here to get over it, I thought you meant the death of the baby's father, but you didn't, right?"

"Oh? What? No, sorry, I'm not explaining it very well. My older half-sister was snatched from her buggy, outside the post office in my mum's home town. She was only six months old. Mum never found her. The police never solved it. I mean, how awful is that?"

Too awful for words, that's what it is. Oh, look out, she's going to carry on.

"I was eleven when mum told dad that she wanted to go back. To the UK I mean. They'd been getting on all right, but more as friends than as a couple. I think that deep down inside it was mum who was more to blame. Dad's a laid back soul, he never kicked up a fuss. But he was shocked when she told him that. See, try and put yourself in her place. I was still pretty young, but old enough to understand to a degree. She always held out the hope that Rebecca would come back, be brought back, or maybe find out that she wasn't the natural child of whoever snatched her and want to find out her real roots. I'm talking about 2012, here, so Rebecca would only have been about fifteen, but it's old enough to get curious, after all. Mum just felt that she was negligent not being in the same home, just in case her baby came searching. She said to me, when she was trying to explain why she had to return to the UK, she said:

"'Chrissy, I can't not be there. I thought I could put it all behind me, but I can't. I just can't. Becca is still out there somewhere, I know it. She's old enough now to start asking questions. What if she's not happy? What if she looks nothing like her parents, or rather those who tried to tell her that they were her parents? Suppose she wheedles it out of them and wants to come and find me. What would I feel like if that happened and I wasn't there?'

"So she said, 'It's time, Chrissy, it's time. I need to go back. I have to. And I want to take you with me.'"

I interject, "What did you think about that? Had you ever been to England?"

"No, of course not. I was raised here as a Greek girl. I went to school here and the only life I know is this one. OK so I learned English from mum as I grew up, but my first language is still Greek. But I'd detected for a long time that something wasn't right. Mum was restless, unsettled. But when you're only just getting into double figures yourself, you don't really understand a lot about these things. Anyway, how many people are there who can understand what it's like to lose a child and never know what happened to her? Now I see it much more clearly, but then, I was only eleven and didn't want to be uprooted from my school, my friends, my dad."

"Must have caused an argument when your mum said she wanted to take you back. Did she? I mean, did you go?"

"Yes, she did take me. It's the only time in my life I can remember seeing dad go ballistic. He never hit my mother, no. But he ranted and raged and got blue in the face. You probably don't know just how much Greek fathers dote on their daughters, do you?"

She doesn't wait for my reply. Not that I have one ready anyway.

"But, in the end, he gave in. I think he knew, though. He knew that I'd want to come back to Crete. And, of course, he was right. All I remember of England is how much I hated it. And I know I'm not being fair, but it's my experience that I can go by, no one else's. At least I could speak English, but from the first day at my new school I was bullied. No one knew me, so the loud mouths started on about me thinking I was something special because I'd come from Greece. I never ever felt that. All I wanted was to get on with people. Maybe find a friend or two. I didn't like the English kids at all. They're so different from the Greeks in so many ways. English kids are all confrontational, aggressive, competitive. They have no respect for their elders either. They have no manners, and all they want to do, even from the age that I was when I got there, eleven, ELEVEN! They want to mess about with the opposite sex and smoke cigarettes. And the language, I couldn't believe it. I thought I'd landed in hell. When I heard twelve-year olds boasting about having sex I was shellshocked. What had my mother brought me to?

"I know they can't all be like that, but that was my experience in the school I was sent to. I was miserable, thoroughly miserable. I couldn't imagine Greek children not showing respect to the teacher, or to their elders generally.

"And then there was the climate. We got back to mum's flat in September, and already I found it cold at night. As the weeks went on I started pining for the sun. I'm not saying that there was none at all, but once we got into November, when over here it's twenty-five degrees and mainly sunny, with the occasional storm, over there we'd have days when the sky was grey from end to end. It was the same grey for hours, even days, and there was fog. I'd never seen fog. It scared me. And frost, and icy surfaces. My feet and hands, my ears and nose were perpetually frozen. I took to staying in my room and crying. Mum tried to cheer me up, but she was torn. When I say, 'my room,' I mean my corner of her bedroom. Because she wouldn't let me use the bedroom where all of Rebecca's stuff was still just as it had been when she'd disappeared. I used to say to mum, 'Look, if she does come home, she won't still be a six month old baby, she'll be a teenager.' But it had no effect. She wouldn't be moved on that subject. It was like I was sharing my mother with this phantom sister who was winning the battle of the half-siblings. The more time went on, the more she became preoccupied with trawling the internet, going out for long walks looking at every child she passed, and occasionally getting into hot water about it when other mothers didn't like the way she'd stare, even follow their kids.

"I didn't last a year. I began to campaign to come home. At first she wouldn't have it. She said she'd lost one child and wouldn't be able to cope if she lost her second. I had to grow up a lot for a child so young. Eventually, though, I persuaded her that she wouldn't be losing me, I'd still be there for her. She'd be able to come over and visit. But I couldn't bear the life there any more. I was becoming emotionally damaged myself."

"And does she come and visit?"

"Yes, she does. She usually comes over in May or June, stays a few weeks, then goes back. She has a deep need to be there, for the reasons I've already explained. Don't get me wrong. She wasn't a bad mother to me, but I understood that she was suffering, suffering from the deep pain of loss, and she couldn't deal with it any other way. There were times, are times, when we laugh. We were good mates on the good times.

"Well, you wanted to hear the story. Bet you wish you hadn't asked now."

"Not at all. It's a tragic story. I can't begin to imagine how your mother must feel. Her whole life has been wrecked by one tiny moment. It's terrible." Right now I feel guilty about having the hots for Chrissy. Here she is baring all about her family's tragedy, and there was I a few minutes ago wondering how to get her and I to become an item. Shallow, or what? It's evident that this tragedy is something that overshadows her entire life.

I mean, here I am, a pretty normal English kid with a nice regular family; mum, dad, and us two kids, Amanda and me. We've had nothing of any note happen to us in all of our lives and now I hear this story from this rather beautiful Greek girl. Can't judge by appearances, can you?

I think to ask her something. "You never said whereabouts in England your mum was from, where you lived for the time you were over there."

"Didn't I? Oh, sorry, it was in Wiltshire, a small place called Lyneham. Don't know if you've heard of it."

Now, life is full of coincidences, right? And it's quite wrong to attach meaning to most of them. But right now I feel like I've just had an electric shock. It may show on my face, because she asks me:

"Jerome? What's the matter? You look like you've seen a ghost."

"When were you there, in Lyneham, exactly? No, wait, you said 2012 to 2013, right?"

"Yes, so?"

"Well I was brought up in Salisbury, only about forty miles from Lyneham."

"Oh, right. Well, it's not that near I suppose."

"No, true. But my mum lived in Lyneham before she married my dad."

"Wow. Now that is a coincidence."

"I mean, she left there in September ninety-eight, when they got married. Dad had a house in Pewsey, which they sold and bought the Salisbury one around the time I was born. But that would have put my mum in Lyneham around the same time as yours when your sister disappeared."

"Wow. Maybe they knew each other."

10. *Lyneham Late August 1997*

When a woman loses her child, it's indescribable how she feels. When she loses her child through sudden infant death syndrome, it's liable to make her inconsolable. If she has a partner to help her through, it may help. If she's all alone and has precious few relatives, all of whom she's lost touch with, it can become an all-consuming burden that makes her lose her powers of reason. She feels that she's somehow to blame. She goes through all the 'if-only' scenarios. If only I'd had her sleep in my bed that night. If only I'd lain her the other way up, given her a dummy, not given her a dummy, checked for wind one more time, not put her 'down' to sleep that afternoon. The list goes on.

She stared at the cot for hours, occasionally nudging the inert infant, hoping beyond hope that the child would stir. It did not. She wept and wrung her hands, she got up and paced around the room, looking this way and that, as if in doing so she'd see something, perhaps someone that would solve this problem for her. She left the child where it was until the following morning, and began to realise that she ought to have called someone. The police? Maybe. A doctor? Probably.

But she hadn't. She began to think about another young single mother who lived just around the corner from her, not more than a hundred and fifty metres along the pavement. She began to resent the fact that this other woman still had her child, whereas her own was dead. She built up a list of imagined reasons why it would be better if the other woman's child were to have a new mother, a new start in life. She created an immoral monster out of a young woman whom she hardly knew, had hardly exchanged a few "hiyahs" with when passing on the roadside. That child still lived and breathed. No one as yet knew that her own was dead. She hadn't phoned anyone.

Surely it would be straightforward. If not easy, not all that difficult either.

She began to formulate an idea.

Before long she was picking up her deceased child, with all the tenderness she could muster, and she wrapped it in a bath towel, making sure to tuck it all around the child's body, so that no toes, fingers or head would be showing. Then she fished around in the cupboard under the kitchen sink for a supermarket shopping bag, one of those 'bags for life' that they go on about. The tough ones with the proper handles, rather than simply a couple of oblong holes punched along the top. Carefully, she slipped the bundle into the carrier bag and placed it on her kitchen table, then looked around again, seeking inspiration.

She went into her modest little hallway and came back with a holdall. She unzipped the fastener all along the top and slipped the child inside, re-zipping it afterwards. Then she waited until evening, went to the hallway again, slipped on her full-length outdoor coat and a pair of ankle high boots, and went out her front door, closing it quietly behind her.

Not half a mile from her flat there was a clutch of allotments, places where enthusiastic gardeners who didn't have enough space at home could grow some vegetables. Most of these allotments had a shed of some sort installed in them. Lots of them had padlocks on their doors, some of which had been jimmied off by petty thieves, looking to steal a tool or two to go and sell down the local pub car park. The woman waited until dusk, and as the light began to fail and it looked to her as if there was no one left tending their vegetable plot, she went to the entranceway, which was a metal gate with a padlock, and tried the lock. It was snapped shut, but it was a simple matter of stepping on to the bars of the gate and swinging a leg over to gain entry to the plot. She was wearing jeans, so it was no problem to climb over in seconds.

Once again, casting her eyes around to check that there was no one within sight, she began walking among the plots, making her way toward each one's shed, to see if she could find one with a door that could be opened. The first was padlocked with two sturdy brass locks. Evidently the person who kept this allotment had been burgled one time too many and wasn't going to be caught as easily again. The second, and the third didn't budge when she tried to pull at them and she began to worry that this wasn't going to be as straightforward as she'd hoped.

Then, she saw it. She couldn't believe her luck, but someone had gone home leaving their garden fork still sticking vertically out of the ground on a newly dug-over patch. The shed on that particular plot looked secure, but there it was, just what she was hoping to find, a sturdy garden fork just waiting to be pulled from the cold earth.

She must have stood not ten metres from the forgotten tool for five minutes at least, hardly moving a muscle. The light faded further and it became evident that the darkness was such that someone passing on the pavement alongside these allotments wouldn't be able to make her out at that distance. People passing in vehicles would most definitely not be aware of her presence.

She went to the fork and pulled it out of the ground. Fortunately it hadn't rained much recently and only a minimal amount of soil clung to the tines of the fork. She had a plastic bag in the coat pocket anyway, and so she slid the business end of the fork into that before slipping the whole thing inside her thick coat. Before long she was letting herself back into her flat. Once she'd closed the door she leaned back against it, heaved a huge sigh and almost punched the air. Only almost. She felt a bit like doing so, but then rationale took over and she began the next phase of her operation.

She waited until around midnight. Fortunately for her it was a dry night, with around sixty percent cloud cover. As it was late, the air was chilly, but stars peeked through between the clouds and it wasn't very windy. Opening her front door again, she took a glance up and down the road. All was quiet. Taking the holdall, she went out to her battered twelve-year-old VW Polo and opened the rear tailgate. Quickly she placed the holdall inside, covered it with a moth-eaten car blanket and darted back to the flat. It was a ground-floor flat in one of those roads where some of the buildings were link, or terraced, houses, and some of them were two up, two-down flats, each with their own external front door. The flat above hers had a stairway leading down to their front door, which was adjacent to hers. All were council-owned.

Quickly grabbing the fork, she went back to the car, placed it in the back with the holdall and closed the tailgate with as little impact as she could manage. Ten minutes later she was driving along a small country lane, heading out towards Hilmarton, then Calne. Once through the sleeping town of Calne she followed the road towards Melksham, heading for Chittoe, knowing that nearby was a beauty spot called Bowden Hill. There she knew she'd find lots of coppices and woodland. On the A342 at

Sandy Lane, there's a stand of trees, almost a small wood, that is not more than a hundred metres from the road. In the middle of this is a pond called Leech Pool. The whole area is enclosed by a wooden fence, with wire built into it to keep too many ramblers from traipsing around in it. There is a small field entranceway between some trees on the lane, where one can pull off the road, kill the lights, and be virtually invisible to any passing traffic, if that is what one so desires.

Pulling into this entranceway, and making sure she drove the car a good ten feet from the road itself, she killed the lights and rolled down her window. There she sat for at least ten minutes, to see if anyone would approach. There was just an outside chance that someone from the village would have seen her drive through, and see her lights go off, thus perhaps wondering if she'd stopped because of a breakdown, a puncture maybe.

When she'd decided that no one knew she was there, she got out, opened the tailgate, retrieved the holdall and the fork, and set off across the hundred metres or so of open field to the small enclosed woodland. She found it easy to get over the wooden fence, and was soon striding into the trees, grateful for the small amount of ambient light from a weak moon that was now trying to peak between the clouds on occasion, but failing most of the time. She dared not use a torch.

Once she'd reached a spot that she considered was almost never trodden by humans, at least not from one year to the next, she set down the holdall, began raking leaves and other detritus from an area of flat ground around three feet by one, and began to dig.

11. Jerome, Crete 2018

Jerome was using WhatsApp to call his mother. It was late in the evening, well after midnight. He'd finished at the taverna half an hour earlier and was now sitting outside one of the bars in the thick of the village, just back from the beach. There was a condensation-covered bottle of Amstel on the table in front of him. It was half-full.

"Mum? Hi! Me. How's things?" It was 10.30pm in Salisbury, UK.

"Same as usual Jerry, same as usual. How about you? Still happy in that taverna where you're working? Or have you slipped away and ended up on some other island by now? Don't tell me you're in some Greek jail."

"No, still here. Plans all gone out the window I'm afraid. I seem to have a pressing reason to hang around here, to be honest."

"Is she pretty?" Mothers know such things about their sons.

"Nope, gorgeous. She's the reason I'm calling you tonight to be honest."

"Oh dear. Sounds serious. I'm not going to be hearing about a shotgun wedding am I? Your father will be furious. It has to be something important, though. I didn't expect to hear from you for a week or two yet."

"All right, all right. I know I should call more often. But you know you'd soon hear if there was anything wrong. No, it's about a conversation we had yesterday. She told me about her parents. Her dad's obviously Greek, a Cretan born and bred, but her mother is English."

"Not so unusual though, is it Jerry? Not these days with all the holiday reps that end up falling for Greek chaps and settling down over there. Is that it, the fact she's British? Surely not enough of a reason to phone your poor neglected mother, is it?"

"Rub it in, why don't you? Look, there's more to it that that, and that's why I was excited to ask you something. Do you remember before you and dad met, when you lived in Lyneham and you were a single mum with Amanda still a baby?"

"I can hardly forget. Not an easy time in my life. I still thank God I went to the Colston Hall that night."

"Yeah, well, do you remember the case of the baby that was snatched from a buggy and never found? The police got nowhere and the case was never resolved. You remember it?"

"Of course. It was massive news here, well, especially in Lyneham. Such things don't happen in small Wiltshire villages and towns. It made the national TV news for a few days."

"Brilliant. I knew you'd have to remember it. Well, you're not going to believe the next bit. I hope you're sitting down."

"Oh dear, and that's the second time I've said that tonight. OK, I'm sitting down, go on."

"The woman whose baby was stolen eventually came out here to Greece. In fact. She settled in the same village where I'm staying, Makrigialos. She's only my landlord's ex, isn't she! And Christina, the girl of my dreams, is only her daughter. Coincidence, or what? I couldn't believe it when she told me. Talk about small world. Can you believe that?"

There was a moment's silence from the other end. Jerome went on:

"Mum? You still there? Should have used the video, shouldn't I?"

"Yes, still here. Just trying to take it in. It's almost uncanny. You said her mother is your landlord's ex, so I'm assuming they're not still together. Have you met her, then? Your girlfriend's mother?"

"No, no. She went back to the UK in 2012. Took Christina with her, but she couldn't stick it. Christina, I mean. Came back here, so her mum now comes over once a year to see her. I missed her by a couple of months this year, it seems. Can you remember anything else about the fallout to that case? Chrissy says the police did a house to house. Did they call on you then?"

"What? Oh, yes, yes, they called. They said they were doing house-to-house enquiries. Two officers came, one woman and a man. They could see I had a baby too and so they asked me questions about your sister. When she was born, could they see the birth certificate, that sort of thing. If I hadn't been able to prove Amanda was mine with her birth certificate, it might have been a bit hairy. But they were quite happy when they heard my story, you know, all about your sister's father not wanting to know. Well, you know the story. We never hid any of it from you."

"Yeah, sure. Did you know what had happened to the mother at all?"

"No, no. Once the story fell off the news we all forgot all about it. Must have been awful for that woman though. Can't imagine how it must feel, the never knowing."

"So you didn't know her then?"

"Me? No, why would I?"

"Well, Lyneham is a small place. Just thought, since you both had babies around the same time, you may have been in the same post-natal class, or whatever they call it. Same doctor's surgery, or whatever."

"I may have seen her around, but we didn't know each other. Sorry to disappoint you, Jerry."

"Ah well. That was my bombshell. But I thought you'd want to hear all about it, since it's something that happened so close to home for you and all that."

"So, you really like this girl then? You're not planning to throw in the towel and give up uni for the life of a Greek taverna owner or anything drastic like that are you? You ought to remember, you're still only nineteen Jerry. It's not a good idea to do anything rash at your age."

"OK, mum, OK. No need for a lecture."

"Give up university? I hope I haven't come into this conversation too late. What's going on then?"

Gavin's voice boomed through the two thousand miles that currently separated his son from his home, and made the boy sit upright. Julie replied:

"No, love no. Least I hope that's not going to happen. Jerry was just telling me about a strange coincidence, that's all. I'll explain when we sign off."

"Hi dad. No, I'm not throwing my life away for a gorgeous Greek goddess just yet. Tell you what though, it's tempting."

"It better not be too tempting, Jerry. Or I'd never have let you go off on this 'expedition' as you call it."

"Come on dad, I am nineteen, you know."

"Jerry, nineteen is barely out of nappies. Now, you have fun, by all means, but make sure you're back here well in time to start university, that's all I'm saying on the matter."

"I'll be home in time, dad, no worries."

Julie said: "I hope you're getting your beauty sleep, Jerry. Must be getting on for one o'clock there isn't it?"

Oh, mum. I don't have to get up 'til around nine or nine-thirty. Stop worrying. I am on holiday, you know."

"Well you keep safe, that's all. Let us know if you learn any more about this English mother of your may-be girlfriend won't you."

'Sure thing."

They closed the call and Jerome drained the remainder of his beer. He strolled back along the sea front, dreaming of doing so with Christina on his arm.

12. Marsha, Crete 1998

Nikos sat down again, and waited for his guest to compose herself. A very slight, warm breeze tickled the foliage of the tree above them. Somewhere an owl could be heard hooting. Two black silhouettes could be seen as a couple strolled along the darkened beach, at the water's edge, their arms linked. They stopped, turned to stand face-on to the sea and their heads tilted until they touched. Here and there, small bats dashed around in the air above their heads, probably seeking their food for the night.

"Someone took her. Forgive me, but do you mean your child was taken by someone in your family? The authorities, maybe? Although I can't imagine why that would happen to someone like you."

"You really don't know me. But no, it wasn't like that. I was negligent, but only for a few minutes. I went into a shop, and left my baby in her stroller outside. I was only minutes, but when I came back out, she was gone."

"Gone? But how?" Such things don't happen in a quiet corner of a Greek island. The scenario didn't compute in Niko's mind.

"If I knew that. If only I knew that. One moment she was there, sleeping in her stroller. The next, it was empty. No one saw anything, no one heard anything. There was no one around anyway. Where I live, you can walk the pavement at some times during the day and not meet a soul. Sometimes you might not even see a vehicle for five or ten minutes, and then a huge truck or a few cars, maybe a motorbike or something, but it's a small town, more a village really, where not much happens. Most of the people that live there either work on the base or commute to Swindon, even further.

"On the base?"

"Lyneham's been an R.A.F. town for decades. It's been right beside a huge military base for longer than I even know. Although it is being decommissioned gradually now, I think. But a lot of civilians work there. Once they're on the base they're not going to be out and about in the roads and housing estates for hours until they come off shift. People who live there don't even notice the Hercules planes that come and go, although they're not so frequent as they used to be.

"But when my baby went, I so wish there had been someone around. If there had been just one other person walking, maybe with their dog or something, maybe they'd have seen him, or her, whoever it was that took my Becca." Marsha dissolved once again into tears. There was nothing for it, Nikos moved his chair closer and slid an arm around her shoulders. She leant into the nape of his neck. She thought, 'I don't even know this man. I only met him this evening. But it feels so good to feel the touch of another human, to feel like someone's there for me. Even though tomorrow he'll probably have forgotten all about this. And I'll be alone again.'

They stayed like this for several minutes. Nikos knew there was nothing he could say. Words weren't what this girl wanted right now anyway. He knew she just wanted comfort, solace, to feel someone supporting her. He tried to resist the feeling that he wanted her. It was only natural. But she was so vulnerable right now. Whatever he was, he wasn't the sort to take advantage of someone in such a vulnerable position. In fact, overriding his sense of attraction to Marsha was his deep sense of helplessness and compassion.

Nikos had a girl in the village whom he'd kind of begun courting. In Greek communities, even in this day and age, there were certain protocols to be observed. Nothing had been spoken or agreed, but she was ten years his junior, par for the course, and he knew that her family would be delighted were he to express an interest. Right now though, at this moment, he could only see Marsha, he smelt her hair, felt the touch of her skin under his fingers as they held her shoulder. He felt the need within her for something, anything, to relieve her pain. Maybe not relieve, but at least ameliorate, or make more tolerable in some way. Who of us can deal with such tragedy alone? Man was made to have a mate, at least that's what he believed.

"*Kyria* Marsha, may I ask, what about your child's father? Where is he?" It had suddenly occurred to Nikos that maybe this was a non-starter as far as any relationship was concerned. Surely she was already married, he thought.

Marsha sniffed, blew her nose on yet another paper serviette, and tried to compose herself. She made as if to sit upright, sending a signal for Nikos to withdraw his arm, although, as he did, she lifted her face to look him in the eye. What was she telling him? In her mind she was saying, 'it's OK. I'm not offended and I'm not averse. I just need to talk some more.'

Nikos met her eyes and saw something positive too. He understood that she wasn't upset with him and didn't find it at all unacceptable what he'd just done. He was relieved beyond measure. He waited, hands now resting on the table, fingers entwined.

"We were engaged to be married. I fell pregnant, yes, but Richard was standing by me. We were about to get it all arranged. But he was killed in a road accident. So it was just me and my bump, which soon became Rebecca, my daughter. I've made quite a mess of my life, as you can see."

"There is nothing in life that can't be healed in some way, surely. You are still young, there is happiness in your future, I'm sure."

"Thanks, I appreciate the thought, but you can't really be sure of that, can you? I don't know how I'm ever going to get over what happened to my baby. It's hard enough getting over Richard, but I suppose I might eventually meet someone who I can fall in love with. Doesn't feel like it right now, though. But my baby...

"It's the not knowing. Is she even still alive? I have to believe she is. I have to. But it's torture not knowing anything, not having any idea what happened on that day. And the worst of it is, you just keep telling yourself, 'Why didn't you take her inside with you? You could have avoided all this if you'd just not left her outside for two minutes.' The guilt never goes away. What can possibly happen to change that? The only possible solution would be to have her back, or at the very least to know she's happy. I don't see either of those things happening if I'm honest."

Nikos looked around for the first time in half an hour. His waitress was clearing away the final detritus from the last couple of tables that had been occupied. The place was now empty, the last few diners having left. He looked at his watch, it was well after 12.30am.

"Tell me, where are you staying? I would like to walk you home, if you wouldn't object."

Registering the merest hint of apprehension on Marsha's face, which elicited some degree of disappointment in him, he decided that it was only to be expected. So he added, quickly,

"Please! I don't mean anything by it and I don't want to be a nuisance to you. But from what you've told me, I am worried about you. I want to be sure you reach your door safely, and hopefully that you'll be able to sleep tonight."

Marsha again made eye contact with her host, gauging his intentions. She wasn't exactly drunk, but she knew that when she stood up she may well be slightly dizzy.

"Yes, OK, thank you. I think I'd like that."

As they walked slowly along the beach road towards her studio complex, she discovered that she was feeling a mixture of two different moods. On the one hand she was relieved to have spoken to someone about what she'd been through those past few months, yet slightly embarrassed that it was to someone that, prior to this evening, she'd never even met. On the other, she was mulling over what she wanted to do. She'd come here with the half-intention of perhaps finding some way to end it all, yet deep down she knew that she had to go on for the sake of her daughter, for whom she so wanted there to be the remote possibility that she'd somehow come back into her life, that there would be a reuniting. She was deeply depressed, yet strangely calm as she walked, this strange man by her side, who seemed to be behaving like the perfect gentleman.

Would it be so wrong if she were to slip an arm through his? Would it send him the wrong signal? Yet, owing to the fact that, if she didn't, she doubted she'd make it all the way back, a distance of around half a kilometre, without stumbling and falling, owing to the fact that her head was struggling in vain against the tendency to swim alarmingly, she took the plunge. She slipped an arm through the crook of his elbow and said,

"Do you mind? I'm sorry, but that drink! I've had Greek wine, Greek brandy and a glass or two of ouzo [this one she remembered], and it's caught up with me. Not that it hasn't all helped. I do feel calmer than I have for a long time, but whether I will tomorrow, I somehow doubt it."

The following morning Marsha sat on her small veranda, a black tea cradled in both hands, fingers entwined around the cup, gazing at the view. It was mid-morning and she had only been up a few minutes. The intense sunlight warmed her body and it made her feel calm. There was a degree of shade from a small wooden canopy, with a few terracotta tiles on top, so her head wasn't in direct sunlight. She thought back to the previous evening and her mind told her that perhaps she ought to go a little easier on the alcohol in future.

Had last night helped? She wasn't sure. She found herself thinking that she was glad that she'd gone into Niko's taverna, glad to have met him, yet her overall feeling now was that she wanted to go home at the end of this holiday. She had decided that her vigil would continue, in the hope that some day the mystery would be solved. She knew that the gnawing loss that she felt would be something that she'd just have to adjust to and live with. It wasn't going to go away, at least not completely.

She'd go home and she'd find herself a job. She'd try and get on with life to the extent that she could, always telling herself that Rebecca would some day return, even if it was years later, because she'd no doubt be told that she'd been brought up by people who weren't her natural parents. Surely they'd tell her, wouldn't they? Yet she had her doubts. It wasn't like she'd been legally adopted, after all. She could only hope that her daughter would see some evidence in her looks, her complexion, her hair colour, her build. There'd surely be something, anything, that would trigger in her some curiosity about her true origins.

The problem was, how long would it take? Of course she would also cling to the idea that someone local may have been the kidnapper and that someone else would blow the whistle. She couldn't forgive herself if she were not around if that happened. Maybe there was someone who saw something, and that someone would eventually decide to go to the police and say something. She even began to think that perhaps she could work out some way of offering a reward, although that would only be possible if she were to find some benefactor who was somewhat better off than her.

As she took a sip of the hot tea, she made a resolve. She'd try and use this two weeks as a restorative break, try and regain her equilibrium and then go back and face her life as it was, make the best of it, struggle on.

Over the course of the next twelve days or so, she found herself gravitating towards Niko's taverna most mornings for coffee, and most evenings for her dinner. Other times she'd lay on a lounger beside the modest pool in the tiny apartment complex, frequently the only person there, and *Kyria* Despoina, the owner, would bring her something from the kitchen, perhaps offer her a cold drink, while she read a book, even slept. She did make longer walks occasionally, but whilst sitting in a beachside bar along the end of the bay, she'd find herself wishing she'd simply gone into Niko's again. She felt alone and sorry for herself. When she sat with Niko, who invariably would join her when she came in, she at least began to feel as though she had someone. In fact, by the time she was only a day from going home to the UK, it had become apparent that there was a feeling developing between them.

On her last evening, she went in, heavy of heart over the fact that she wouldn't be seeing her new friend again for quite a long while, yet also desperate to be at home, in case the unexpected happened. Maybe that young policewoman, what was her name again? Drysdale, Helen Drysdale, that was it. Maybe she's been trying to get in touch and has some momentous news. Marsha clung to a slim thread of hope.

Sitting at her favourite table, staring at the beach and the crystal blue sea just a few metres away, she felt a hand on her shoulder. Nikos kissed the top of her head and sat down, taking hold of her hand as he did so.

"So, my little English sparrow, you are going to leave me. How will I fill my evenings now? Who shall I take my coffee with tomorrow morning, and all the mornings after that?"

Marsha, self deprecating as usual, replied: "You managed perfectly well before I came, I'm sure. You'll soon find another bereft and vulnerable woman to charm."

She didn't mean that, and he knew it. He tried to look hurt, nevertheless.

"You can be cruel, Marsha, you know that? You mean you haven't seen how you and I have grown close this past couple of weeks? You haven't noticed how much I love your company? You think I haven't developed a deep fondness for you? That I don't feel some of your pain?"

"A deep fondness. Is that what it is Niko?" She regretted saying this the moment the words tripped off of her lips. Yet it triggered a response the like of which she knew she'd been hoping for.

"Marsha, Marsha, this isn't the end of you and I. I believe you know it. Yes, two weeks ago we didn't know each other. Yet we have spent many hours together since then, and you have opened your heart to me. You know I think I'm falling in love with you. No, correct that, I should have said, I have fallen in love with you. I want you to come back, and soon."

This caused Marsha to begin crying. Tears seeped from the corners of her eyes. She couldn't help but tell herself that she felt the same, and yet, what about the distance? The logistics? The expense? Was this just a silly holiday romance? Was she behaving like an eighteen-year-old? Yet this man, Nikos; he was around five years older than her, not a young, flighty, sex-mad teenager. And he'd behaved like the perfect gentleman the whole time. In fact, right now she was hoping that he'd not do so any more. He began to fulfil her wish. He reached to her face with the other and, since his right still held hers across the table, and wiped the tears from her cheeks. He tucked a strand of her hair behind an ear and said:

"So? What do you say? Are you going to leave here and never return? Or will you come back? Marsha, if you say you'll come back, I'll be here and waiting. In fact, since I know you're not well off for cash right now, I'll pay your air fare if you will come again, and come again soon. You can stay here, upstairs in one of my studios. We can really think about where this might go. I will come to Heraklion, to the airport, to collect you.

"But I must tell you one thing. I am not the joking kind when it comes to situations like this. I have enough experience in life to know what I want. Right now, I want you.

"There, I've said it. Whatever crisis you are facing, and you've been more than open with me about it, I want to be there with you to help you through."

He stopped, looked her in the eyes, waited for her to say something.

"I'll come back." She said.

13. Lyneham August 1997

I must be meticulous about this. If anything goes wrong I'll be caught. I can't let that happen. She must be mine, it's only right.

I must begin by shadowing her all the time for a week at least. Get to know all of her movements. Make my plans, get everything ready. My baby's coming back to me. I know it.

I know it.

I don't have long. My neighbours know I keep myself to myself, but if they begin to notice I'm not taking the stroller out, they'll smell a rat. I must go out at the usual times. I can stuff the blanket in the stroller, but if someone wants to talk, maybe coo over the baby, I'll be rumbled. No. Meticulous planning, it can't be flawed in any way.

No one knows about the scooter. I haven't brought it home. It was easy enough to buy it. Found it in the want ads in the local free paper. It's on its last legs, but I only want it for one run. The most important thing is, it has one of those top boxes on the back that's plenty big enough for a few minutes dash. Paid a few quid cash for it and I haven't sent the registration document off to Swansea. The seller was only too glad to be shot of it, but it goes, and that's what counts. Once it's done its job it'll soon be in a ditch for someone to discover a few days later, hopefully longer. I know a place not more than twenty minutes walk from here. Should be easy enough. I've been keeping it behind some garages a few streets away. If it gets vandalised, then tough. I'll have to revise the plan. But around here, well I doubt anyone even goes round where I've parked it anyway. And at least the local kids aren't quite so wanton as they are in town.

It should be OK.

14. Lyneham August-September 1997

The young woman pads the seat of her stroller with a pillow, tucks the baby blanket all around it, until she's happy that it looks realistic enough from a few feet away. She makes sure that the grapefruit with the baby's hat on it isn't showing any yellow skin, just the hat peeps out above the blanket. The stroller is in the hallway, just inside the front door, which is white PVC with a frosted glass panel occupying almost 50% of its surface area.

She peeps from her window at Marsha's front door. She lives that close. Door-to-door, it's no more than fifty metres between the two homes. She glances back at the clock on her lounge wall, and looks anxiously, expectantly, back out through the window. Sure enough, almost to the minute, the door opens and her quarry steps out, manoeuvring the stroller over the front doorstep.

The woman waits until Marsha is just rounding the corner at the end of the street and hustles her own stroller out through the front door. She walks briskly just far enough to be able to see Marsha from a distance. She stays far enough back so that Marsha can't hear her, and also so that she can stop and quickly be out of view if necessary. There is a little light traffic on the road beside the pavement anyway, a few vans, cars, the occasional lorry, just enough to provide sufficient background noise to mask the sound of her stroller following the woman in front. No one driving past even gives either woman a second glance. They're all too busy worrying about their working day.

The woman following checks her watch periodically. She tails Marsha for over half an hour, first to the post office, then to the local supermarket. Where she walks on by when Marsha goes in, comes past again two or three times, and then follows Marsha as she makes her way home.

Confident that she hasn't been rumbled, the woman quickly walks, almost at a trot, to her own front door and lets herself inside. This goes on daily for over a week, then to the end of a second week.

The woman was confident now of the schedule that her quarry followed. She just needed to wait in patient anticipation. The third week gave her the straw of hope that she'd been waiting for. Marsha left the baby outside while she popped into the post office on the Thursday morning. She emerged, confident that her baby would be where she'd left her, which, of course, she was.

Time to move the scooter. Across the road from the filling station, which is just in front of the post office, there's a small church hall with a modest car park. There's never anything parked there on a weekday morning. There are a few shrubs and a couple of trees around the perimeter, just enough to hide a motor scooter behind, so as not to attract anyone's attention. At around one o'clock in the morning on a Wednesday night/Thursday morning in early September, she leaves her front door wearing a black tracksuit and trainers. She sprints a couple of blocks to the garages where she'd left the scooter, hoping it'll start without a problem.

She sits astride the scooter, pushes the key into the well-worn ignition slot and turns it. Pushing the start button on the handlebar she heaves a sigh of relief as the little fifty cc engine spurts into life, so quietly as to not even be audible from the nearest house, which is thirty metres or more away, the other side of the garages. She twists the grip and speeds off, rounding a few bends and on to the main road through the village. She doesn't turn on the lights. Within minutes she's turning into the church car park and pulls up in the far corner, behind an unpruned shrub. Quickly she turns the engine off, leaves the key in the ignition and jumps off. Within three minutes she's sprinted back to her front door and let herself in.

Next morning she is again ready and waiting as her neighbour along the road comes out to make the short walk to the post office. The woman watching knows that just this once she can't take her own stroller, she has to trust to luck. When she makes the snatch too, she'll have around thirty seconds to run around the back of the petrol station, so as not to be visible from the pay booth, across the road, praying (to whom, exactly?) that, just for those few moments, there will be no traffic, and over to the scooter, which will hopefully still be there with the key already in the ignition.

As her quarry approaches the post office, the woman is closer than she's ever been before. She knows that time is crucial for this very risky part of the plan to work.

"Don't look round. Don't look round, please!" She mutters to herself.

'YES!" She exclaims inwardly as Marsha hesitates, then decides to leave the stroller outside. Within seconds the follower sprints to the stroller, slips the child out, overjoyed to discover that it is sleeping soundly, drops it delicately into a supermarket 'bag-for-life' which she's pulled out from a pocket and runs around the back of the filling station. Is there any traffic?

She's just about to come out from behind the building and expose herself to the road when a red Audi approaches from the Wootton Bassett direction. She steps back, alarmed, heart pounding, hoping that the baby in the bag won't wake and cry out. The car is soon gone around the roundabout and off towards Chippenham. She goes for it. Within ten seconds the child is inside the top-box and the scooter engine has sputtered to life. The woman guns the twist throttle and, almost colliding with a tree, shoots out of the parking area, on to the road and off towards her own street, just around the next corner.

Once again she knows that her street is usually as quiet as a church mouse at this time of the morning, but there's always a chance that someone will be passing. She pulls up right outside her own front door, right beside her battered old car, leaps from the machine and opens the door. She turns to go back to the scooter and opens the top-box. Quickly she extracts the child in the shopping bag and runs into the hallway, where she dashes through to the bedroom, takes the child out of the bag and places it in her own baby's ready-prepared cot. The child is now awake and grizzling a little.

The woman knows how little time she has to get the scooter away, before anyone local notices it. She quickly shoves a ready-prepared dummy into the baby's mouth, one that's been sweetened with a little honey, and dashes back through the hallway and out to the waiting machine, whose engine is still ticking over.

She leaps on to the machine and hares off like a mad thing. Ten minutes later she's run the scooter into a roadside ditch down a small country lane, a ditch that's heavily overgrown, since fortunately for her, it's early September now, and the countryside is full of copious greenery, and started back to the village, running as fast as her legs will carry her.

Once back in her own road she slows to a walk, trying to look relaxed, and wanting desperately for the child not to have begun screaming. She sees a postman coming along the other side of the road. He spots her and shouts a "Morning! Nice day! Just the right weather for a jog, eh?"

"She nods, waves back and, even though inside she's wracked with nervous tension, tries to walk the last few meters to her front door looking like she has all the time in the world, and lets herself in.

She can't believe her luck. The baby is grizzling, but not bawling. She kicks off her trainers in the hallway and walks into the bedroom, and up to the cot. She picks the child up, cradles it against her chest and neck, pats its back and says:

"Sssh. It's all right. You're home now."

And, to the sound of a distant police siren, she adds, "And mummy's not going to let anything bad happen to you. I'm never going to let you go."

15. Jerome, Crete 2018

As the days turned into weeks, Jerome was delighted to find that his landlord-cum-boss' daughter began to stick to him like a persistent limpet. He could hardly but turn around and she'd be there. She'd find opportunities, too, to touch him, usually trying to make it lighthearted, but betraying what Jerome could only interpret as the symptoms of a crush. She loved to put an arm through his, drape herself over his shoulders when he was sitting at the table, ruffle his hair whenever she could.

In short, he completely abandoned any vague plan he'd had to go island-hopping. He was besotted too, of course.

Nikos didn't seemed to mind in the least that his daughter was 'joined at the hip' to this young Englishman. He had no major aspirations for Christina, only that she be happy and marry well. When all is said and done, most Greek fathers, especially in rural communities, are content to see their daughters married off, as long as it's to someone that is a good provider. He'd talked with Jerome and knew that he was going to university to read history. If he became a teacher, maybe even a lecturer, then he'd do nicely. He liked Jerome anyway, and he wasn't at all worried about Christina becoming attached to a non-Greek. After all, hadn't he himself married an Englishwoman?

That was the only thing that occasionally put him in a reflective, even melancholy mood. He still loved Marsha. He'd tried to understand why she had to leave, to go back to the UK to be in approximately the same place as she'd been when her baby had disappeared, but it didn't mean he wanted things that way. Although he'd more than sympathised with Marsha over such a plight as hers, he'd still lived in hope that she'd get over the growing urge that eventually defeated her to go back, in the slim hope that her lost daughter would some day come searching for her roots.

They'd had almost twelve years together before Marsha had gone back to the UK. He didn't regret so much as a moment. Even now, six years after she'd gone back, he still entertained the hope that, each time she came over to visit, she'd decide to stay. But he'd grown used to the disappointment and could no longer muster up the stomach for a fight over it. When she first came back to visit he would try, but it always degenerated into an emotionally charged kind of meltdown on her part. Yet in all honesty, he'd tell her, he hadn't so much as looked at anyone else.

He enjoyed so much having Christina around, and secretly wished that she would marry someone who'd be willing to take on the business. He was now fifty-two and was ready to ease back a gear or two. He was still in very good health, even though his waistline wasn't quite what it was. He often thought about whether he'd been too limited in his aspirations. Yet after some consideration, would always come back to the fact that there was in all probability no other life that would have brought him any more contentment, or more satisfaction than the one he'd led. Had it not been for Marsha's unique circumstances, she told him, and he knew she'd meant it, that she'd never have had to leave him. She didn't do it out of lack of love, or even out of selfishness, but simply because she had no other choice. True she'd become very difficult to live with in the last couple of years before she went, but he knew the reason for that, even if it didn't make it any easier to bear.

Would he have liked to have had a son? Probably. Yet what had he to complain about? Not all that much, apart from the fact that, if they did become serious about each other, Jerome was still virtually certain to want to have Christina move to the UK when he left at the end of the season. That was the only difficulty he found about their friendship. And that was all it had been up until now, but would not be for much longer, he suspected. There was still a little time, maybe he could be persuaded to throw in his lot with them here. If it did get to a serious enough pitch, and Nikos had to admit that they were still quite young really to be making such decisions, yet if it did reach the stage where they could hardly bear to be parted from each other, he'd be in a position to make a very attractive offer to Jerome if he were to decide to stay on Crete.

He knew an allegorical story that a American had once told him over a late night Metaxa session after a meal in the taverna. The man's name now escaped him, but he was sure it had been something like Alvin, or Ethan, or something. Anyway, he'd been here with his wife and two teenage children on what was likely to become their last family holiday together before the kids decided that it was no longer cool to go on 'vacation with mom and dad,' as he'd put it. It concerned a rich American businessman on holiday in the West Indies. Strolling along an impossibly beautiful stretch of beach one evening, just before sundown, he'd passed a multi-coloured shack, apparently built from driftwood, beneath a few palm trees, outside of which an old black man was sitting, grilling a fish on a stick over an open fire. Close by was a modest launch with an outboard, pulled up on to the beach and secured by a rope stretching to the trunk of the nearest palm.

The American tourist struck up a conversation with the man.

"Hey!"

"Hey, man."

"That your boat over there?"

Yeh, man."

"You use it just for fishing, maybe? Or would you take me out on it, so I can fish a while too?"

"I take people out man, sure. You wanna go, we'll go."

Next day, the two men are sitting contentedly on the boat, a mile or two offshore, their rods hanging lazily from their hands, a cold-box of beers right beside them. The tourist can't resist offering some advice.

"You know, you could do more with this boat. Why don't you advertise? I mean, there's nothing in my hotel about you, and it's only yards along the beach. If you were to advertise, you could probably increase your income by quite a lot of bucks."

"And what would I do then, man?"

"Well, who knows, in a year or two, you might have several boats, employ a couple of guys, maybe even form a small company."

"Yeah, and what then, man?"

"The sky's the limit. If you worked hard, you could expand to other islands, in five years probably have an office in Miami or somewhere."

"And what would I do then, man?"

"Well, you know, a lot of the big corporations started off small, just like you. Who knows where you could go. You'd probably make a million, then be able to retire early, in your fifties or something, live the good life."

"And what would the good life be like man?"

Well, I don't know. You could probably sell out to some other big company and retire somewhere, well, ...somewhere like this." Already the man realised that he was shooting himself in the foot. The Black guy next says:

"I already here, man."

Nikos decided it would probably be a good idea to tell this story to Jerry some day, see how he reacts.

Jerome and Christina were sitting on the sunbed under the shade erected for the 'staff member' who looks after the sun beds, the very same one they'd sat on when Christina had told him about her mother's tragic past. About half the umbrellas were in use and Jerome had recently done a 'round' to be sure everyone present had either paid, or ordered a drink. That was the deal, order a drink or something to eat, and if you spent over five Euros per person, you got the sun bed for free.

"So, Jerry, you haven't told me very much about your family. Give me the gen."

"It's not very interesting."

"Still, I'd like to hear it anyway."

"Well, you already know I grew up in Salisbury. Dad's a big wheel in a bank. We moved there when I was born, near enough, because dad got a promotion which involved him moving from the Swindon Branch to the Salisbury one. My parents had been living in Pewsey from when they got married, which is a village not much closer to Swindon than it is to Salisbury, but they decided to move anyway, so dad wouldn't be commuting along country roads all the time.

"When they met, mum was living in Lyneham, and you already know that coincidence. She told me she'd read about what happened to your mum, but that she didn't know her really. I thought it a bit odd, to be honest, because Lyneham's not very big. But there you go, can't expect everyone to know everyone. She did say that it dropped off the news fairly quickly, when the police failed to come up with anything.

"Oh, and she said that the house-to-house enquiry reached her door. She had to show Mandy's birth certificate, just routine I suppose, in the circumstances. I'd imagine that mum never left Mandy anywhere unattended after what happened though. Kind of freaks you out when something like that happens so near to home."

"So, how old is your sister?"

"Mandy's twenty-one. She's a beauty therapist and masseuse. She's given me the treatment once or twice, when she was still training."

"What, makeup and manicure, that kind of thing?"

This elicited a grab from Jerome. He turned and grabbed Christina with both hands, picked her up, which wasn't difficult, and began to trot down to the water's edge, while she made as if to thump his chest in mock outrage. She was only wearing her bikini, and he his swimming shorts. Reaching the sea, he ran in up to his waist and threw her as far as he could, laughing all the while.

She didn't come up for around twenty seconds, just enough for Jerome to start to worry, but then he felt her hands around his ankles, as she wasn't visible owing to the foam cause by the splash and Jerome's legs running through the water. He was toppled over by her tug and pretty soon they were both under water, she quickly throwing her arms around him and drawing him to her. Thus came their first kiss, and Jerome was in seventh heaven.

Walking back up the beach to the sun bed and their towels, they both knew that the dynamic between them had shifted. Jerome now felt a slight embarrassment, mixed with a charge of excitement over what may follow, while Christina slipped an arm through his.

"What does Amanda look like, Jerry?" She asked, trying to sound as uninterested as possible.

They both knew why she'd asked that question. The instant she said the words, Christina regretted it. She'd wished she hadn't asked. For they both knew the implications. To ask what Amanda looks like was to suggest that, if there were a resemblance between either herself and Jerry's sister, or between her mother Marsha and Amanda, then it would point the finger at Julie, Jerome's mother. They'd both been in Lyneham at the same time, and Amanda was the same age as Rebecca would be now, if she was still alive.

The dynamic changed once again, and only minutes after it had done so before, but this time for the worst, at least for the time being.

Arriving back at the sun bed under the awning, Christina withdrew her arm and picked up her towel. She began rubbing herself down, while Jerome did the same with his own towel. Neither spoke for a minute or two, each acutely aware of the other and how they were reacting to this newly awkward situation.

"Sorry." Said Christina. "I didn't mean anything by that. It didn't come out right."

Jerome thought about it. At first, replying to her apology with a forced smile, he thought how offensive the idea was. Why, there had to have been a couple of dozen women around Lyneham with young babies at the time. And anyway, like the police even conjectured, Rebecca would more likely have been stolen to order and spirited away to some distant place, where it would be all but impossible to find her.

Yet, he couldn't help but see where Christina was coming from. Was he showing unswerving loyalty to his mother when he ought at least to consider the possibility that it had been her? Yet how did she explain that she'd been through the whole process of pregnancy and childbirth herself, she had the birth certificate for goodness sake. How, or why would she want to steal a baby when she already had her own? As far as he was aware, Jerome only had the one sister, not two.

As the two of them sat down beside each other again, Jerome said:

"Look, it's no problem. I'm sorry if it looked like I took offence. I suppose my initial reaction was shock that you might even think that my sister could actually be your sister and somehow my mother had been the one to steal her. But it wouldn't make sense anyway. I mean, Mand has a birth certificate and mum went through the whole process of giving birth, so it wouldn't make any sense to think that she'd stolen your half-sister, would it? I read much too much into your question.

"It's me who should say sorry, not you. It's only natural that you'd want to build up a mental picture of my sister, including what she looks like. I don't know what possessed me. Do you forgive me?"

"Of course. But do you forgive me?"

"Nothing to forgive."

"Then how will you show me that?"

He did, with a lingering kiss on the mouth.

A third change in the dynamic between them in a matter of five minutes. Jerome said:

"She's tall, about five eight. Don't ask me what that is in metres and stuff."

"It's OK, I am half English remember."

"Yeah, forgot that. Well, she has dark hair, wavy I'd say, and, although I suppose I've never thought about it before, she's pretty, beautiful even. Not as beautiful as you though. She has green eyes."

Now it was Jerome's turn to be embarrassed. He blushed. But then, so did Christina.

"You think I'm beautiful, then?" She looked at him sideways, smiling.

Now he was tongue-tied. So he slid an arm around her and pulled her to him.

He replied, "What do you think?" Then he kissed her again.

A few metres away, in the shade at the front of the building, at the back of the dining terrace, Nikos looked on with interest. He well remembered the way it used to be. His own mother was married at sixteen and others he knew had been married a couple of years earlier. In the more remote rural areas, things were still like that. It was rapidly changing now though, largely due to the advent of television and, more latterly, the internet. 'Young women in remote villages these days,' he thought to himself, 'are no longer screened off from the outside world.' Although he was not so sure if that was a good thing or not. Not much he could do about it though. So he was more amused than concerned to see the goings on between his daughter and his useful summer 'guest.'

He had admit, though, to being more than a little curious about what they talked about.

16. Near Bowden Hill, Late July 2018

A middle aged woman in shorts and wellington boots, was walking her Jack Russell across the fields near Sandy Lane, a village on the A342 in Wiltshire. It was a good summer, with warm weather and infrequent rainfall so she didn't need a thick coat or jacket, yet the boots were a precaution, as she was walking through fields and woodland. A thickish fleece was enough to make her work up a sweat as she strove to keep up with the enthusiastic dog running ahead of her.

This part of Wiltshire is a beauty spot, and could well be described as a typical English rural idyll. The village is situated near the gentle slope that ascends to Bowden Hill, not far to the West. Scattered about the countryside here are coppices and small patches of woodland, some of which are fenced in to conserve them against too much footfall from walkers. Some of these enclosed areas haven't been walked in for many years, possibly decades.

It was early evening, at that time of year when the evenings seem to go on forever. After all, it was little over a month past the longest day of the year. It was the season when the blackbirds are still singing, just about, maybe for a couple more weeks. Wrens and robins, chaffinches and chiffchaffs also provided the musical backdrop, as well as the occasional pheasant. Buzzards too, cried from high above, their eerie high-pitched tone causing hearers to look up and search the sky.

About a hundred metres across a field from the quiet road leading from the thatched cottaged, chocolate box village of Sandy Lane towards Chittoe Park, there's one of the aforementioned coppices, surrounded by a sturdy wooden fence, backed with wire mesh, in the centre of which lies a small lake. The lake, which could probably better be described as a large pond, goes by the name of Leech Pool. Rarely does anyone, apart from those charged with the care of the countryside, go near the place.

The dog walker approached the fence, with the purpose of skirting around it and heading on across the countryside and on up gentle Bowden Hill, from where she planned to circle back around to her car, parked on the road near Sandy Lane's pub, the imposing, yet very welcoming George Inn, which almost resembled a manor house. As she walked alongside the fence, she was annoyed by the fact that her feisty dog, Dandy, found a way under the fence and darted into the thick of the coppice, becoming lost to sight.

"Dandy! Dandy!! Come ON! Get back here!!"

Dandy did not oblige. Rather, his owner could hear him scuppering about and then the sound of paws scratching the ground drifted to her ears from somewhere within. She called him a few more times, but he wouldn't come out. There was nothing for it, she'd have to scale the fence and go in after him. She was probably in her early fifties, not slim, but then not overweight either. She was a regular walker and her stamina was good.

With a final heave she got herself to the top bar of the fence and jumped down on to the thickly weeded ground among the trees on the other side, where she began thrashing her way through the undergrowth, dappled early evening sunshine occasionally dazzling her eyes.

Snapping off lower twigs and thrashing away the occasional cobweb, after twenty five metres or so, she saw the Jack Russell, which was completely absorbed in its pursuit of pawing the ground in a small clearing. Here the weeds were not so high and the sun reached the floor without hindrance from the tangled branches of the beech, oak and horse chestnut above, all of which were still verdant, since autumn was yet a few weeks away from beginning its miraculous transformation from green to gold, red and copper.

"What are you doing Dandy? What's so interesting, eh?"

She reached the dog and tried to pull him away from his work, but it was a hard-fought struggle. He wined as she held him by his collar high enough to stop his paws from reaching the soil. There was something there, something that one wouldn't expect to find in a clearing in a small untouched coppice in a Wiltshire beauty spot.

It was what looked very much like the remains of an old towel.

17. Marsha, Late July 2018

Sitting on her sofa in front of the TV on the evening of Friday July 28th 2018, Marsha had a tray on her lap and was munching a baguette filled with salad and cold chicken. On the table in front of the settee was a glass of fruit juice, beside her slipper-clad feet.

She fiddled with the TV remote as the six o'clock news began on the BBC.

"Good evening. Our top story tonight: The body of a young baby has been discovered by a woman walking her dog in a remote beauty spot in Wiltshire. Police say the body seems to have been there a long time, possibly decades, but forensics are still digging up all of the remains and preparing them to be sent to the laboratory for examination. They want to be sure that there was only the one body, which up until now it looks like is the correct assumption."

While Marsha watched, her hand now inched from her mouth, her arm having stopped half-way when this headline was announced, the TV picture cut from the studio to a coppice in the middle of a large field, which was surrounded by Police tape, one or two vans close by and with a large tent evidently having been erected near the fence. The reporter was standing a few metres away and about to give more information about the story.

"Last night, a Mrs. Enid Cadwallader, from the Wiltshire town of Calne, was walking her Jack Russell past this coppice behind me, when she says the dog took an unexpected turn toward the fence and burrowed through under the wire meshing. She tried to get the dog to return to her, but it refused, causing her to have to scale the fence and go in after it. She is reported as saying, 'He doesn't do this kind of thing. He's a spirited dog with a lot of energy, but he's usually very obedient and likes to stay close to me when he's off the lead. So I suppose I knew that something unusual was in there.'

"She says that for some inexplicable reason the dog was trying to scratch away the soil in a small clearing, not far from Leech Pool, the small lake which is situated in the centre of this coppice. When she managed to pull the dog off, eventually securing his lead to a bush nearby, she scraped away a little more of the soil to discover the remains of an old towel, and visibly poking through the towel was what looked like a small bone. At this point she had no idea what it might mean, but was far too – as she herself put it – 'lily-livered' to go any further. She then called the police and waited for them to arrive, when she then gave them a statement.

"The police say that the towel was very rotted, but still identifiable as a bath towel, and that the bones proved to be those of a small infant, not more than six or eight months old. Evidently, the shallow grave had finally come close to the surface after years of erosion, including rainfall that had worn away the slight mound that had been left by whoever dug the hole. In the undergrowth nearby, the police have also found an old garden fork with a rotted wooden handle, which could well have been the tool used to dig the hole.

"As of yet, there is no word as to how long the baby's body could have lain there, but the police are confident that a close examination will determine pretty accurately when it was buried..."

The reporter then gave their own name and the picture switched back to the newsreader in the studio.

Marsha dropped her baguette, which came apart on her lap, lettuce, tomato, mayonnaise and chicken pieces going everywhere. She switched off the TV with the remote and sat, staring at the blank screen and struggling with a mind gone riot.

She'd always been able to convince herself that her Rebecca was still alive somewhere, that she'd been spirited off and given a new identity. That she'd grown up none the wiser and was, hopefully, some day going to find out that her family wasn't really hers, that her birth mother was somewhere else, and she'd want to go and find her.

But what if whoever stole her was a local girl after all? What if the thief panicked when her neighbours got suspicious? What if it meant that she had to get rid of the baby after all, for fear of being caught? She might have simply smothered the child and gone off to this remote beauty spot to bury her, to hopefully escape discovery, and hence punishment? There were so many 'what ifs,' but she had to believe that, once the police laboratory was able to determine when the baby had died, or at least have been buried, they might yet come to call, even if it was twenty-one years since Rebecca disappeared. She'd heard that the police never close cases like hers, they simply leave them on the back-burner until new evidence comes to light, if it ever does.

And if this baby did prove to be Rebecca, how would she deal with it? Perhaps, despite the intense pain, it might lead to some kind of closure. The not knowing was the worst of it, surely. Twenty one years of hope. Twenty one years of conjecture, of imaginings, of staring at every other baby she ever saw, even though Rebecca, had she been alive, would very soon not have still been so small. It didn't seem to matter, the passage of time. It was like her baby had been frozen in a moment; that, until she could be found, she'd remain a six-month-old infant, in suspended animation somehow. All those years of trying to picture what she'd look like now, what would have been her style, her abilities at school. Twenty-one years of delusion, if this child were indeed her.

Whilst her mind would tell her this, her heart still led her to look at every baby stroller, every mother changing her baby in the toilets at a local café.

A thought struck her, ought she to phone the police, remind them of her case? Surely they'd have it all still on file somewhere. It was very doubtful if the same detective would be around to pursue it, or that young policewoman, Helen Drysdale. But whoever was now serving in the same capacity may well be glad to hear from her. But then again, maybe a dozen other women would also be ringing them up, some of them genuine, some of them those sick types that waste police time. Marsha herself was now forty-seven, that young policewoman would be somewhere near that too, and the detective, well he must surely have retired by now. She almost reached for the phone, but stopped short.

'Yes, yes, that was it. At least wait until they announce how long that baby's been there. Maybe it's only ten years, maybe it's thirty years. No point getting too agitated until you hear,' she told herself.

But that didn't stop the tears from flowing. Out from her tear ducts they came, and they flowed copiously, they flowed like a river and she found herself reaching for a box of tissues, the one she kept on the lower shelf of her coffee table. Her job as a dental receptionist was steady, and her position secure. She had a good boss and had worked for him for many years now, yet she couldn't see herself going in to work the next day. She felt nailed to the sofa, it was rather like the way she'd been when Rebecca first disappeared, she was losing all ability to function as it all came flooding back, fresh as if it were yesterday in her mind and heart, the latter of which was now once more rent in two. In fact the pain was so intense that she pressed a fist into her sternum, in a vain attempt to dull the aching. It didn't work.

She sat there motionless until the clock on her wall said ten o'clock. She grabbed the remote and once again began to watch the BBC news bulletin. She hung on every word, but very little had changed since the six o'clock report. The only appreciable difference was that the police had now confirmed that it appears that there was only the one body, there were no others. They'd also taken the fork away for examination, because perhaps that too would yield some clues. Although after so many years lying there, there was no chance of any fingerprints being extractable.

So, apart from getting up and going to the bathroom once or twice, Marsha sat on that sofa until eight o'clock the next morning, when she mustered up the strength to call her employer. The phone had rung at around seven am, when she usually got up to get ready for work, and she'd seen the number on the caller ID. It had been Christina, in Crete. More than likely she'd seen the news there too and wanted to talk to her mother, to see if she was OK. Marsha hadn't the strength to talk to her other daughter right now. Her boss told her not to worry, they'd manage for today. He'd call her that evening to see how she was. She normally only worked a few hours on a Saturday anyway.

She knew he would call. He was that kind of boss.

At around eleven am, her mobile phone rang, the call this time showing as a local number that she didn't recognise. She didn't answer it. Half an hour later her doorbell chimed. She got up and stared along the hallway, and could see through the frosted glass that it looked like two police officers standing there. A feeling of cold dread came over her and she struggled to walk along the hallway, yet she knew that it was the only way. What had they come to tell her? Did they know it was her baby that had been found?

She reached the front door, ran a hand through her dishevelled hair, grasped the latch and opened it.

"Good morning ma'am, are you Marsha Travers?"

"Yes, yes, I am. Come in."

"Thank you." They stepped inside, a couple of young officers, one male, one female. She thought, 'They look so young, like teenagers.'

"Ms. Travers, you'll no doubt have seen the story on the TV of the baby they found up in the wood near Sandy Lane?"

"Yes, I saw it." She could think of no other words with which to continue. She led them through to her lounge, where the remains of last night's dropped baguette still adorned the sofa, the rug and the coffee table. "I'm sorry about the mess. I'm afraid I was a little unsettled last night. It's Rebecca, isn't it."

"No, no, that's not what we've come to tell you. Well, let me qualify that. We don't want to upset you more than is necessary Ms. Travers, but, as of yet we don't know the identity of the victim, but we do know that the lab says it was likely around twenty years, give or take a couple either way, that it had lain there. This would place it in the 'window' of your baby's disappearance.

"Now, of course we were quick to go back over past cases, and yours stuck out as a very, very likely candidate to have some connection with this find, but what we need, in order to confirm the child's identity, is a DNA test. That's why we've come, we'd be grateful if you'd consent to provide us with some saliva in a small glass bottle, which we have brought with us. With that and a few cells from the bones that were discovered, we can know within a few hours, a day or two at most, whether the child was yours, or is entirely disconnected with your case.

"Would you be willing to provide the sample we request, Ms. Travers?"

Marsha didn't bother to correct them since, although she no longer lived in Crete with Nikos, they were still married, and her surname had been Papadakis for some eighteen years.

"Yes, yes, of course." She replied. The young woman officer produced a sterile plastic ziplock bag, within which was a small glass phial with a plastic lid. Inside that was a cotton bud.

"All we need is for you to wipe the cotton bud along the inside of your mouth, along the cheek if you like, and then to pop the whole thing into this glass tube. The top goes straight back on and it's isolated from contamination until it gets to the lab. That's it."

The young officer handed Marsha the phial and she did as she'd been asked. When the bag was once again sealed, the two officers got up to leave.

"Look, Ms. Travers. It may not mean a lot, but we really hope this is not a match, we really do." They both gave a half smile and turned to walk back along the hallway to the front door. As the male officer opened the door, he turned and added a final thought:

"We did attempt to call your mobile number earlier, as we had it on file from when you first got it. Is it still the same number, or have you changed it?"

"No, no, I haven't changed it officer. I'm sorry, now I know it's you I'll answer it next time."

They both smiled in thanks, slightly doffed their hats and went off along the path to their waiting car.

'How odd,' thought Marsha. 'That a little glass tube may mean the difference between hope and hopelessness, between a glimmer of light and total darkness.'

Her phone was ringing from the lounge. She went straight to it and saw that it was her daughter Christina again. This time she swiped the screen to answer the call. Her dear daughter's voice spoke tinnily in her ear as she held the device up to the side of her head.

"Mama? How are you. I take it you've seen the news. I saw it last night. What's happening? Do you know anything?"

Marsha explained the visit from the two police officers.

"That's good isn't it? I mean it will probably be someone else's baby, right? Why would someone steal a baby only to kill it? Doesn't make sense. It can't be Rebecca then, can it? Keep strong mama, it's bound to be business as usual. There is still hope."

Behind her daughter's voice she could hear an English person muttering a few words, a male.

"Is that your 'friend' Jerry with you?" asked Marsha.

"Yes, of course. You know, I told you, didn't I, that his mum could easily have known you. His sister is about the same age as Becca would be, you know all that. The fact that she lived in Lyneham when you did. Still can't understand how your paths never crossed."

"I don't believe I've told you Chrissie, that I do remember another young single mum living just along the road from me. Maybe that was her, I don't know. We never really talked, apart from an occasional good morning. You'll have to ask your boyfriend where his mum lived exactly. I think the one I saw now and then used to jog a little too.

"Anyway, look, as soon as I hear from the police about the DNA results, I'll phone you. Don't you worry about me, OK? I'm fine."

She wasn't at all. And her daughter knew that perfectly well.

18. Marsha, Late July 2018

Marsha watched the TV daytime news on the Sunday, to see if there was anything new reported, even though she knew that there would be no announcement as to the baby's identity until she'd been privately informed. As the bulletin began, she found herself almost unbearably stressed.

"Police have announced that they are looking into links between what's being called the 'Baby in the Wood' case and an unsolved disappearance from twenty-one years ago. The case of the six-month-old snatched from outside a quiet rural post office in the heart of Wiltshire was never solved, and the police say the case is still open. It's understood that officers have visited the disappeared child's mother in the past twenty-four hours to take a DNA sample, to see if there's a match with her and the remains that were discovered on Friday, not more than eleven miles, or eighteen minutes by car, away. A police spokesman told BBC News that the baby in the wood does appear to have been there for

approximately the right period of time to match the time of the Lyneham baby's disappearance. The results of the DNA test are expected either late on Monday, tomorrow, or early on Tuesday morning."

That was all they said, and Marsha switched off her TV. As she did so, her mobile chimed, revealing that someone was trying to make a video call using Viber. She looked at the device and saw her husband's face. She tapped the screen to answer the call.

Nikos' face appeared before her, brow furrowed, as he began,

"Marsha, how are you? We've heard the news. In fact, it even got mentioned on Greek TV news today, because they knew that you'd moved out here some time after Rebecca disappeared. I'm expecting some TV reporter or other to come knocking on our door any time soon. They're probably going to want to 'expand' the 'human interest' side of the story."

"I'm not too good Nik, have to admit. It's hard having no one here to lean on."

"I'm..."

"No! I'm not blaming you, or Chrissy, it's just hard, that's all there is to it. I know I chose to come back here. I know you'd still have me back. I don't deserve it, but I know you're still hoping that I'll come back. I can't bear the waiting, but I suppose, if it's the worst, then I may at least be cut free from it. All the ties that keep me here, in the pathetic hope that my baby'll come back to me somehow, would be cut. Perhaps I would be able to finally forget this place and come and live with you again."

"Look, Marsha..."

"I know I made it hard for you towards the end. You knew what you were taking on with me, though, Nik, right? And I couldn't explain it then, and I can't now, except to say that I have no choice in this. While I can cling on to the faintest trace of hope that she'll knock my door one day, I have to be here. I can't go anywhere else, I can't. I can't..."

As she spoke, the words were coming harder, and her self control was slipping away. She wept. She had wept so many times, so many tears over the past twenty-one years. Would there ever be an end to it? Nikos was torn to shreds at the other end, as he watched the screen image of his wife begin to shake, as her hand lost all semblance of stability. She had to put her phone down on the table, while she grabbed at tissues with both hands. Nikos found himself staring at the ceiling light fitting, two thousand miles away, all the while hearing his wife's sobs. He was in pieces too, yet knew he could never regret having fallen in love with this woman, and having tried to bring her some relief, some solace.

"Marsha, I could come over. I know it's the season, and I'm really busy, but you can't be on your own now, not with this on your shoulders. I think Chrissy and Jerry could cope with the place while I'm away. They'd manage. He's proved to be such a help that boy. I really would like him to stay on, make it all legal. And chef and the Ukrainian girl are both capable.

"Marsha? Talk to me. Shall I come? It's high season, I could get a flight from Heraklion, be with you in a few hours. What do you say? Marsha?"

The sound of sobbing continued, but he saw the image blur again as her face came back into view.

"No, Niko, No. You need to be there. Who'd do the buying? What would happen if the VAT people came calling? Have you thought of that? You can't come now. You can't come until November." She was referring to the fact that November would be the first month of winter, when the taverna would be shut down and people in the area who didn't have olives to harvest would be free to do other things, like travel, for instance.

"Look, I have to go, I think I'm going to go to bed and see if I can sleep a while. I do love you Niko, remember that. You saved me, you know that?"

"Marsha, Look..." But she cut the call. He tried to reconnect, but she'd put her phone on silent and left it on the coffee table while she'd gone into the kitchen to make a hot drink to take to bed with her.

In Makrigialos, Nikos went on-line. He was looking for a flight. He glanced out toward the brilliant light beyond the taverna's beach terrace. There on the beach he could see his daughter, sitting beside Jerome, as she always seemed to be now, the both of them deep in conversation, her arm draped casually around his neck.

They too, were talking about this latest development in Chrissy's mother's tragic life.

"What if, and I know it's maybe far-fetched, right? But what if it happened another way?" said Christina. "What if that baby died somehow, so the parents buried it and went and stole my half-sister to replace it."

"Yeah, that is a bit..."

"No, wait, Jerry. Doesn't it make things all neat for them? I mean, I've been thinking this past twenty-four hours. If they'd had a cot death, Sudden Infant Death Syndrome, or whatever, what if that happened and they knew about mum and her baby? If they lived nearby and could study her for a week or two, maybe longer. They could have planned the snatch. If they didn't tell anyone that their baby had died, and they were out and about, with what appeared to be their child in the neighbourhood, then who'd be the wiser?"

"Yeah, but Chrissy..."

"It's brilliant when you think about it. I mean, if the police came knocking when they did the house-to-house search, they'd be able to produce a birth certificate and everything, wouldn't they? No one would think of doing a DNA test, because everything would be in order. It might be callous where my mother's loss was concerned, but you have to admit it's a clever plan."

"Yebbut, don't midwives do follow-up on new babies in the UK? They might not have the same system here, but over there, surely the midwife doing a home-call, the doctor's surgery or someone would spot something suspicious."

"I know this, mum told me. The midwife only calls for up to ten days after a baby is born. If everything goes well, that's it. If the people who did this, assuming that's what happened, then moved away, then the doctors and nurses at their new surgery would be none the wiser, would they? I'm going to tell mum about this, see what she..."

"Chrissy, OK, maybe you have something, but maybe it's best to at least wait for the DNA results before going off on this. Perish the thought, but if that baby does turn out to be your missing half-sister, then that would be an end to the matter, apart from the police trying again to find out who'd put her there."

Back in Lyneham, Marsha was lying under her duvet, shivering, although it was summer. Her mind was unable to tear itself away from her wild imaginings about that poor child in the woods. Was it buried while still alive by some young girl in a panic? If so, what would it have gone through, being placed in the ground wrapped tightly in a bath towel? Even if it had already died, all she could do was imagine the insects, the grubs, the mammals in the wild. The days, turning to weeks as that poor lost child lay there, in its shallow grave, with no one to grieve for it. The days when it rained, snowed even? The months, the years.

And if it were to turn out to be her own child, her sweet, dimpled little Becca? How would she react? How would she find a way to go on, to put this all behind her finally, after all those years of conjecture.

As she lay there, fretting, biting her lower lip until it became swollen, her pillow becoming wet with her tears, she finally, after a couple of hours, fell asleep from sheer exhaustion.

But she dreamt of bats flying through woodland clearings, of a baby's cries in the wild, lonely countryside, and no one to hear it. No one to pay it any mind. She dreamed of four-legged creatures in the pitch dark, sniffing around on the ground immediately above that poor forgotten child.

And her other daughter, out there on a beach in Crete?

Christina began to wonder about her boyfriend's mother. Wasn't there just too much about her history to leave it un-researched? Hadn't she been a single mother living within a very short distance from Marsha? Of course she'd deny ever knowing Marsha, if she were the guilty party. Stood to reason didn't it?

'Yes,' thought Christina. 'Jerry's mum would surely have known my mother. So, if she'd had nothing to do with this, surely she'd have acknowledged knowing Marsha when Jerry told her about meeting me. But she said she never knew mama. That must suggest that she's covering something up. It wasn't all that long after the snatch that she married Jerry's dad and moved away, so convenient for her.'

Yet how to broach this with Jerry, that was the problem. Ought she even to do so at all? Maybe she could wait, and she had to admit it would be difficult, but maybe she ought to wait until she eventually got to meet this Julie or, more importantly, Jerry's sister Amanda. She hadn't seen Jerry video-calling his sister, so she hadn't been able to see her face. What if there was a resemblance?

'God,' she thought. 'How am I going to feel if Amanda turns out looking like mama, or even like me?' The more she mulled all this over, the more she became convinced that there was something to her theory. Maybe Jerry's coming here was more than coincidence. Maybe it was fate's way of revealing a terrible deception and, eventually, seeing it all put to rights?

Christina was young, yet she believed her feelings for Jerry to be genuine. Maybe they were, who knew? Young girls getting into a lasting relationship at her age have made it work. Equally, people twice her age 'falling in love' have soon fallen out again. If it turned out that Jerry's mother had been the one who'd stolen her own half-sister before she was born, what would that do to her relationship with Jerry? Would it survive such a crisis? Christina believed it would, but she couldn't be sure about just how Jerome would react. He'd been a bit prickly when she'd simply asked what Amanda looked like before, at least initially. But she was sure that, whatever was the case, he didn't know about it. She was sure that his mother had never revealed what she'd done to either Jerry or to his dad Gavin. She had no proof of that, but she just felt it deep down.

How to go about finding out the truth, that was her biggest dilemma right now. First and foremost, though, she had to get to at least see Amanda, better still, to meet her face to face. If she were able to do that, she believed that she'd know.

Instantly, she'd know.

Yet, if Amanda resembled either her or her mother, why hadn't Jerry seen that right from the start? 'Why hasn't he told me,' thought Christina, 'that I reminded him of his mum, or his sister, or both? But then,' she thought on, 'boys don't see these things, especially when the likelihood of all this isn't apparent to them.'

No, that wasn't any reason not to think that Julie was guilty. Christina, from that moment on, was on a mission. She'd get to the bottom of all this.

And in the end, they'd all thank her for it.

Next morning, Monday July 31st, Marsha was in her dressing gown, once more on the sofa, clutching a mug of coffee, but not drinking much of it. It was around eleven am and her mobile phone chimed into life. She saw the number and knew it was the police calling. She stared at it for a second, not wanting to know the result, yet needing to know it. She knew she had to answer it. Picking it up, almost as if it were infected with some deadly virus, she tapped the screen to answer the call.

The nice lady on the other end told her that the lab had come through with the result. They'd worked over the weekend and that was why it was earlier than expected. Pressure from the media, that kind of thing, the lady said. The baby was not Marsha's Rebecca. It was 99% certain that it was no relation whatsoever. Marsha thanked the caller, who said that an F.L.O. would be around to see her, to see if they could offer any support and explain what the police would do now.

Marsha thanked the lady officer and put the phone down. She truly didn't know whether to be glad or not. Had it been Rebecca, she could have laid the whole thing to rest. Painful though it would have been, she'd have been able to close this whole chapter of her life, one that had plagued her for over twenty years. Now, though, it would be more of the same. The not knowing, the speculation, the clinging to threads of hope, it would all go on as before. She didn't know how to feel. She was numb.

Later that day the doorbell rang and she once again opened it to the police. This time it was a lone policewoman, a young thing who introduced herself as PC Janet Green. Once they were both seated in the lounge, PC Green began.

"Marsha, if I can call you by your first name..."

"Of course."

"Marsha, now we have a new case that's been opened owing to this discovery. There will be new enquiries and a new appeal for witnesses, anyone who may be able to shed some light on this, anyone who can remember that long ago seeing something, hearing anything, that they might have thought suspicious and didn't think worthy of reporting to the police at the time. Perhaps someone from Sandy Lane saw a vehicle parked in a farm gate that they didn't recognise as local, perhaps someone knew someone had had a baby, and then it disappeared.

"We must also pursue another avenue of thought. Has it struck you that the person who buried this baby may have been the one who stole yours? In a disturbed state of mind sometimes, a mother in such a situation will do very irrational things. So if you can, and please don't feel pressurised, but if you can, try and visualise the road you lived in back then and who else lived nearby. Was there anyone you knew, even only to say hello to, who might perhaps be a possible suspect? If you can put your finger on anything, it may help with our enquiries.

"I know it's a long shot, and I don't pretend to understand what you're going through, but I'd like to think that we might, we just might be able to get somewhere. It has happened before, you know. Cases like this have been re-opened due to some unexpected development and it's led to a conviction, or to an outcome that's solved a long-lasting mystery."

PC Green got up to leave, fingering her cap, she said, as she made for the hallway. "You know, it's precisely because of cases like yours that I joined the force. I wasn't the type, I'm still not, to see myself chasing villains down back alleys. No, but trying to get to the bottom of a case that causes deep hurt to someone, now that appeals to me. To think that I might make even a small difference to someone's life, that's why I joined.

"I'll see myself out. But I'll be back in touch." She smiled weakly, and left.

19. Christina, August 2018

The more she thought about it, the more Christina persuaded herself that Jerome's mother Julie could well have been the baby-snatcher. There were so many things going for her theory. She was a single mother living in the same small country town as Marsha at the same time. She'd told Jerome that she didn't remember Marsha, and yet how unlikely that would have been, at least in Christina's mind. She hadn't met Jerome's father Gavin until months after the snatch, giving her ample time to get baby Rebecca to adjust and think of her as her real mother, after all she was only about six months old when stolen. Julie could so easily have fended off the police when they called during their house enquiries. She was a single mother, yes, but she had her baby and she had the birth certificate to show for it. There had been no body discovered and so the police would have thought, 'Well, she has one child, so where is the second? If she'd stolen Rebecca, what possible motive could she have had?'

The whole scenario became more and more likely in Christina's mind. If only they could do a DNA test on Julie, that would prove it conclusively.

Christina was very besotted with Jerome, of that there was no doubt. She really didn't want to endanger their relationship, but she couldn't shake off the doubts in her mind, and began to seek ways of broaching the subject without engendering irritation in him. Their relationship was still very innocent from the point of view of many British youths. This was understandable when one considers the environment in which Christina was growing up.

Jerome would no doubt have liked to progress it further, but he knew that he didn't want to spoil his relationship with Niko either. His life this summer was proving much nicer than he'd expected, and he got a real buzz out of seeing some of the tourists who became regulars at the taverna, whether it be under the umbrellas on the beach, or in the restaurant area, going through their agonies about having to fly home at the end of their holiday, while he stayed right where he was. It was something special not to have to cut his stay short owing to time constraints, or financial ones. He'd hardly spent a penny for several weeks and was saving up the tips and the extra cash that Nikos would slip him when he was in a generous mood which, much to Jerome's delight, was quite frequently.

Jerome's ego was boosted by the attentions he received from Christina and, although their relationship hadn't progressed much beyond kissing and throwing arms around each other, plus the occasionally boisterous wrestling match in the sea, he was fine with that, because his life in general was simply ideal, even Arcadian. He liked that word, he'd only recently come to understand its meaning.

The young Englishman was, though, for the present, entirely ignorant of his girlfriend's growing fixation with his mother's past.

Christina lay awake during the night, unable to sleep for theorising over the possible outcomes, were it to be true about Julie, Amanda and her own half-sister, Rebecca. Her mental gymnastics over the whole case led her down all sorts of avenues. Before Jerry had turned up, Rebecca had simply been some ethereal being that existed in a kind of half-reality. Something that could not exist outside of her mother's mind, although affecting her deeply. Now, since Jerome had arrived and she'd learned of his mother's history, and thus his older sister's, she found herself imagining more and more frequently what her own older sister would look like, what she was doing, where she was living. She didn't really consider the possibility that Rebecca could be dead. And now that her father had spoken to Marsha, and then received a text from her telling him that the remains of the baby found in the woods in Wiltshire were not a DNA match, Christina was all the more desperate to see Amanda, to study her features and see if there were indications, clues as to whether her theory was correct.

She had to tread carefully, but told herself that she had to try something.

In the heat of the middle of the day, she took Jerome yet another cold beer from the fridge, as he lay sprawled on the sunbed under the beach shade, ostensibly on 'umbrella' duty, yet with his earphones in and some thrashing music no doubt assailing his brain. He was barely awake, yet became aware of the deepening shadow as Christina came to stand over him. She was very tempted to rest the bottom of the beer bottle on the centre of his chest, but wasn't in the mood to be picked up and carried at a pace down to the sea to be thrown in – yet again. And this despite the thrill it usually gave her from the close body contact they both enjoyed during the process.

He opened his eyes, saw the beer and slowly swung his legs around to sit up. She sat down beside him as he pulled his phones from his ears and passed him the condensation-covered bottle, its top already removed.

"So," she began, "Does Mandy work for herself, or for a company?"

"Oh she works for a spa. They're all the rage in the UK these days. Women drop in during their lunch breaks, after work, on their days off, all believing that to have an Indian Head massage, or some ridiculously expensive beauty treatment or other that they'll stave off growing old. Can't see it makes any difference myself, but they pay small fortunes for the privilege. Mandy wears a white coat and looks all official while she lights candles and rubs oil all over people. Still, she's happy, and it pays well."

'Great!' thought Christina, 'He hasn't sussed.' She pressed her advantage: "Does she get much paid holiday leave then?"

"Oh, a few weeks a year. Pretty much par for the course in England, why?"

"I just thought, with you over here for the summer, it would be a good opportunity for her to come over for a week or two. It would be dead cheap for her, 'cause she could stay here, of course. Would she want to come, do you think? Does she maybe have a boyfriend, or something that would affect her freedom to come at the drop of a hat?"

"She has to book her time off to fit in with the other girls. I don't even know what she'd planned for this year. Last year she had two holidays, one she went to Vegas and the other Phuket. Anyway, I don't see her that often to be honest."

"She doesn't live at home with you then?"

"Nah, she moved out the year before last. She's in Bath now, in a swish flat near the city centre. I think the spa is in one of those posh Georgian terraces or crescents. Nice place. Did you go when you were over there?"

"No. But I've seen the photos. I'd like to go some time, if I had someone to act as my guide, you know..."

"Oh, I think that could be arranged."

"So, does she have a man then?"

"I don't think she does, not right now. She's had a few relationships, but seems determined not to be tied down just yet. She's got a bunch of friends. They do a lot together, including holidays and stuff."

Although Christina was aching to keep this going in a particular direction, she couldn't help herself at hearing that, so she asked, "And what about you, Jerry? You want to stay a free spirit, like your sister?"

"Oh, I don't know. There may be one or two reasons why I might be different from Mandy on that score."

"And what might they be, then?"

"Well, I could be looking at one right now."

With that he slid an arm around her back and pulled her to him. They kissed and she slid her arm around him too, enjoying the feel of his hot skin under her fingertips. She rested her head on his shoulder.

"You don't think I'm too young then?"

"Too young for what?" He was teasing her now, and she knew it.

"Too young to make decisions about what I'm going to do with my life. I mean, I finished school this year. I don't know what I want to do, except I don't really want to be away from here, from dad. I can't think of anything that would make me want to spend years away. It's so perfect here."

'Let's tease him back,' she thought.

"What if some prince charming were to woo you away with promises of seeing the world, then?"

"Well, I don't know. I suppose if he was good-looking enough..."

"Counts me out then."

"Not at all. In fact, it very much counts you in." She replied.

And with that, she decided to abandon her strategy for the moment. Too much other pressing business.

A couple of days later, they were alone at the breakfast table. Nikos had explained that he had to go to England for a few days. After all that had taken place during the past week, he'd decided that he had to go and support Marsha, to give her someone to lean on. He knew that there was no way she'd be able to come over to Crete right now. There was, after all, a new spate of police activity since the discovery of the body of the baby and Marsha's expectations and aspirations were stimulated anew after years of simply lurking at the back of her mind and somewhere deep in her damaged heart.

It was Jerome, Christina, chef Manolis and the foreign girl whose name Jerry could never remember, left to hold the fort. Christina decided to have another go.

"Why don't you call your sister, invite her over. We could have a good time for a week or two. Who knows, I may make a good friend and you'll be left all on your lonesome for a few days."

Jerome stared at Christina for a few seconds. Was he picking up the vibe from her? Did he smell a rat? Then he spoke:

"OK, I'll ring her. But I doubt she'll be able to change her plans any time soon. After all, it's already August. But I suppose it would be a good idea. At least she wouldn't be able to have a go at me when I go back for not having asked her to come, I suppose."

Those words, 'when I go back,' they stabbed Christina in the heart, rather unexpectedly. She began to think about the fact that, in something like seven or eight weeks, this could all be over. She found herself sick at the thought.

"So, you will be going back then. At the end of the season I mean?"

"Well, I have to I suppose. I should be starting at uni. To be honest, until I said that, I'd quite managed to put it out of my mind."

"How will you feel, when it comes time to go?" She couldn't help it, she went on, "About me I mean?"

"Oh, Chrissy, Chrissy. Let's not think about it. It's ages away yet. Might never come."

"But it will, won't it. If we're getting involved, serious I mean, now, how are we going to feel almost two months on from here?"

Now Jerome felt the pain, deep inside. He hadn't expected this when he'd set out for what he'd expected to be a hedonistic, no-strings kind of summer. What had he got himself into? Yet, despite all the uncertainty, the possible heartache further down the line, he was glad.

"We'll work something out, I'm sure. If we still feel like this in October, we'll have to work something out, won't we?" He was trying as much to reassure himself as he was Christina.

"I hope so, Jerry. I hope so."

She got up, cleared some of the breakfast things, and went into the kitchen.

Marsha heard the doorbell, it was early evening. She walked along the hallway, seeing the silhouette through the frosted glass, feeling some familiarity with it, yet not coming to any conclusion. There was just something, but nothing she could put a finger on, about that shape. She opened the door, expecting it to be a cold caller, but was stunned to see her husband standing there, holding a small travel bag in one hand, which he immediately dropped as he stepped forward to take Marsha in his arms.

Nikos had never been to England, yet he'd managed to work out how to find Marsha's modest little flat, and one way or another, by plane, bus and taxi, got himself there. He thanked a distant God that he had a passport, which he'd used to travel to America once, some years ago, to visit some people who'd patronised his taverna while on holiday in Makrigialos and insisted he come and see them in Minnesota.

As he'd travelled, he'd come to the realisation that somehow, in some way, he would have to get back together with Marsha. After what had gone on recently, and how she'd been once again put through the mill, all the reasons why he'd fallen in love with her twenty years ago were still valid.

He noticed how she gave herself to his embrace, which was a good sign. They stayed that way, on her doorstep, for a full two or three minutes, as she descended into tears. But these were tears more of relief than of pain. They flowed because she realised too, that, even though she'd told him not to come, she was so glad that he had. She could not go on without someone to help her through, without a shoulder on which to lean. No more could she deal with this alone, and she didn't want to anyway.

Eventually, she felt his embrace loosen a little, and she stood back to allow him to enter the hallway. She led him through to the kitchen and then into the bedroom, he closing the door behind them.

Next morning she awoke to find her head resting on her husband's bare chest and it felt good. It felt right and she realised that she hadn't felt so safe in years. She lifted her head to see that he was already awake, his hand stroking the back of her head. He smiled and said:

"My darling, this is long overdue."

"I know," she replied, "I know."

"I've called Amanda by the way." Jerome said this as he found Christina in one of the upstairs studios, cleaning it for some new arrivals due later in the day. Her hair was all falling out of its pony tail and she was wearing a pair of rubber gloves. She stared at him, half smiling, waiting for him to go on.

"Well, she's coming. She had a bit of leave due, and hadn't taken it. As luck would have it, no one else is off next week, so she's going to see if she can get a flight for Wednesday the 8th. So, you'll get to meet my sister, then you can lay all your suspicions to rest, little lady."

She felt a moment's alarm as he said this, but saw that he was smiling as he spoke. She was hugely relieved that he seemed to not hold it against her, but rather, she hoped, understood her doubts and fears.

Despite the wet rubber gloves, she ran to him, jumped on to him, wrapping her bare legs around him, and planted a big kiss on his nose.

Jerome found himself hoping that his sister would indeed not prove to look anything like his girlfriend's mother.

For he too, almost to his own surprise, had a modicum of doubt in his mind.

20. Marsha and Nikos, 2018

Nikos and Marsha had spent a couple of days talking, talking some more, then more again. They had both come to realise that they wanted to be together, if it weren't for the small matter of whether Rebecca would ever come looking for her birth-mother, and, if so, could Marsha cope with living anywhere other than Lyneham?

Nikos was sure they could work something out. Maybe if they left information at the post office about Marsha's whereabouts, or gave it to the local police. Surely Rebecca would think to enquire in either or both places, wouldn't she, if she came looking? Then there was the possibility of putting something on-line. Maybe Marsha could start a blog and explain the whole scenario to whoever out there might want to read about it. This idea did actually appeal to Marsha, since she felt that there'd for certain be others in similar circumstances who may want to exchange thoughts, encouragement, etc. Plus, surely if Rebecca had any clues as to where to look, she'd go Googling and then almost certainly arrive at Marsha's blog. Nikos considered this a possible breakthrough idea.

Marsha had to admit that, despite having told Nikos not to come, she was extremely grateful that he had. He'd already spoken to Manoli, his chef, plus the 'kids,' as he now called Jerry and Christina, and everything seemed to be OK at the taverna. In fact, Christina was enjoying front-of-house duty and Manolis had expressed the view that she was probably a better draw to passing potential diners than her dad was. Easier on the eye for starters. It had only been a few nights, but Manolis was sure things were becoming busier during the evenings.

Jerry was a bit miffed at Christina being tied to the front door for a few hours, but, on the other hand, they'd already enjoyed a couple of intimate evenings taking moonlight dips, as well as hanging out at one or two of the music bars at the other end of the bay well into the small hours. Ulrika, the Finnish waitress, was doing OK at table and Jerry was making sure he kept all debris cleared quickly after diners left.

On the morning of Saturday August eleventh, PC Green turned up again, to bring Marsha up to speed on the investigation. The TV news had made scant reference to the case after the initial furore had blown over. Sitting down in the lounge, having been introduced to Marsha's Greek husband, PC Green began:

"Well, I'm afraid things aren't progressing very fast, sadly. There was an appeal made for anyone who may have been in the area of Sandy Lane around twenty to twenty-one years ago and remembered anything out of the ordinary, but no one has come forward. It was nigh on impossible to pinpoint an exact date when the child had been buried, so it was decided to focus on the dates relating to baby Rebecca's disappearance. Working on the assumption that the person or persons who buried the child had then gone on to steal Rebecca, they'd arrived at somewhere around late August to early September 1997, since, as you know only too well, your baby was stolen on September 18th. Those were the dates that they tried to put into peoples' minds, yet still no luck.

"Well, that is if you discount the idiot that rang in to say he'd seen the aliens land and take off again. There's always one, I'm afraid, sometimes several. Sick they are, when you consider the pain that victims are going through.

"We've interviewed the landlord and staff of the pub in the village, some of whom are now retired, but the landlord's still the same person, well – couple, as it happens. But they knew nothing. They said they don't remember anyone coming in who looked like they were overly nervous, or didn't come from the local area.

"I'm sure you'll agree that it's very difficult for people to isolate what they did or didn't see during a couple of weeks over twenty years ago. It's usually only possible if you can relate the dates to something memorable in their lives. That way, sometimes, other stuff is still in there and can be brought back to mind. As it happens, there was a momentous event around the time we're looking at. On August 31st, 1997, Princess Diana had that car crash in Paris and died soon afterwards. A lot of people remember what they were doing when they heard that. All through the next couple of weeks the story dominated the news. So it is just possible that someone will yet remember something that they thought was out of the ordinary by relating it to the sad news about Diana, but there are no guarantees, I'm afraid."

Marsha and Nikos continued to sit, hands entwined, as they listened. They could see that the young policewoman wasn't finished yet.

"We do have one or two other lines of enquiry. For example, we discovered that, according to the electoral role, plus the records of the house-to-house enquiries that were made following the incident – sorry to make it sound so matter-of-fact, but that's how we refer to it – there were one or two other single mothers living in the vicinity when it took place. When the initial enquiries were made, everything seemed to be in order with each of these other mothers, but with this new discovery, there is the possibility that one of these, or even a couple with a young baby, lost theirs for whatever reason, and then stole baby Rebecca to replace her.

"It could have been 'Cot Death,' for instance. Someone, especially a young mother on her own, without the emotional support of a partner, could well have become unbalanced enough to do something like this. So we are following that up now, and will be trying to trace those other mothers, even couples, who were living near you at the time. If they'll consent to a DNA test, it will clear them if they're innocent. Of course, if they're guilty they will object to a DNA test. That alone, of course doesn't prove guilt, and they have the right not to cooperate, but it will probably make us look very closely at their daughter and their circumstances in order to try and prove the thing one way or another.

"I must stress, that someone who's innocent may object to a DNA test. I can't really get why they would, but there are people out there who are very suspicious of such things, believing that maybe their personal DNA will go into some permanent database and some day be used against them, or something like that. Some may just simply take offence at the whole idea, protesting that they think it's insulting that they are even implicated. Then there are those who perhaps don't want their partner discovering that the child isn't actually his. In our experience, though, once we explain that it's our duty to explore every avenue, however unlikely, the majority will come round.

"But, once again, no guarantees I'm afraid."

The PC closed a small file she had before her and stood up. Marsha said:

"You wouldn't like a cup of tea or something, before you go?"

"No, thank you anyway. I have a busy day and ought to get on, but I really wanted you to know that we're doing our best and that, as far as I'm concerned, we'll leave no stone unturned. I'll see myself out, don't worry."

Both Marsha and Nikos now spoke over each other as they thanked the young PC for coming and at least holding out the hope that there may yet be a breakthrough. They heard the door close and looked at each other. Nikos spoke first.

"It sounds like there may be something. I'm impressed that they seem to be able to check those others who were living near you in similar circumstances. That's got to be a high probability, I'd say."

"Yeah, well, I've been through all this before. But thanks. I need someone to make me look at the positives, not the negatives.

"Mind you, and I nearly forgot with all this going on, Chrissy did tell me something when we talked a week or two back that I thought was really weird. You have that young lad staying with you, helping out, and seems he and Chrissy are getting on like a house on fire, right?"

"Yes, Jerry, Jerome. Unusual name for a young *Anglos* I thought. He's a nice boy. I could do with one like him."

"Well, didn't his mother live in Lyneham at the time too? Chrissy said he has an older sister who'd be about Becca's age. And she wasn't with anyone at the time, his mother that is. Jerry's dad came on the scene later. I bet it was her."

"Whoa, whoa, Marsha, you don't know that. Hold on a little. Let's not go running away with an idea and then get disappointed when we find out it's all wrong. You could get into serious trouble if you go making accusations."

"There'd be no harm in telling the PC about her, though, would there? I mean, OK, if it isn't her, then what's she got to worry about?"

Marsha picked up her phone and stabbed at the screen.

"What are you doing?" asked Nikos, although he thought he already knew the answer.

"I'm calling PC Green."

21. Christina, August 2018

Jerome was driving Niko's pickup around the periphery of Heraklion airport and getting quite stressed out. There were buses and coaches everywhere, people crossing in front of him towing wheeled cases, and then stopping to go back for a toddler or two. There were policemen in short-sleeved shirts and smart caps with shiny peaks looking like it wouldn't be a good idea to mess with them, as they all carried arms, and it was the first time Jerome had driven so far on the other side of the road, and the first time he'd experienced Greek drivers.

He was starting to get seriously stressed out about where he could pull over, going round each of two roundabouts that were only about fifty metres apart, and back again. He pulled out his mobile phone and stabbed at it to call his sister, whom he reckoned must be at least at baggage reclaim by now, hopefully on her way out of the building.

"Hello Jerry! You outside? I'll be out in a minute, I've got my case. Where are you?"

"In driving hell. No, sorry. Anyway, great. When you come out head up across the car park and you'll see a couple of roundabouts, one's got a lot of car hire offices near it. If you end up at that one don't go any further to your right, walk back the other way. I'm in a dark red Toyota pickup, belongs to the boss, I'll shove the flashers on and pull over and you jump in smartish, OK?"

"No problem bruv. Can't wait to see you."

No sooner had he thrown his mobile down on the console between the seats, than he saw his sister, looking amazing in a pair of white canvas pumps, tailored white shorts and navy strappy sun-top, towing a bright red wheelie-case with a rigid extendable handle. She also had a small rucksack on her back, also bright red. She looked like she'd just stepped off of a yacht.

Jerome tooted to get her attention, whereupon she looked around, saw him, waved and jumped up and down on the roadside. He was soon able to skid to a halt, jump out, throw her suitcase into the back and open her door for her. Within thirty seconds they were on their way back up the link road to route 90, the national road, which was a modern dual-carriageway at least for a few kilometres back in the direction of Agios Nikolaos.

"Great idea, baby bruv. I wouldn't have thought of it, but now I'm here, bring it on. How's it hanging?"

"All good Mand, all good. I can't believe my luck to be honest. It's very tempting to just stay here and never go back for uni, or anything."

"Wow, you are smitten! And not just with this young cutie you've told me about. Looking forward to meeting her and dishing the dirt on you."

"Now, c'mon Mand, I'm..."

"Jerry. You know I'm only teasing."

A look of relief spread across his features. He always was slow to get his sister's humour.

"...Probably." She added, a look of mocking slyness painting itself on her face. She reached across and tousled his hair. "So, how long does it take to get to this little paradise you've found, then?"

"About two hours, depending on the traffic. The road to Ag. Nik. is pretty good, then it becomes a little more patchy after that, but it's not too bad, mainly. The coast road east from Ierapetra's OK. Traffic's nothing compared to back home, anyway.

"We'll be there well in time for you to get settled in your room, then for us all to eat a meal together this evening. You're gonna love the location, Mand. It's stunning."

In the early evening Christina was setting the last of the tables in expectation of the evening sitting. She'd told Ulrika to sit out front for a change. The Finnish girl was well able to charm any passers-by. She glanced at her watch and reckoned that Jerry and his sister ought to be appearing any time soon. She'd got to play it cool. If there did seem to be any striking resemblance with Amanda to her own mother, she needed to hold her horses. She still wasn't sure how she ought to handle this whole 'investigation,' as she called it to herself, without messing everything up. She decided that she'd have to get to know Amanda, hopefully win her confidence, so that she'd then be able to probe deeper without Amanda becoming suspicious. Whatever she did, she didn't want to mention anything about what happened to her mother's first child at all.

And that would be difficult. After all, if Amanda had been talking to her own mum, she'd probably have heard about the conversation that Julie had had with Jerry about the stealing of Rebecca. It would be very likely that she'd already know about the Wiltshire connection. She was just going to have to see what happened. But she decided that, whatever direction their conversations took, she wasn't going to be the one to start on about that subject until their friendship was firmly established, always assuming that it would be.

Another aspect of all this that bothered Christina, although not enough to want to call her 'investigation' off, was that she had to remember that Amanda was innocent in all of this anyway. Whether she was, in fact, Chrissy's long-lost sister, or no relation whatsoever, she would obviously believe the latter. Chrissy, at least to begin with, didn't want to start her down the road of doubting her origins until she felt that the evidence was really convincing. Already, of course, to Chrissy it was. But she had to try and understand how someone unbiased would view what she had, which was simply the fact that Jerome and Amanda's mum had lived in Lyneham at the same time as someone had stolen her older sister from outside the post office, that she had been a single mum too and that she had denied knowing Marsha, which, to Chrissy, seemed very unlikely.

The pickup turned off the road and parked up beside the taverna building. Chrissy went around the side of the building to greet the arrivals. When Amanda got out of the pickup she couldn't immediately see any obviously familiar facial features, although her hair was rather like the natural colour of her mother's, before she started getting it out of a bottle, that is. But then, mousy-blonde wasn't all that rare in the UK, when all said and done.

The girls squealed from delight as they ran towards each other, both excited to finally be meeting the other, but for very different reasons. Jerome grabbed Amanda's case from the back of the vehicle and, after having given them a couple of minutes to prattle on (as he viewed it), he interjected.

"Let's get you settled in your studio upstairs, then you can freshen up if you want to, and come down and chill for the rest of the evening. You'll have plenty of time tonight to get acquainted."

Both girls gave him a look of disdain, which morphed into a mock grimace of "*get you*," before Amanda broke from Christina's embrace and went to follow her brother up the outdoor staircase that led to their rooms. As she ascended the stairs, she looked over at Christina and gave her a huge smile, before adding:

"See you soon! You're every bit as beautiful as my kid brother makes out, by the way." She then winked, as she knew that this would embarrass Jerome, and disappeared behind the rendered, whitewashed stone wall that served as a bannister.

Jerome came back into the restaurant a minute or two later, obviously keen to hear Chrissy's first impressions.

"So, what do you think of my big sis, then?"

"She's gorgeous, Much better looking than you had me believe. Does she look like your mum?"

The moment she'd said the words, she worried. Would he take that the wrong way too? She knew that eggshells were everywhere right then. Seeing a look of possible suspicion on his face, she hastily went on, "because, if she does, your mother must be a stunner too."

"I don't think I've ever shown you any photos, have I?" Jerome asked.

"No, you haven't. I was beginning to think you had…" She was going to say 'something to hide,' merely as a joke, but realised it wouldn't have gone down the right way.

"Had what, Chrissy?"

Now what was she to do? She'd already dug a couple of shallow holes, but was now in danger of digging a full-scale man-trap and falling into it herself. And Amanda had only just arrived. Time to go on the attack, she decided.

"You know what, English boy? You're in danger of becoming paranoid." With that she gave him a big kiss on the lips and started adjusting the cutlery on the nearest table.

Jerome visibly relaxed his shoulders, "Sorry Chrissy, I shouldn't be so suspicious, should I? Look."

With that he pulled out his mobile phone and began swiping the screen. When he was ready he thrust it toward Christina, screen towards her. She stopped huffing on a knife, wiped it with a clean white napkin, and extended a hand to steady the screen so she could examine the photo it was displaying.

"Your mother, right? Julie?"

"Yup. Taken about last April, so only a few months old. It's in the back garden of our house in Salisbury. She loves gardening, as you can see behind her."

"Nice looking woman. How old is she now, then?"

"Mum must be forty-seven. Dad's not much older, you want to see a picture of him too, see where I get my good looks from?"

"Of course."

Jerome retracted the phone and swiped a few more times, then showed it to her again.

"That was taken at some dinner they went to, to do with dad's work. He likes dressing up in his dinner suit. Makes him feel like James Bond, I reckon."

"Oh, yes, smart-looking guy. I wouldn't say you were a lot like him. But you do have similar hair, except yours hasn't gone grey at the temples yet. I'll soon sort that out." She giggled. "So, who does Amanda take after, character-wise I mean?"

She was taking a bit of a risk here, but she couldn't help herself. Jerome hesitated, seemed as if he thought better of something, and answered,

"If I'm honest, I'd say she's more like mum, after all, dad's not her birth father, remember?"

"Oh yes, sorry, forgot about that." She decided that she'd got away with that one. "Did your mum ever talk about Amanda's father? Must have been pretty hard for her. Your dad's obviously a caring man to have taken on a young baby along with his new girlfriend like that."

"She did tell me a bit some years ago. Not a great deal, except that his name was Phil and he worked for a printer's in Swindon. She thought he'd stick by her, but when she told him she was pregnant, he cleared off. I think she found out that he was the sort who two-timed his girlfriends anyway, so it looked like he never learned to have a sense of responsibility. She thought she loved him at the time, but soon 'got real,' as she put it, once his true colours came out.

"Did I tell you how she and dad met?"

"No, only that she had Amanda when she'd lived in Lyneham. Didn't know my mum though."

"Well, it's not that interesting a story. They both liked the same band that was playing in Bristol at the Colston Hall. They met in the bar, he took her home, since they both lived quite a drive away, and the rest is history. Mand was only a baby, and he adopted her legally when my parents got married. She knows the truth, but, as far as she's concerned, Gavin Pillinger is her dad, since he brought her up, and she has no recollection of him not ever being there for her. I think she knows the name of her birth father, but, to be honest, I'm not sure about that. I do remember some years ago, I must have been about ten, and Mand twelve, when mum and dad sat us all down out on the patio one evening and told us the whole story. Mandy didn't bat an eyelid. I think it affected me more than her, and

I'm the son of both of them. You never know how stuff is going to affect you emotionally, do you?

"To be honest, too, I don't recall my sister ever referring to the subject again. She's legally dad's daughter anyway, and so what happened in the year or so when mum fell for her, gave birth and then met dad seems to not be of any importance to her at all. I take my hat off to her, really. She's a strong girl."

With that a few drops of water landed on both of their heads, causing them to look up. Amanda was drying her hair with a towel, whilst standing at the parapet of her balcony. Looking down at Jerome and Christina, she called out,

"Wow, Bruv. You were not wrong. I can't think of a better view to have from a balcony. It's so, ...well, so beautiful. No wonder you don't want to leave."

Jerome looked at Christina when his sister said this. She returned his look, betraying the hurt that she was going to feel when that day came for him to set off back to his real life. 'If only he could be persuaded to stay.' She thought.

Not much later Amanda came down, dressed in a loose cotton blouse over a pair of denim shorts. Her feet were bare. Christina fussed over her and settled both her and Jerome at the best table at the edge of the dining terrace, close enough that they could rise and step straight on to the beach from there. She told them that this was to be Jerry's night off, and that she was going to make sure they were fed like royalty, while they'd be able to talk until they dropped once they were all settled at the table, wining and dining, so to speak.

She was true to her word and soon the table was groaning under all the dishes, not to mention a carafe of house wine and a couple of beers for Jerome. Christina could hardly contain her curiosity and found she was trying very hard not to stare at Amanda, trying to see if there was anything that might indicate that they were related.

And there was something. There was, she was sure. It was something about the nose, the shape of the eyes, even the way Amanda moved her head. Christina was sure of it. The indications were there. They weren't striking, but they were there. Amanda had hardly arrived and Christina was bursting to dig deeper. She was desperate to ask again about the circumstances surrounding Amanda's birth and where exactly she and her mother had lived when she was a baby. She might not recall too much herself, but there was always the chance that Julie had told her things, information, maybe even let slip one or two indications about what had happened.

As the evening wore on and she watched the two half-siblings talking, she became conscious that she was making Amanda feel uncomfortable. She was in danger of causing a major upset, yet seemed driven on by an internal urge. She burned to relieve her mother of all the heartache, the mystery, of not knowing. She was restless, agitated, needing to get it all out into the open. She even found herself seeing Jerome's arrival here, in Markrigialos of all places, as some kind of sign that she was the one who was meant to solve the twenty-one-year-old puzzle that had wrecked her mother's life, placed a severe strain on her parents' marriage. How come he came here, when he could have ended up in any one of a hundred islands? Christina's case was becoming watertight, if only in her mind. Fate had decreed that she solve this riddle. So she reasoned.

"Christina? You in there?" Suddenly Christina became aware that she'd gone off into a reverie about it all and that Amanda was trying to talk to her. How long she'd been trying to elicit a response, Christina didn't know, but she could only hope that it hadn't been too long.

"Yes, sorry. I was miles away."

"You did look a bit, well, like the lights were on but no one was home. I was asking, do you miss your mum? It can't be easy with her being over there and you and your dad being here. Jerry's told me about what happened all those years ago. I can't imagine how hard it must have been."

She paused, waiting for Christina's response. Which was difficult for the half-Greek, because all she could do was see her long lost sister in that face, even if the likeness was slightly tenuous.

"Yes, but mama says that she has no choice. She has to be there because one day, some day, she believes that Rebecca will come looking for her birth-mother."

Amanda found it odd that Christina referred to her mum as '*mama*,' but put it down to the fact she was raised in Greece. Greek girls probably called their mums '*mama*.'

"Wow. Seems so unlikely, but I suppose I've no idea how I'd feel if it happened to me."

Christina knew that she had to do something to get out of this situation. If she stayed there another minute she'd be bound to really upset both Jerry and his sister. She pushed her chair back and stood up.

"Anyway!" she declared, "I'd better get a few things done. Dad being away and all that. You guys stay here, I'll bring you some water melon to round things out with." She added the last bit with a weak attempt at a warm smile.

Before either of the others could remonstrate, Christina had hurried off to the kitchen, arms laden with a selection of the debris from their meal together.

"Jerry," said Amanda, "She's lovely, she really is. But I can't help thinking there's something just a little odd with her. I mean she seemed to stare at me for minutes at a time. Is that a Greek thing, then? Or am I just being silly?"

"Well, usually she isn't like this. But, based on what you've seen, I'd have come to the same conclusion."

He wasn't inclined to tell Amanda about Chrissy's wild theories just yet. But he knew, from tonight's experience, that they hadn't been laid to rest. He could only hope that Amanda hadn't been doing the sums too, and realised what was preoccupying her young hostess.

22. Nikos, August 2018

Nikos found a flight to go home to Crete on Saturday 11th. He hated to leave Marsha again, but knew that in the middle of the season, he couldn't expect the kids to manage the taverna for long. He was very pleased, though, that he'd made the effort to come, because it had enabled he and Marsha to resolve a number of things.

Marsha had returned to live in Wiltshire back in 2012, six years earlier. The reason, despite their having had other minor differences, was obvious. She couldn't bear to be anywhere else, because of the uncertainty over her lost child. She'd been back to visit every year, but only for a week or two at a time, but this visit had confirmed to both of them that they wanted to be back together, however they could arrange it. It did seem to Marsha that a website, a blog, plus leaving some contact details with the post office, which was now run by different people, and the police, was the way forward. Sally, who'd been behind the desk in the post office on that awful day back in 1997, was long gone. They were, however, a nice couple there now and they knew the story. They'd be happy to keep Marsha's contact details to hand, they told her, were the improbable ever to happen and a grown-up Rebecca walked in through the door asking if they knew where to find her.

So Nikos was flying home feeling slightly more settled, mulling over the prospect of having Marsha back in Makrigialo with him some time in the not-too-distant future. It would be good for Christina too, of course, to have her mum on hand all of the time. He knew that she missed Marsha really badly sometimes, especially when she had 'female' things to talk over. A dad, especially a Greek dad, wasn't well equipped for such occasions.

As he stared out of the aircraft window and watched England shrink beneath him, his thoughts transferred to what little he knew about Jerome, his mother, and the suspicions that Marsha entertained about her. He'd be seeing Jerome again in just a few hours, and had to fight to persuade himself that, first and foremost, the boy wasn't guilty of anything. He also knew, having talked several times with Chrissy, that Jerome's sister would be there too, when he got back. She too, even if she were Marsha's lost child, was completely innocent. The only guilty party would be their mother, whose name escaped him for the time being.

He'd now seen for himself how small Lyneham was. Surely, when Marsha was walking around with her small baby in a buggy, she'd have come across Jerome's mother somewhere. And wouldn't they even have attended some kind of post-natal clinic or something? It was difficult to believe that they didn't know each other. OK, so Marsha didn't know the other woman, but she had told Niko in the past couple of days of one or two other women of similar age that she remembered seeing around the place leading up to the time of the snatch, and even afterwards. With a little research, maybe on the electoral roles or something, she could probably discover who they were, after all, she did say that one in particular definitely lived in her street, even though they'd never exchanged more than a nod and a smile as they passed each other by. Could this have been Jerome's mother? After all, she now knew for certain that she'd lived nearby.

Nikos was a Greek, and, like the majority of his countrymen, he was superstitious. He, like his daughter, although as yet unbeknown to him, was beginning to draw the same conclusion. Why had Jerome landed right there, not only in Makrigialo, but at his very taverna? There was no way that he could accept the randomness of existence. Like so many people who don't really think it through, he saw meaning in most things that happened, believed that things happened for a reason. Despite the fact that so much works against such a belief, it doesn't appear to stop millions believing such things, although those millions are primarily in the developed countries, where they can have the luxury of such self-delusion. If you're a refugee on an inflatable in the middle of the ocean, you don't have such luxury, for you it's simply a matter of survival.

But Nikos, as he watched Europe passing thousands of feet below him, became more and more convinced that Jerome's mother was the culprit. She'd have to be called to account. There would have to be a DNA test or something. Quite how all of this might be accomplished was still unresolved.

His plane landed at Heraklion just twenty minutes late, not at all bad for a charter flight in August. Coming through passport control and customs was quick and easy, since he had no hold baggage. He knew that Jerome would be out there waiting for him in the pickup.

Jerome, now a man of some experience in picking up someone from the airport at Heraklion, having done it 'all of once,' was parked where he shouldn't be with his hazards flashing. He was learning fast. In Greece you can stop your vehicle anywhere you want to, just as long as you switch on your flashers. No one will bother you then. Oh, they might sound their horns, thrust an open hand, fingers outstretched, in your direction (an insult far worse than the one or two fingered gestures of offence used in the UK), but they'd pass on, fretting, muttering, whatever.

Nikos spotted the pickup the moment he emerged into the warm evening air, and ran at a trot to get in. Jerome started up the engine, switched off the hazards and they were away. Nikos, carry-bag on his lap, spoke first.

"Everything OK at the restaurant Jerry? It hasn't burnt down or anything?"

"All A-OK, Niko, nothing to worry about. Apart from the earthquake that brought the balconies crashing down on the dining terrace."

For just a millisecond Nikos registered alarm, before jabbing Jerome in the side with a fist and bursting out laughing. "You and your English humour, eh?"

Jerome smiled broadly and pulled into the main national route's traffic, accelerating fast. He knew how to handle the pickup now, and he already knew that his girlfriend's dad was also a mad driver, and so wouldn't be bothered if he were to gun it a little.

"You know, Jerry, you really ought to think seriously about what you want to do with your life. I mean, yes, it's OK going off to study history and all, but what practical use is that when you get your degree, or diploma, or whatever it is you get at the end?"

"Well, I could teach, become a lecturer myself, attach myself to some museum or other, become a consultant for archeologists doing digs, I could even..."

"OK, OK, I get that. But what about your quality of life? What is it that makes a man truly happy, did you think of that? I mean, look at me. I never went to university, but I have no real money worries, I have a wonderful place to live, and my stress levels are low. Well, apart from when the VAT men come inspecting now and again. But, you know what I'm saying, right? I'm fifty-two now, a time when a lot of my countrymen retire. I need someone to pass my business on to some day and I'm not likely to be having a son at my time of life now. I think you know how fond I've become of you in these weeks that you've been with us, don't you?"

Jerome could hardly believe what he was hearing. Was Nikos offering to leave the business to him, which would obviously mean that he accepted that there was something special between him and Chrissy?

"What are you saying, Niko, spell it out, please. If you don't mind."

"Jerry, Chrissy loves you, I can see that. OK, so she's young, but my grandmother was married at fourteen. She and my *pappou* had a wonderful relationship, and my own mother, too, was married at sixteen. Sometimes you have to grab what life puts before you. I see in you someone who has a nice way with people. You don't run a successful restaurant if you don't know how to make people happy. Ask yourself, where do you want to be in twenty years' time, eh?

"You could be the owner of a restaurant on the beach on a Greek island, with a beautiful wife and a couple (I hope!) of also beautiful children. If you think about that, you and I could work at it together for, say five or six years, until you've learned to speak Greek and how to do the basic paperwork. I'd be beside you every step of the way. The accountant does most of the work anyway, and Chrissy is very bright with things like that. What more could you want out of life, eh?"

Jerome's mouth was open wide, but nothing was coming out.

"I got to say, Jerry, I shall be very sad if you leave us at the end of the season. Very, very sad. But Chrissy? *Christos kai panagia mou*, she'll be suicidal. A lot of people work thirty, forty years to end up living somewhere like my village, you know Jerry. There are *Anglezoi* living around us now and they're all old. You could be here forever from your younger years, with a very beautiful wife beside you. I know, she's my daughter, but you agree she's very beautiful, don't you?"

"No question about it. I've never seen another girl as beautiful as Chrissy. But, it's a huge step you're asking me to consider. I need to think about this a while. My dad would probably go ballistic."

"You think so? Doesn't he know a good investment when he sees one? You tell me he's a banker. He ought to prefer you to make a career choice like this. I mean, what guarantees do you have to earn a living once you finish at university?"

"Good point. Have to admit that. Bloody hell Niko, I'm flabbergasted, have to say."

Nikos was quite pleased that he'd broached the subject. He knew he'd have to allow Jerry some time to chew this over, but he had the hope that it might just work out well for he and Christina. Now, though, he had something else on his mind, and wasn't too sure about quite how to bring it up.

"Jerry, me and Marsha, we're going to start again. We're going to get back together."

"What? Really? That's wonderful news. Chrissy'll be beside herself. Does that mean that Marsha will be coming back to Crete, then?"

"Hopefully, yes. We haven't worked out the details yet, but we believe that a blog or website of some kind will be enough for her daughter to find her, if ever she learns of her past and wants to look for her birth-mother. And we could leave her contact details with the people in the post office and with the police. It should work enough for Marsha to make the move and cope emotionally, don't you think?

"Sure I do. There are no negatives as far as I can see."

"Can I ask you something else? And before you answer, let me explain. You know how much I think of you Jerry, it's clear from what I've just proposed, right?"

"Of course. And I'm flattered, but you're making me nervous now."

"Well, there's no easy way to say this, but you know that your mother was around when Marsha's baby was snatched, right? And, don't get me wro..."

"Oh, god. This again. Chrissy's been on about this too. It's rather hurtful to be honest. I thought we'd laid it to rest. But I'll admit, I've had my suspicions since Amanda arrived. Chrissy's been acting a bit odd, staring at Mandy and asking odd questions. I'm not stupid, but I hope my sister hasn't sussed anything. It's all getting a bit wearing now. Can't you just leave it? I don't want to talk about this."

"Jerry, look. Give me a moment, please. Try and put yourself in our place, well, Marsha and Chrissy's place. Wouldn't you clutch at any straw you could find? Ask yourself if you can understand how a mother would feel, having her six-month-old baby stolen and never ever finding out what happened, who did it, where the child is now, if she's even still alive. I've struggled to deal with my wife's emotions over all of this, but I have to admit that I can't begin to imagine what she's been through, what she's still going through.

"Jerry, first of all, remember: Chrissy and her mother are not accusing you of anything. They know you weren't even born when it happened. They know that your sister is innocent too. But to have it proved beyond doubt that your sister is really your mother's daughter, well, wouldn't that really be the only way to solve this once and for all? You know what could have happened, in your heart you know.

"A mother, like yours, has a child that dies. She loses her mental balance and sees another woman with a child of similar age. In a moment of madness, it's quite believable that she might dispose of her dead baby and steal another. Think how watertight it would be. She'd have a birth certificate to prove that she has a daughter. No one would be any the wiser. We're not even saying that the woman who'd do this is evil, only that she could easily have lost her reason and balance for a while. That baby that they found in the countryside, it was buried about the same time as Marsha's baby was taken. It seems such a reasonable explanation. All I ask is that you think about it for a while, and you'll see why Chrissy, Marsha and I, yes me too, now I've talked with Marsha about it, we think that it would be only the right thing to do for your mother to be persuaded to have a DNA test. That's all. Once it proves that your sister is really your mother's daughter, that would close the matter. It would still leave us with no explanation about what happened to baby Rebecca, but at least it would clear away any unpleasant suspicions that might otherwise linger between us and your family. No, not your family, your mother, no one else.

"Please, Jerry, think about that. With you on our side, we could maybe persuade your mother to help us here. Yes, that's the way to look at it. She'd be helping close out one of the lines of enquiry if you like. Doesn't that make sense?"

Despite all his yearning to counter Niko's argument, deep down Jerome had to admit to himself, however unpalatable it felt, that Nikos was right. But there was something more.

"You do realise that, if mum agreed to the DNA test, then Amanda would have to as well? I mean, let's just suppose for a moment, that mum tests positive with that baby whose remains were found. It still wouldn't prove that she'd stolen the baby. The only way to prove that would be for my sister to agree to a test too. I'm not sure I can see that happening. I don't know if it's right to drag her into this, after all, she's only ever known dad as her father, and had an uneventful, balanced upbringing. Are we prepared for how she might be wrecked if all this has to be done? Who'd answer for it if she was emotionally damaged by it all?"

Now it was Nikos' turn to doubt, to hesitate. Yet he still felt that the thing had to be pursued. He responded:

"Jerry, you know something? There are lots of situations in life that no one wants, no one finds easy to deal with. But that doesn't mean that they don't have to be investigated. Sometimes, whatever the consequences might be, matters have to be seen through to the end. It's not nice, it's not something that those involved have to be comfortable with, but it's necessary. If there's no other way, then there's no other way."

Jerome once again winced, frowned, internally struggling with the logic of it all, yet fearful of the potential outcome. Nikos added one more thing.

"I have to tell you something else, too."

"Oh no, what?"

"Marsha has already phoned the police to tell them about your mother having lived nearby when the baby was taken. She's told them about the fact that your mother was a single parent with a few-month-old daughter living in the near vicinity. I fear that it won't take long for the police to trace your mother and come knocking at your parent's house anyway, asking if she would be willing to cooperate with their enquiry."

"So, it's already hit the fan, then." answered Jerome.

23. Julie, August 2018

Julie Pillinger hadn't worked for some years. Her husband's income was more than adequate and she was very happy being a 'domestic engineer' and full-time parent. The only problem with the latter of those two was that children eventually grow up.

So she'd begun looking around for some way to occupy her time, now that Jerome was getting near to going off to university and his older sister Amanda had already moved into her own flat in Bath, twenty-eight miles away. Like a lot of women on the wrong side of forty-five, she'd spent twenty years and more entirely serving the interests of her husband and children, and it had left her feeling a significant measure of disquiet about all the time she was now beginning to have on her hands.

She stared at herself in the full length mirror, mounted on the inside of one of her wardrobe doors. That waist wasn't what it used to be. And that jowl. Ought she to think about a facelift? She did give it some thought, but decided that, one: she didn't want the pain, and two: she didn't want to face all the explanations she would have to give to all and sundry once she was ready to again face the world. A third reason was that to maybe cut down on the amount of sherry that passes her lips might also be an easier option.

No, the only thing for it was to get to the local private sports club and start playing badminton, maybe swimming or something too. She had the time, of that there was no doubt. She mused disconsolately that if only she were young enough to have another baby. But, no, that part of her life was gone. The hot flushes, every time she suffered one, were like a sarcastic reminder of that irreversible fact. She decided that, if she were to go through with this, she'd need some moral support. So she phoned Daphne, Trevor's wife. Trevor worked with her husband Gavin in the bank, and the two couples had taken several holidays together, usually on huge cruise boats in the Caribbean, or around the Canary islands in wintertime. The two couples were also prone, during the summer months, to sitting together under the parasols around their patio tables, sipping malt whiskies or gins and tonic and putting the world to rights.

Daphne was up for it, and they'd both gone to join the club. Then they'd gone off to town shopping for the appropriate attire for playing badminton and the right costumes for women of a certain age to wear while doing laps in the pool.

"No point" Daphne had said, as they'd walked out of a major sport retailer's store doors, "in not looking the part. Dressing right is half the battle!"

Julie had agreed, as if they'd needed any persuading, that they ought to shell out for a few short, white plaid skirts and a couple of polo shirts to go with them, not to mention a couple of expensive, top-of-the-range racquets. They also spent a king's ransom on the right kind of shoes for playing badminton. Once again, it would make them feel like they were serious, not to mention accepted, by the already existing fraternity that functioned on the badminton ladder (singles and doubles) in the club. Oh, and sweatbands for the wrists, they had to have those.

It was while she was standing once again before her bedroom mirror, dressed in full badminton garb and swinging her racquet about, that the doorbell rang unexpectedly at 11.30am on August 16th, a Thursday.

Cursing, she went downstairs to open the door. There was no time to change.

She was somewhat taken aback to find two police officers standing on the step in the not insubstantial front porch of the house.

"Oh, can I help you officers? Is there some problem?"

"Mrs Pillinger by any chance?" Enquired the female of the two officers. The other was a male.

"Yes, of course. But…"

"Do you think we may come inside?" The male officer asked, in a manner as to suggest that it would be a very good idea to comply.

Julie walked them along the hallway and out through to the back and the huge conservatory that extended the kitchen out into the garden, at the garden end of which sat a rather expensive set of lounge furniture, affording anyone who was lucky enough to sit there a beautiful view of an immaculately manicured garden, that seemed to go on for ever, and contained three mature oak trees at least fifty metres away from the house.

Extending her hand as an invitation for the officers to sit down, she said:

"Can I get you anything? Tea, perhaps, coffee?"

Once again, the female officer spoke: "No, no thank you. We just need to ask you a few questions in relation to a case we're currently pursuing, if that would be all right?" She phrased that last part as a question.

Julie was suddenly conscious of the fact she was dressed as if she were just about to go on to the badminton court. She asked if she might be excused just for a moment, and the two officers answered in unison, "By all means."

She dashed upstairs and soon returned wearing her robe, its cord drawn tight to hold it together over the badminton clothes. "What can I do for you? This is rather a surprise. Has something happened in the area, a robbery perhaps? Do you want to know if I've seen anything suspicious?" With that she also sat down on one of the sumptuous armchairs.

"Well, it has to do with a case that was unsolved from over twenty years ago. Plus there has been a recent event, by that I mean new evidence, that has come to light that leads us along a new path of inquiry. We were hoping that your memory of events some time ago will help us progress with this investigation."

"But of course, but I can't for a minute imagine what this might be about. What case was this?"

"On September 18th, 1997, you may recall the case of a six-month-old baby being stolen from a baby stroller outside the local post office in Lyneham, as you were also living there at the time, is that correct Mrs. Pillinger?"

Although it was very evident that these officers were trying not to alarm her, Julie could sense an underlying current that made her deeply uneasy.

"I'm not sure. Wait a minute, let me think. Yes, I do remember something about that. It was on the TV news, even nationally if I remember correctly, but they never got to the bottom of it. As I recall, they called it 'The Post Office Snatch', is that it? Is that the case you're referring to?"

"Yes, quite right. The thing is, owing to some very recent developments, we want to interview a number of people who lived in the vicinity at the time, with a view to hopefully helping them to recall anything that might aid us to pursue this case to a successful conclusion."

Julie felt an unwelcome heat run up her spine, and shifted in her seat. She replied, "Well, naturally, if there's anything I can do to help. But I'll be honest, it's all rather a long time ago now."

"You see, at the time the baby disappeared, there were, according to the electoral role and parish records, only four other women of similar age to the victim living close by who were also single mothers, plus a number of couples who also had babies of about the same age. You, of course, were one of those single mothers.

"The victim had lived in Pound Close, and seems to recall knowing you. Well, not knowing you, exactly, but having seen you around and occasionally fleetingly greeting as you passed on the pavement, that kind of thing. Do you have much recollection yourself of Mrs. Pavlidis, who at the time would have been Miss Travers?"

"No, not really. I wouldn't recognise her now, if that's what you were hoping. As you said, we never knew each other enough to be on friendly terms. I know it's a shame, but we tended to keep ourselves to ourselves in that area at the time. I'm not sure what else I can say to help you really.

"But, you mentioned recent developments. May I ask what they are?"

The male officer was doing most of the talking, while his colleague was making short notes on a pad, occasionally sucking the top of her pen between times. "You will have seen, no doubt, the news just under three weeks ago, about the body of a small baby having been discovered in a fenced coppice not far from the village of Sandy Lane, about ten miles from Lyneham?"

"Of course. Awful. I was shocked that such a thing had taken place. Didn't they say that the baby had been there a very long time?"

"Indeed. In fact the lab dated the remains, which were wrapped in what was left of an old bath towel, to around the same time that the Post Office Snatch had occurred."

"But, forgive me, officer, how would it relate to the stolen baby? I mean, it wouldn't seem to make sense to steal a baby, only to kill it, would it?"

"I'm coming to the link Mrs. Pillinger. You see, the more likely scenario would be that someone's child died, lets' say from SIDS, or 'Cot Death,' as it's often known. Now, if that someone had been a single mother, already emotionally fragile after having given birth so recently, then it's quite feasible that she could have, let's say, 'flipped,' as it were. Often, a person in such an emotional turmoil can have a breakdown, certainly can begin to reason irrationally. For example, seeing another woman, perhaps a close neighbour, still walking her infant could push such a woman over the edge. Experts say that in such a circumstance, it would be entirely possible that the woman whose baby had died could begin to reason that she deserves to have the other woman's living child. She might even believe that she'd be the better mother, that the other woman didn't deserve to keep her baby. Or she might not even have considered the other woman's feelings, merely her own and her need to continue to nurse a baby, which she'd very quickly come to believe was hers, once she'd made the snatch.

"Of course, much of this is conjecture, for the present."

Was that a very slight sigh of relief that the officers witnessed in this woman? Perhaps. Perhaps not. Julie asked:

"So, if that's the case, what are you doing here, if you don't mind me asking? You are aware, I'm sure, from your 'research', that I had a daughter, and that I still have a daughter, Amanda. The police came around doing house-to-house enquiries after that baby was stolen. They interviewed me at the time and I showed them Mandy's birth certificate. You're surely not accusing me of anything, are you?"

"Not now, no. But you'll understand, Mrs. Pillinger, that we have to pursue every line of enquiry, however doubtful. You see, the baby that was found in the wood near Sandy Lane wasn't a DNA match for the baby that was stolen. We've only recently compared the DNA from a voluntary sample provided by the mother whose baby disappeared, and it's not a match. This, then would fit with the current theory that I've just outlined to you."

"I'm afraid you've quite lost me now, officer."

"Well, if I can cut to the quick, then. If those few women who were living in the area at the time would be willing to supply us with a DNA sample, we could very easily and quickly eliminate them from the enquiry."

A definite look of alarm this time. Both officers saw it.

"You see, let's suppose that someone in your circumstances, for example, did the switch as I've just outlined. That would mean that the baby in the woods would match their DNA, and the DNA of her daughter, the girl she'd raised as such, would be a match for Mrs. Pavlidis, wouldn't it?

"And conversely, if someone in your circumstances were to test negative on both counts, mother and daughter, then you'd be in the clear. That would be it, as far as you/she were concerned."

A look of full realisation came over Julie's face at this point.

"Are you telling me that I have to supply you with a DNA sample? Is that it?"

"Not at all. As things stand, we can't compel you to do so. We can only ask that you consider cooperating, because, if you're in the clear, and we're sure you are Mrs. Pillinger, you have nothing to hide, nothing to be afraid of, do you?"

The officers both now fell silent. The female officer suddenly found her pad to be extremely interesting and worthy of study, while the male kept eye contact with Julie, waiting to see if she'd blink, or look away. He knew how to read people, or so he thought.

"Do I need to consult a solicitor?"

"What? No, of course not. All we're asking, is that you consider giving us a sample of your DNA. Nothing more. Assuming it tests negative, job done. And, of course, we'd invite your daughter, who isn't a minor any more, right? We'd invite her also to do the same."

"And what if I have other reasons to refuse, would that make me a suspect in all of this?"

"Mrs. Pillinger, the only way we can compel someone to supply us with a sample, is if we were to arrest them. A refusal to supply a sample is not an admission of guilt. Although, I must say, I'd find it hard to understand why anyone wouldn't want to help us with our enquiries."

"Right. So, let me get this straight. I'm not a suspect, I'm a potential witness. Right?"

"Well, if I'm honest, I'd have to say that you do fall into both categories. That's why a sample would resolve the position for you, of course. It's not a reason for you to become concerned. I should add that, in cases like this, all kinds of people are viewed as suspects, until we eliminate them one-by-one from the enquiry. No stone unturned, I'm sure you understand."

"But, what if I have personal reasons for not wanting to give you a sample of my DNA?"

"I can't comment on that. Look, maybe we should give you a while to think about this. What say we come back and see you in a few days, give you a chance to maybe talk with your family, especially your daughter, would that be acceptable?"

'No, it would not.' Thought Julie, although she chose not to voice that opinion. Right now, all she wanted was for these two police officers to leave her house. So she replied:

"Yes, of course. Whatever you say. Now, if you don't mind, I am rather busy right now." Saying this she rose and gestured as if to say that it was time they left. They both rose in response.

When they were once again standing on the front porch, with Julie poised to close the door behind them, the female officer turned to add one last comment.

"Mrs. Pillinger, I hope you'll see this from our standpoint. We have no option but to pursue every possibility in every case. It's nothing personal, you understand?"

Julie simply nodded. They smiled, just slightly, and turned to walk to their car.

What to do now, that was Julie's problem. Before the police officers arrived, she'd been just about to phone Daphne to sort out their first visit to the badminton club, to see just how bad they were at the sport. Now, she couldn't bring herself to pick up her phone. There was an awful lot going around in her mind. There was no way she could bring herself to ask Amanda to give a DNA sample. She'd been so happy that for years and years everything had gone smoothly in the family. Amanda saw Gavin as her dad, even though in the back of her mind she knew that he hadn't been her natural father. How could Julie drag this all up now and throw her daughter's origins into doubt? Plus, there was still another, pressing reason why she feared DNA testing, and it was so pressing that she just couldn't accept it, couldn't take the risk.

No, she'd exercise her right to refuse. There was, after all, nothing the police could do if she did, was there? She went back upstairs to the bedroom to change. Suddenly she felt rather silly all dressed up for the badminton court.

No, whatever they said, she'd have to refuse a DNA test, at all costs. She believed that her family's happiness depended on it.

With all of this, and her other main worry occupying her mind, she quite forgot that the officers had told her that, if they were to arrest someone, they would then have the right to insist on a DNA test, precisely in order to obtain essential evidence.

24. Jerome, 16th August 2018

He'd mulled over Niko's words for a few days, and as yet Jerome didn't know that already the police had been to see his mother. By coincidence, he decided to call her the same evening.

From the time that they'd arrived back in Makrigialo, Nikos hadn't mentioned the conversation they'd had on the drive back from the airport, and had put on a normal face once he was back in control at the taverna. He'd greeted Amanda with a genuine warmth, and on the surface everything looked rosy.

Except that to Jerome, somehow, everything was now different. He still loved Christina, yet had to fight the unpleasant feeling that she'd somehow been the reason for all of this blowing up. Chrissy had started on about how much of a coincidence it was that his mother Julie had lived around the corner from Marsha at the time of the snatch and, to his way of thinking, from that moment on it had started a ball rolling, a snowball that was gathering momentum and size, and it seemed to him that there was no way of stopping it until it hit the bottom of the mountain, with who-knew-what consequences.

He was still very much enamoured with the place and the way of life, except, in the pit of his stomach, he couldn't shake off the doubts about his mother, and what she may have done all those years ago. He now found himself casting sideways glances at his sister, to see if there was any way in which she might resemble Chrissy. After all, if his mother had truly done this awful thing, then that would make the girls half-sisters, however weird that might be. He couldn't see anything obvious, but he also knew that it didn't prove anything. He thought continually about this whole issue of DNA testing, how it would either lay it all to rest, or truly wreck everything. It may mean that Chrissy's mother could finally find some kind of happiness, and yet it would also wreck his own family from within. Why, his mother would probably go to prison. How on earth would his father deal with that?

And how, too, would Amanda deal with it? He couldn't begin to imagine what confusion it would kick off in her mind. He thought, 'Imagine if me and Chrissy do stay together, maybe get married some day, then my legal sister would also be my sister-in-law.'

His head hurt simply at the concept.

Then there was the whole issue of the proposal that Nikos had put to Jerome about staying around and making his home there, eventually becoming, in effect, Niko's heir. It was a tremendous opportunity, and yet a daunting challenge at the same time. It was enough to contemplate all the implications of that, without all this about the case of the baby-snatch and how it might involve his mother. Just days ago he'd been over the moon about how his carefree summer was working out. Now he'd feared that he'd walked into an uproar of potential family disaster and recrimination.

And so, he made the decision to call his mother. He hadn't talked to her in a while anyway. He still hoped not to speak to his father, because he wanted to further mull over all the possibilities of Chrissy, the taverna, and his future before doing that. He truly had no idea how his dad would react. Perhaps he'd be pleased, and yet he might also go ballistic.

So Jerome called his mother on his phone, without using video.

She answered within two rings. It was around 7.00pm in the UK, 9.00pm in Crete. There was a lull in the work at the taverna, and anyway, he didn't do a great deal mid-evening, apart from clearing tables, and there wasn't a lot to be done in that regard for an hour or so.

"Hi Mum, how are things?"

"Hello Jerry. To be honest, I don't really know."

"That's a bit weird, isn't it? What don't you know, then? Has something happened? You haven't broken your leg or anything? Is dad OK?"

Gavin was a member of the local Freemasons' lodge, so Jerome knew it was a pretty safe bet that if his mother hadn't gone to some function or other with him, then he'd be out during the evening anyway, giving Jerome the chance to talk to his mum without fear of Gavin overhearing and wanting to interfere.

"He's fine. Out as usual. No, Jerry, it's been a strange day. I'm not sure I know what to tell you really."

"Maybe I can help. Nikos told me that Chrissy's mum had told the police about you, once she'd found out who you were, following me and Chrissy having compared notes about the time when you'd both lived in Lyneham. So let me guess, have you had a visit from the police, maybe?"

"Spot on, Jerry, and it wasn't a very enjoyable experience."

"So, what did they say? Surely they're only following up every lead, however tenuously it may be linked to the case?"

Julie hadn't thought that she would, and she certainly hadn't planned this, but she went on to explain to her son all about the visit from the two officers. She left nothing out. She knew that there was no one else she could hope to be able to confide in. So it had to be her son, and it made her feel a small measure of relief, once she'd unburdened all of it.

Jerome said, once his mother had finished, and had begun sounding like she may be going to cry, "So you haven't told them if you're going to do the DNA test, then?"

"No, not yet. But I can't Jerry, I just can't."

This was slightly worrying for Jerome. Even though he'd resisted at the beginning, Niko's words were really beginning to sound right to him. Surely the test would exonerate his mum, and thus they could lay it to rest and get on with their lives.

"Why? Or is that a silly question? Is it because you'd have to get Mand to do one too?"

There was a slight pause here, as his mother's thoughts had changed direction somewhat. Quite without warning, she burst out,

"Oh Jerry, why did you have to end up there of all places? If you'd gone anywhere else, anywhere at all, this would never have happened. I can't believe you went to the same place where that woman's daughter lived!"

The distress in her voice told Jerry all he needed to know. He may only have been nineteen, but he thought he knew what was happening in his mother's mind, and he didn't like the implications one bit.

Resisting the temptation to rebuke his mother with an 'Oh, so it's all MY fault now, is it?' He took a deep breath, and tried to remain conciliatory. "Look, mum, nobody can predict stuff like this. It just happens. Life's full of odd coincidences, you know that. I mean, why did you go to that concert in Bristol on the night you did? If you hadn't gone, then you'd never have met dad, would you? Or, what if you'd gone, but not stayed in the bar when the main act came on? Only in that case you'll say you were glad you did, right? We can't go through life looking for someone or something to blame for the stuff that happens. It's just the nature of things.

"And anyway, I know you won't like me saying it, but I can't quite get what the problem is. I believe in you. You're my mother, I trust you. Surely you're innocent and, if so, why not just do the test and have done with it? In a couple of days the police will rule you out and pass on to someone else they can suspect, don't you see that?"

"It's not as simple as that Jerry. You don't understand."

"No, too right I don't." He was, finally, starting to lose it himself now. "Then make me. Mum, tell me what's such a big deal with doing the test."

"I can't Jerry. I just can't. But you have to believe me. Please, believe me! There's a good reason why I can't do the test, but it's not what you think, honestly and truly."

"What DO I think, then, mum? Is my trust in you, is my believing you, misplaced after all? Where do we go from here if you don't do the test?"

"For a start, how do I explain this to your father? He knows nothing about all of this yet."

"SO? If you're not guilty of stealing someone else's child, what's the big deal with telling dad? I still don't get it. Don't you owe it to me, your son, to explain yourself?"

Jerry, as he'd become more heated, had retreated down the beach towards the water's edge, so as not to be heard by the girls and Niko in the restaurant. But that hadn't stopped Chrissy and Amanda from noticing his gesticulations as he became more agitated. The terrace was about half-full with diners, mainly holidaymakers, enjoying the impossibly beautiful setting of a quiet Cretan beach on a hot, summer's evening. They were so wrapped up in their whole Grecian experience that they failed to notice the young man a few metres away, getting heated over a phone conversation.

Chrissy went to the back of the inside section of the dining area, which was totally devoid of diners at this time of the year, and went behind the desk to crank up the *bouzouki* music just a tad on the hi-fi, just to be sure that the diners didn't even begin to notice the agitated young man. Her father was having an involved discussion with the chef, Manoli, so that was all right then. One of the guests, a man in his forties by the looks of him, obviously well oiled with retsina, responded to the music by pushing back his chair, getting up and trying to do a Zorba's dance. His wife or partner was having none of his efforts to drag her up from the table too. The other couple seated at their table responded in different ways. The man evidently enjoyed the spectacle and wanted it to become more raucous. His partner, on the other hand, was clearly embarrassed by their friend's antics and stared around her to gauge the reaction of other diners. No one was giving a monkey's toss.

Amanda was due to fly home in two days. She too noticed her brother's wild gesticulations as he threw his free arm around in frustration while pacing back and forth along the water's edge and remonstrating with his mother. She decided that she ought to go and see if she could do anything to help. She had a pretty good idea what they were talking about, so she thought. She didn't know how far off-beam she was, though.

As she felt the warm sand pushing through her toes, she approached her brother, just in time to hear him say,

"Dad's going to have to know sooner or later."

"Jerry? Is everything OK?" His sister asked, from a distance of around two metres. She was trying to make it seem as though she was concerned, yet hadn't heard anything. Fortunately for him, she hadn't heard the previous comment about what his mother may or may not have done twenty one years earlier.

Amanda was slightly perturbed to see her brother turn towards her and show an expression of horror. She still felt she knew, though, what this was all about. So she said:

"Jerry, why not let me explain to dad? I'm sure he'll come around once he sees how much of an opportunity this is for you. Going to uni isn't everything, I'm sure that dad knows how many graduates are cleaning windows or fixing lattes nowadays."

Jerry, in that split-second, knew that his sister had misunderstood the nature of his conversation with his mother. He hoped that his mother had heard Mandy's words.

"No, look, it's OK Mand, I can handle this. Go back and chat to Chrissy. I'll be back in a minute."

She hesitated, then turned and walked back up the beach. Chrissy had stopped, a pile of plates and cutlery in her arms after having cleared a table, and was standing waiting for Amanda to get close enough to talk. She had a much better idea about what it was her boyfriend was probably discussing.

"What's the problem? Is he all right?"

"Oh, I think so. You must know how tricky he's going to find all of this…"

At that point Christina experienced a moment of doubt. Was Amanda now appraised of the facts, then? Did she know what her possible past may now be? Amanda went on, allaying Christina's fears on that score.

"I can twist dad around my finger much better than my little brother. I'm sure he'll come around. Frankly, once he gets a look at you, he'll be as smitten as Jerry is anyway."

Meanwhile, further down the beach, at the water's edge, Jerome was concluding his conversation with his mother.

"Look, mum. It comes down to this. You either fill me in on your little secret, or I'm forced to re-think my whole defence of you. I don't like it one bit, but you're going to make me think very bad things about my own mother. Now think on it, please!"

With that he closed the call and shoved the phone into his back pocket. He turned to face the sea, slammed a fist into the other hand's open palm and began to cry.

25. Julie, Still 16th August 2018

It was late when Gavin came home. At around 11.45pm Julie heard his car pull up outside and his key entering the front door lock. After she'd talked to the police, she'd changed into some pyjamas and her towelling bathrobe, the one that was really warm when she wrapped it around herself. For some reason, even though it was August and not particularly cold, she felt chilled.

She had no idea how she was going to act normally when he came in. Not only had the police unnerved her, but her conversation with Jerome had not gone at all well, and she felt as though everyone was against her. As yet, she had no idea whether her son had spoken to Amanda about his fears. She hadn't had time to bring that up before Jerome had closed the call. She was never one to drink brandy, but had hit the drinks cabinet and was now on her third from her husband's bottle of Van Ryn's 12 Year Old Distiller's Reserve. Gavin was nothing if not a brandy aficionado.

She stood up from the sofa in the conservatory and went to the kitchen worktop, seeking some way of seeming to be at ease, but it wasn't working.

Gavin appeared at the kitchen door, looked at her standing there, saw the glass still in her hand, and knew things weren't quite right.

"You OK? Sorry I'm late, but you know how it is with these things. Still, no other functions for a few days now. Tomorrow's Friday, what say we go out to eat, eh? I fancy Italian, you up for it?" Yes, he knew that something was bothering her, but was trying not to make it too obvious. He knew her well enough to wait a while. She'd want to unburden herself soon enough.

This time, though, he couldn't begin to imagine quite how serious the problem was. Nodding towards her hand, the one still holding the brandy balloon, he asked:

"Dutch courage? You don't usually imbibe. Out of gin? Or is there something that's got to you today? C'mon love, tell Gavvy." He walked up to her, prised the stem of the balloon lightly from her hand, placed it on the slate worktop, and put his arms around her.

Julie had intended to show a brave face. She didn't want to let on. She'd hoped that she'd have been able to keep it from him. But she couldn't help herself. She burst into tears and buried her head in his shoulder.

"Oooh, now, now, love. Can't be all that bad, surely? Missing the kids, maybe? I know you wish Mandy was still at home. I suppose it is the first time that they've both been away for this length of time. Have you spoken with them today? Is that it? Maybe that old motherly instinct is getting the better of you." He was trying to make light of things, but not very successfully.

After she didn't reply, but simply went on sniffling, he pulled his handkerchief from his trouser pocket and pressed it into her hand, gently lifting it by her wrist to help her wipe her eyes. Still she couldn't speak. In truth, she couldn't think of anything to say that wouldn't give the whole thing away within seconds. He guided her to the solid oak kitchen table, pulled out a traditional beech dining chair and settled her into it. He then walked around the table. Took off his tux, loosened his bowtie and sat down. After looking at his wife for a few moments, still with no words coming from her, he got up again, went into the other room and returned a few moments later with a brandy for himself, plus the bottle, which he placed on the table between them. Then he thought for a second, went back to the worktop and brought her glass over, placing it before her on the table.

"Look, Jules, if it means that much to you, I'll acquiesce if you like. I'm not going to say I like the idea of you working, but if it would make you feel better to get a part-time job again, maybe fill your days a little, I'll agree, how's that?

"I mean, I don't want you doing a Georgie Fame wife act on me, now do I?"

This was a not-all-together tasteful attempt at levity. He was referring to the fact that the singer's wife had committed suicide, so the given wisdom was, back in 1993, by jumping from the Clifton Suspension Bridge in Bristol, after having lost all will to live once her children had grown up and flown the nest. The story had left a lasting impression on Gavin and he'd spent all the years watching his children grow up worrying about how Julie was going to cope once they too had left home. Julie had so enjoyed every moment of their upbringing, the family holidays, the dressing of grazed knees, the school concerts, even the tedious parent-teacher evenings at school, she'd simply been born to raise children. He knew deep down that, if she were able to have another now, then she'd jump at the chance, but it hadn't happened after Jerome, and they'd had to be content with the two. Gavin found that suited him just fine, but he knew that Julie, had she been able to choose, would have loved another one or two, ...or even three.

"Sorry, darling. I shouldn't be flippant. Well, are you going to talk to me, then? I'm listening, you know."

Julie found it all the more difficult to begin, because right at that moment it infuriated her just how good a husband Gavin had been. He always did listen. He rarely raised his voice. Right from way back in 1998, when they'd met and eventually married, she'd marvelled at how he took to Amanda, even though she wasn't his. She didn't deserve him, which made it all the more difficult to tell him what was on her mind now.

Gavin swilled the brandy around in his glass, studying it for a few seconds, before gulping the whole thing down and pouring himself another.

"It's late." He said. "You want to sleep on it, huh?"

She shook her head. This was the first indication that she'd given him since he'd come home that she might just summon the will to begin talking to him about what was on her mind. She opened her mouth as if to speak, then closed it again.

"Oh boy," said Gavin, "it's really that bad, eh? Look, come on love, I'm willing to sit here until you are ready, but I can't help you until you help me." He offered an encouraging smile. Julie found that hard too. 'He won't be smiling in a few more minutes,' she thought to herself.

He reached across and stroked his wife's cheek. Yes, she'd put a little weight on in recent years, but to him she was still as beautiful as the day he'd first set eyes on her in that bar in the Colston Hall. He couldn't criticise anyway. After all, his waistline wasn't what it was, and wasn't likely ever to be so again.

Finally, she felt she could speak. There was nothing else for it. She knew that it would have to come out sooner or later. She composed herself, then, in one breath, she blurted out:

"The police came today. They suspect me of being a child-snatcher."

Gavin did a double-take. His first reaction was to be dumbfounded. Surely he hadn't heard right. It was his turn to open his mouth and not say anything. When he did look like speaking, she stopped him.

"No, Gav, don't say anything. I have to explain it all. There's no point in holding any of it back. You'll hate me for it. Let me tell it all, then you can say what you want."

Julie took a large gulp from the brandy in front of her, then began.

"You know about the baby-stroller snatch case in Lyneham not long before we met, don't you?" She elicited a nod from Gavin, and an indication that he was going to reply, and so hastily continued:

"Well, not long afterwards the police came doing house-to-house enquiries. They could see that I was a single parent, like the woman whose baby had been stolen, Marsha Travers, and so they wanted to see proof that Amanda was mine. Of course I showed them her birth certificate. I didn't have two babies in the house - they made sure of that - and so they left me and went on along the street, and I thought they were satisfied that I was in the clear. End of story, or so I thought."

She was struggling to keep the nausea down, but went on. "When Jerome got to that place where he's staying now, on Crete, Mackery-something-or-other, well, the daughter of the man he's working for is the daughter of the same woman." Here, Gavin's face registered surprise, as she'd have expected. "See, apparently, the woman had gone out to Greece some months after the baby was stolen and, cutting a long story short, ended up marrying the Greek man who ran the taverna where she would eat. They had a daughter, and she's the one Jerry's soft on. How strange is that, that of all the places in the world, Jerry should end up there? They got to talking and it came out that her mother had been the one, and Jerry told the girl, Christina, about me having lived nearby at the time."

"I can see how that would have come as a shock. It's a huge coincidence, but how does that upset you so, love?"

"I haven't got there yet. Wait, Gavin. You heard that story a couple of weeks back about the baby they found buried over near Sandy Lane?"

"Of course, it was all over the news for a while. What's that got to do with us, with you?"

"Well, the police have been putting two and two together. They say that the baby in the wood was buried about the time that the other one was stolen. They seem to think that whoever buried that baby, which they'd probably lost with Cot Death or something, then went and stole Marsha Travers' child to replace her own.

"Now do you see why they came to see me?"

"I'm a bit slow. You said that they saw Mandy's birth certificate. So how come they came to see you now, twenty-one years later?"

Julie again had to fight to keep her composure. She managed to go on.

"They're looking again at everyone who'd lived in the Lyneham area at the time, to see if any of them may have been the possible perpetrator. Now do you get it? They say I could have been the one whose baby died, and then went and stole the other baby. They say that Amanda might not be mine but in fact the child that was stolen from Ms. Travers. Gavin, I'm a suspect."

That was all she could manage before cracking up again. Gavin sat back in his chair, loosened his shirt collar, and stared at the ceiling for a moment. Then he said:

"Wait a minute. Why couldn't that baby they found have been the one that was stolen? I mean, maybe it died after whoever'd stolen it couldn't look after it properly or something. Why should that cast suspicion on you?"

"The news said, maybe you missed it, that DNA testing had proven that the baby they found a couple of weeks ago wasn't Marsha Travers' baby." Now Julie suddenly realised that she was painting herself into a corner. She hadn't wanted to even mention DNA tests. It had slipped out as she tried to respond to her husband's logical question. She gulped and couldn't think of a way out. Before she could think of anything, her husband said:

"Well there you are then. It's simple. All you have to do to prove your innocence is provide a DNA test, and you'll be in the clear. Amanda too I suppose, when you come to think of it. Thinking it through, if you're proven not to be the mother of the baby in the wood, then they'll still probably want to be sure of Amanda's origins, yeah? So, surely it's no big deal."

"I'm not giving them DNA, Gavin. I'm not."

Her husband now exhibited a flummoxed look. "What? Why ever not?"

"It's complicated. But they can't insist that someone provides DNA. It has to be voluntary. Not giving DNA isn't proof of guilt Gavin. People have their reasons."

"And what would yours be, then?"

Now she knew that what she said next would drive a wedge between them, "I can't tell you. All I can ask is that you believe me."

26. Amanda, 16th August 2018

Amanda couldn't stop keeping one eye on her brother, and it alarmed her when he evidently concluded his phone call home and, instead of coming back into the taverna, sat down on the beach, his back to her and facing the sea, and appeared to be in some distress.

There was nothing for it. She had to go down to the water's edge and see if she could find out what was so wrong.

She arrived at his side and sat down next to him. He was crying. The thumb and index finger of his right hand were pressed into either eye to try and stem the tears. Sliding an arm around his shoulder, she said:

"That bad, eh? I told you, though, bruv. Leave it to me. He'll see reason. If it's truly what you want to do, I don't see what's wrong with it. I mean, what an adventure. How amazing that you should come here and all this to happen. There are people who'd give their eye teeth for such a coincidence. As careers go, there's not much wrong with it. I mean, to find a lovely wife and a share in a good business both at the same time, and to be still only nineteen, what's not to like?

"You know dad," she rocked him towards her and away again to emphasise her point, "He's a softie. You just need to know the right moment to bring things up with him. I mean, you wait, give him a few months and he'll be bragging to all his Freemason friends about how his boy's running a restaurant in Crete."

The fact that his sister hadn't cottoned on made Jerome all the more miserable. He'd really wanted to keep Chrissy's suspicions from Amanda, but after this conversation with his mother, he felt as though circumstances, not him, were driving things irrevocably forward. There would soon be no way to keep all of this from her. The sooner she knew the better. As he struggled with his thoughts, and she carried on reassuring him about a situation that hadn't even arisen yet, he felt like he was the passenger on a vehicle that was now out of control.

He shook his head several times, as if by doing so, it would clarify the situation for him, perhaps show him the way forward. It didn't work. Lifting his head a little, and staring out at the vast, twinkling sea, he arrived at a kind of resolve. There was a distant yacht passing in the twilight, its sails billowing. For a fleeting moment, he wanted desperately to be on it.

One way or the other, his sister would have to know what her mother may have been guilty of. She'd have to know about Julie's attitude towards the possibility of a DNA test. She'd have to know that her brother suspected that she may really be the daughter of his girlfriend's British mother. Either way, it would shatter what had been for Amanda an almost seamless upbringing of security and love. It would start her down a road of having to discover her origins. At the very least she'd probably want to now know who her birth-father was, maybe try and find out if he was still living, and, if so, how to get in touch with him. The whole dynamic of the

Pillinger family would shift and never be the same again. At least, that was now how he perceived things.

Amanda misunderstood his shakes of the head.

"Come on, Jerry. You know what I'm saying's right. Think about it."

"You don't know, Mand. You don't. It isn't what you think." He couldn't go on for the moment. He was trying to frame the words.

"What don't I know? Jerry, if I don't know dad, who does?"

"This isn't about dad. I haven't even talked to him about Chrissy, Niko, the business, my future, none of it. It's not that, Mand."

'Then what is it, Jerry? What can be so bad that you're all upset like this? It's not just thinking about leaving Chrissy at the end of the seaso…"

"Mand, listen, OK? I know you mean well. I know you're trying to help. But until you know what's going on, you can't. Even when you do, you probably won't be able to help. Rather, it's you who'll be upset."

"Now you're scaring me. What's going on then, Jerry? What can be so bad that you have tears running down your face. That's not the brother I know. I can only imagine that mum's got cancer or something. Is that it? Yes, of course, she's told you and she hasn't told me. Oh, God, what type is it? Breast cancer probably, or cervical. Oh God, what are we going to do. How on earth…?"

"Mand, please. Stop second guessing me. Mum hasn't got anything wrong with her. Not physically, anyway." He heaved a massive sigh, and went on. It was time. "She's had a visit from the police, Mand. She's suspected of a very serious crime."

Amanda thought for a second. Then replied, slowly, as if trying to understand the words in a foreign language: "Suspected of a very serious crime. That's impossible, surely. I can't imagine that mum…"

"Mand, please, let me explain. I was hoping not to have to, but there's no alternative now. Things have gone too far. You remember when you were a baby, only months old?"

"Well, obviously not exactly. But I know what you mean. You mean when she lived on her own with me before she met dad, right?"

"Yes, right. Have you ever talked in depth with mum about that time? How she was feeling about your real father? If there were any indications that she was uncomfortable talking about it, would you remember that?"

'I've no idea what you're driving at Jerry. But, well, yes, years ago, as you'll know anyway, they told us about how they'd met when I was about eleven months old, but why is that relevant to what's happening now? If you're going to start on about my birth-father, forget it. Dad's raised me from a baby, he's my legal father and, in every practical way, he is my dad. I believe that the person who brings you up, looks after you, pats your back when you cry, plays with you on your swing, all that stuff that parents do, the one that does that is your father in every way that really counts, or means anything.

"And I still don't get why this ought to be connected to you being so upset now."

Jerome took yet another deep breath, sighed and continued:

"Look, Mand, you remember the baby snatch case, in Lyneham, September 1997?"

"Well, I know about it, of course. But I was a tiny baby, so it was before I was old enough to know about such things." She sat there, a puzzled look creasing her brow.

"Well, apparently, the police are linking it with that baby that was discovered buried in the wood over near Sandy lane and Bowden Hill, about three weeks ago."

Jerome searched his sister's eyes, to see if perhaps the penny was dropping. Still no signs.

"Look, Mand, they believe that whoever buried that baby may well have been the one to snatch the other one, the one from Lyneham post office. That snatch happened while mum lived alone with you in a flat in Lyneham, not ten minutes walk from the post office. Although it's a possibility that the child was 'stolen to order' and spirited away to some east European country, the fuzz think that it's more likely this scenario: that the local woman's baby dies, she becomes unhinged, and so steals a baby off of someone else.

"So they're reopening the original case and re-examining all the women they interviewed back then, and our mum had a visit when they were doing house-to-house enquiries. When they called on her back then, she only had you, and your birth certificate to prove it."

"So, slam dunk. Why's that a bother now?"

"Well, look at it from their standpoint. Our mother could have – she could have – well, let's suppose for a moment that her daughter died from cot death. Then she could have been the one who stole the other child and brought her up as her own. Yes, she had a birth certificate to show for you, but what if... Well, what if..."

Amanda's face contorted. Jerome knew that she'd finally cottoned on. And it wasn't sitting well with her. She exclaimed, "What if I were the child that was stolen, that's what you're saying isn't it? You think mum stole me after her own baby died?! What kind of a woman would do such a thing? What would that make me, anyway?"

Now it was Amanda's turn to become emotional. She began to fill up, and Jerome, now feeling stronger for having blurted all of this out, slid his arm around her.

"Look, Mand. I refused to believe it too. You do know, don't you, that Chrissy's mum was the woman whose baby was stolen, right?"

"Which explains why Chrissy keeps staring at me. She's looking to see if I look like anyone on her mother's side, right? How could she...?"

"Don't blame Chrissy, Amanda, please. She's an innocent party in all of this, as you are. You have to try and imagine how it's been for her and her mother for twenty-one years now, well, twenty-one for her mum, and all of her life for Chrissy, or at least, as far back as she can remember. And when Chrissy first threw this side-ball at me, I refused point-blank to believe it."

"So do I. I can't imagine our mum being so calculating, so callous, so selfish."

"Yes, but Mand, I've spoken with mum this evening, as you know. And now I don't know what to think."

"Why? What could she possibly have said that made you doubt her?"

"She refuses to give the police a DNA sample. Why would she do that if she's innocent?"

His sister didn't answer this time, she was crying too much.

27. Amanda, 17th August 2018

She only had one day before flying home. Following the momentous, outrageous, fearsome news from her brother, she hadn't slept at all well that Thursday night. Amanda struggled to comprehend what it might all mean. She'd be flying home, but at least not going to her parents' house in Salisbury. No, she'd be going back to her apartment in Bath. She knew, though, that her mother would want to talk to her, no doubt to beg for her belief, her trust, her confidence.

Yet how could she give that to her mother, when she, like her brother, failed to understand why Julie was refusing to give a DNA sample, which could easily prove her innocence, assuming that she was, of course, innocent? Amanda had arisen at two in the morning and gone down to the water line, where she'd walked several hundred metres along the beach and back again, contemplating who she may really be. She'd always been secure in the belief that at least her mother was really her birth-mother. What if it turned out that she wasn't? That would mean that she and Jerome weren't blood relatives at all. It would mean instead that Christina was her half-sister. At least she'd be able to meet her birth-mother, if that was what Marsha turned out to be. Would they get along? How would they be with each other after twenty-one years?

She knew that she couldn't begin to try and understand what Chrissy's mother had suffered. Had it all been due to her own assumed-mother's callousness? And had it really been callousness, or the deeds of someone who wasn't functioning correctly from an emotional or mental standpoint? Would that have made it more forgivable, if so? Right now, she felt that if it all turned out to be true, she'd never want to see her assumed mother again. But then, what about her father, her legal father anyway, Gavin? How on earth would he come to terms with it? She had no doubts that she loved her dad, for he'd been everything that a good father ought to be for her. Would he cope if Julie were to be tried and found guilty?

There was just too much hanging on it all, too many factors to take into consideration at once. She truly understood at that moment what it meant to say one's brain hurts.

She felt strongly that she didn't want to see her mother at all. Yet, on the other hand, she also felt that she might be the one to talk Julie into the DNA test. Ought she to do that, if only for her father's sake? What if the DNA test showed that she and her mother were indeed not related? She soon came to understand that she too would have to give a DNA sample. That ought to show beyond doubt who she was, where she came from. If her mother were to object to her supplying DNA, would she go against her mother's wishes anyway? She rather believed that she would. The possibility of her mother's DNA matching with that poor child that had been found in the wood was horrifying, for it would reveal that her mother had done something that she considered unthinkable. She'd had a baby, it had died, she'd told no one, buried it unceremoniously and stolen another, 'That was me,' thought Amanda, to replace her. That would mean that she was a second Amanda, the first having died and been secretly buried somewhere where the guilty party had assumed she'd never be found. The thought of her being a substitute for the deceased child chilled her to the bone.

What possible reason, or reasons, could her mother have for refusing to supply DNA anyway? It was hard to imagine anything other than the fact that Julie had done this thing and knew that the test would prove beyond doubt that she was guilty.

As Amanda eventually climbed back on to her bed and pulled the single white sheet over her, at something approaching four o'clock in the morning, she also found herself dreading meeting up with Christina in the morning. How would their relationship now have changed? Did Chrissy already believe all of this, or was she willing to still believe that it might not have been Julie who'd stolen her older sister and wrecked her mother's life?

When she finally did wake up, after finally having fallen into a troubled sleep as the sun was rising at around 6.40am, she found herself in a state of anxiety about seeing Christina. It was around ten, and she heard the sounds of voices, cutlery and crockery from the kitchen below, signalling that Jerome, Nikos and Chrissy were probably taking breakfast.

She rose, showered and threw something on. She knew she'd have to go down and face the others, so she kind of did so on automatic pilot. Had she been able to do so, she'd have curled into a ball and slept until arriving home to Bath, but, alas, this wasn't an option.

When she walked into the room below, to see the other three sitting together around the table, a selection of dishes and glasses, cups and condiments on the table before them, she hesitated at the door. Christina, however, got up, ran to her and threw her arms around her.

"Mandy," she said, "Whatever happens, whatever's true and

whatever's not, you and I aren't guilty of anything. Look, you're either going to be my real sister, or probably [and saying this she threw a glance over her shoulder at Jerome] my sister-in-law, so let's be sure of one thing, we're mates, OK?"

Amanda nodded, grateful for the 'olive branch' as she saw it. Walking arm-in-arm with Christina, she went and sat at the table, where both Jerome and Nikos extended an arm to squeeze her hands. By the time half an hour had passed they were all much more relaxed. They were able, by talking about things, to focus their minds on the fact that everything now hung on Julie, and what she, or the police, were likely to do about the situation. They all assured Amanda too, that whatever the outcome might be, they'd be close, always, whatever their family relationship turned out to be.

That Friday passed without much more talking. There wasn't a lot that could be said anyway. They all fell into a groove, the one that Christina and Jerome had been following for weeks by now, of preparing the taverna for the lunchtime clientele, then clearing up and doing the same for the evening. Nikos went off to Ierapetra for more supplies, and Amanda was able to steal a couple of hours on a sun bed during the afternoon, where she was grateful for the fact that, between swims to cool off, she was able to doze quite a lot. Ulrika had brought her a couple of cool cans to drink as well. It seemed everyone felt that she was the primary victim in all of this, and deserved some special consideration.

As the evening drew on and the light began to fade, at somewhere around a quarter past eight, Chrissy and Amanda were sitting together at the back of the restaurant. Nikos and Jerome were fussing in the kitchen with chef Manoli. Ulrika was servicing the early diners.

Chrissy said: "May I tell you something that I hope doesn't upset you Mandy?" Without waiting for the reply, but seeing from Amanda's expression that it was OK to go on, she added:

"You know I kind of stared when you first came here? Well, now you know what I was looking for. I don't think I've shown you a photo of my mum, have I?"

Amanda shook her head. Chrissy drew out her phone and swiped at its screen. Then she showed it to Amanda. Amanda stared at the face on the screen. She was looking at a woman who looked in good shape, probably early forties, no grey in her hair, which was shoulder length and of similar colour to hers. It was a head and shoulders shot. Chrissy withdrew it just for a moment, saying, "That was taken four years ago. My mum, as you obviously realise. Here's one of us two together."

She swiped a few times and then showed Amanda another shot, this time of Christina, arms entwined with the woman she'd seen in the other photo. The two looked very much alike, although Amanda could see the Greek heritage of her father in Chrissy's features too. She stared again at Marsha, using her thumb and finger to expand the photo to a closer view. She moved the photo around on the screen, examining that face, looking for clues, much as Chrissy had done with her own face when she'd first arrived.

They were there. There wasn't a striking resemblance, but there was something, something Amanda couldn't quite put her finger on, but she found herself seeing something, much as Christina had done when looking at her, days earlier. Was she seeing it because she expected something to be there? Christina had asked herself the same question. Were they both being subjective? Neither could be sure, yet both thought they saw something.

Amanda then began to re-examine in her own mind her mother Julie's features. Had she ever thought to look closely to see any family resemblance there? She obviously wasn't going to have any of her dad's features, but she felt she ought to have some of her mother's.

Try as she might, she couldn't see anything. Neither could she be sure that she and Jerome resembled each other as much as she felt they ought to, if they were truly half-brother and sister. At times like this, sometimes people don't see things because they don't expect to see them.

No, Amanda was becoming convinced of her mother's guilt. And she didn't like it one bit.

28. Julie, August 2018

Gavin and Julie hadn't had a good night. After their conversation about the visit from the police, and Julie's attitude toward giving a DNA sample, Gavin had gone quiet. Julie had asked that he believe her, and to accept that she had some cock-and-bull reason for not giving a sample. But he couldn't understand it, and it made him furious. Hadn't they always been honest with each other? Didn't they have a good marriage? Weren't many of their friends and acquaintances always going on about how close they still were, even after twenty years together?

Gavin wasn't the type to blow up, to shout and scream. He just went quiet. And so they hadn't exchanged more than a few perfunctory words since the conversation had ended the previous night. After his breakfast of muesli and chopped fruit, accompanied by strong filter coffee, plus one or two vitamin pills, he grabbed the car keys and his brief case and headed out the door to go to work. It was a Friday, the day when he usually knocked off early, because nothing ever got done in banking circles on a Friday afternoon, at least, not in his field. Fridays were squash-playing days, or, in summer time, as they were now, golf would be high on the agenda after work, and before going home, via the local pub. Gavin and Trevor were joined at the hip when it came to what they did to unwind. As, indeed were Trevor's wife Daphne and Julie.

Julie was left sitting at the kitchen island fingering the handle of her mug of herbal tea. She was disconsolate, miserable, frightened even. She'd not intended to mention about the DNA business, but now realised that that had been an unrealistic hope. What was going to happen now? She was sure that Amanda would know by now, since she was out there in Crete with Jerome. How would she be taking all of this?

What's more, she wondered how she'd get out of this situation without causing any more upset in the family.

It hardly seemed possible that it was still less than twenty-four hours since the police had come calling, so much had happened between her and her son, her and her husband. She knew deep down that neither truly believed her, and she knew it was because she was refusing to give a sample of DNA. The police officers had said that they'd give her a few days to think about it. When would they be back again? How would she handle it when they reappeared?

She really had no idea.

Meanwhile, the police were actively researching the three other women who'd lived in Lyneham during the time of the snatch. Two of them had been eliminated from the enquiry, and the other, who proved slightly more difficult to trace, had since died, although not that long before. Her daughter was still alive somewhere, and they were pursuing that line of enquiry, in the hope that, once they'd been able to make contact with her, she too would either test positive, or also be eliminated.

Amanda flew home on Saturday the 18th, and didn't call her mum. Gavin continued to simply live in the same house as Julie, but without talking, except when he had to, and she sank further into a pit of depression.

On Wednesday, August 22nd, the police again appeared at the front door. It was around 9.30am and Julie had only just got dressed, although she hadn't planned to do anything apart from pig out on daytime TV. She hadn't called Daphne, and Daphne hadn't called to see if she was OK. Julie put this down to Gavin probably having talked to Trevor and so, she believed, yet more of those in her immediate circle were closing her out. Things were getting decidedly unpleasant. She was miserable, and the arrival of the same two officers did nothing to change that for the better.

She led them into the conservatory, much as she had done the previous week. And so they began.

"Mrs Pillinger, may we ask, have you changed your mind about giving a sample of DNA, so we can sort this out quickly and avoid any more unnecessary distress?"

"I can't. No, I just can't. But I didn't do it. Please believe me."

"Well, we're going to ask you to come with us down to the police station, if you wouldn't mind. There we can take a proper statement and..."

"Are you arresting me now?"

"No, no. But, of course, your willing cooperation will go a long way to persuading us that you have nothing to hide."

"Can I call my solicitor?"

"Of course, if that's what you wish. But for the time being we simply want you to accompany us, so that we can go over a few things that we have on file, and clarify a few matters. If it's of any help, you can call your solicitor at any time when you're at the station, no problem."

Julie realised that she had no alternative. She went to collect a jacket from her wardrobe, and slipped on a pair of shoes from the hall cupboard, and allowed the officers to lead her out to their waiting car, which was parked on her driveway, in full view of the neighbours. It was a leafy suburban street and, as chance would have it, Mr. Anstee, her nearest neighbour, had chosen that moment to cut his lawn. He lifted his straw fedora to her as she caught his eye, before watching her climb into the police car. His eyes didn't leave that car until it turned the corner a hundred yards away and disappeared from view. Then Mr. Anstee, the local retiree with too much time on his hands, whipped out a mobile phone and called someone.

Once they arrived at the police station, Julie was ushered into a private room, where, within minutes, she was asked to provide fingerprint samples. Just routine, they told her. She was already in a state of panic, and the face of her retired neighbour was all she could see in her head, so this didn't help at all.

The officers left her in the private room for about ten minutes. Their conversation away from her ears revolved around their desire to try and knock her confidence, to see if she'd crack. If she was the guilty party in the baby-snatch case from all those years ago, then she'll have been thinking for a very long time that she got away with it. They needed her to feel a degree of fear. Leaving someone alone in a police interview room was always a good gambit.

After a full ten minutes, a detective entered the room, followed by the female uniformed officer that had been to the house. He sat across the table from Julie and asked,

"Mrs. Pillinger, before we begin, would you like a drink, maybe?

Tea, coffee?"

"Water, please, just water. Can I call my lawyer now?"

The detective had been hoping that she'd maybe not want to do this so soon, but it was what it was, and he acquiesced. He slid a desk phone on the table towards her and sat back. She barely lost eye contact with him all the time she was calling her solicitor, a woman called Margaret Browning.

"She'll be here in half an hour."

"Would you mind if we began anyway? It's just routine, Mrs. Pillinger, we need you to help us, that's all."

"Are we 'off the record' then, as you people say on the TV dramas?"

"Well, TV dramas are quite a long way from the real world, but I know what you mean and, yes, OK, let's say that, until your solicitor gets here, we are. You see, we were able to trace the other three single mothers who'd been living near you when young Rebecca Travers was stolen. Two of them have been eliminated from the enquiry, and the third, well, sadly she died last July, from a brain haemorrhage. Her daughter's believed to be living in the Swindon area, so we're following that one up. One of the other women had been in Bristol at the time of the snatch, and we were able to verify that. She'd been visiting relatives. The other was sick and had a sister staying with her for about a week, helping with the baby, that kind of thing. That just leaves you."

Here he stopped, and made no attempt to go on. He wanted to apply the pressure without being able to be accused of doing so with aggressive questioning, especially as they were waiting for the solicitor to arrive, and she'd blow a gasket if anything underhand had been tried.

At that moment a young officer knocked, was invited to enter, and brought in a plastic cup of water for Julie. The detective thanked him and waited until he'd gone again. Julie decided to speak. The detective had hoped that she would.

"Couldn't that baby have been stolen by someone who took her out of the area? I mean, we hear about professional organisations doing this kind of thing. Surely they could have taken the child away so fast that it could have been in London, even a boat across the channel, before the police had even got into gear?"

"Mrs. Pillinger, whilst what you say would have been a possibility in some cases, in this one it doesn't look likely. You see, there had been a young petrol pump attendant on duty in the booth of the petrol station in front of the post office that morning. She said she didn't see anything, nothing at all. Now, if you recall, the location of the post office in relation to the forecourt is such that, this attendant, even though not paying much attention to what was going on around her, would definitely have seen if a car had sped away from the post office. Instead, she said she'd seen, according to her statement, nothing. No people, no vehicles. That would mean that for the baby to have been taken when it was, it had to be someone who went on foot around behind the forecourt office, and out on to the road from there. Either way, there would have been a vehicle involved if it was an organised snatch, and one way or the other, the young attendant would have seen something.

"So, you see, we're much more inclined to believe that this case is connected to the baby recently found in the wood out near Sandy Lane village.

"Can you, and I know it's a long shot, but can you recall anything about your movements on that day? Yes, it was a long time ago, but since the case hit the TV news that very evening, a lot of people seeing that report would remember that day more clearly than they otherwise might have."

"I think it's time I waited for my solicitor, don't you?" Julie at least had watched enough TV dramas to know the best way to protect herself from being led into a verbal trap.

They sat there, looking across the table at each other for another twelve minutes, during which time both Julie and the female officer crossed and uncrossed their legs numerous times. To Julie, it seemed like a year, when finally there was a knock and, without waiting for an answer, in walked her solicitor, Margaret Browning, fifty-something, prim, with her hair in a no-nonsense bun at the back of her head. She was clutching an attaché case under one arm. She greeted the detective,

"D.I. Stephens, always a pleasure. I hope you haven't started without me."

"Ms. Browning, so nice to see you again." He said this in a manner that clearly indicated that the opposite was, in fact, the case.

And so the interview began again, this time with the correct formalities, including the recording facility. Once or twice the solicitor advised Julie not to answer a question, but, much to the detective's delight, she strongly advised Julie to give a DNA sample, as it would clear matters up once and for all.

By the time the interview was over, the policeman had decided to let Julie sweat just a little longer, and so allowed her to leave and go home. But he wasn't at all convinced of her innocence. There had to be a connection between the baby snatch from all those years ago, and the body of the baby of about the same age found in the Wiltshire wood.

And he was going to find it.

That evening, the 'baby in the wood' case was back at the top of the news. The TV reporters even turning up in Gavin and Julie's road and filming the front of their house. Of course, their next door neighbour, Mr. Anstee, was only too pleased to tell the great British public what he'd seen. The report on the BBC Six O'clock News began:

"The police in Wiltshire have again appealed for help in the case of the 'baby

in the wood,' the body which was discovered just outside the village of Sandy Lane on Thursday July 27th. Detective Inspector Stephens, of the Wiltshire Constabulary, says that police are convinced there is a connection between this case and the one of the baby that was snatched from outside the Lyneham post office back in September 1997. There was a significant development today, when a woman was taken into police custody in order to, as the police state, 'assist with our enquiries.' The woman is apparently a Mrs. Julie Pillinger, from Britford, just outside of Salisbury in Wiltshire. Our reporter James Allen is at the scene."

Cut to the scene in the leafy lane where the Pillingers live, and a reporter standing with an elderly man wearing a straw fedora and looking very pleased with himself. The reporter begins:

"So, Mr. Andrew Anstee, you're a neighbour of Mrs. Pillinger's, correct?'

"That's right. I live next door. I was just out cutting the lawn when this police car pulls up in next door's drive. Before I knew it they were ushering Mrs P. into the car and it was off down the lane."

"And how well would you say you know the couple, Mr. Anstee?"

"Oh, I've lived next door to them for years. They're not the most sociable of neighbours, I'd say. But they've never given me any cause for concern. Until now, that is."

At this, much to the evident dismay of Mr. Anstee, the camera moved away, taking him out of shot, and focussed once again on the reporter's head and shoulders.

"It's understood that, after a couple of hours Mrs. Pillinger was released without charge and returned home. She has so far refused to meet reporters outside the home, or offer a statement of any kind. It appears that she was a single mother, living in Lyneham, at the time of the baby snatch in 1997. According to our sources, but the police haven't confirmed or denied this, they are working on the theory that perhaps a woman's child died and, rather than

report the death, she chose to dispose of the body and steal another child from someone else.

"The investigation continues.

"James Allen, BBC News."

Julie sat on her sofa, sipping whisky and crying uncontrollably as she watched the Six O'clock News. Gavin hadn't come home, and she could only conclude that he'd got wind of the goings on somehow, and was in no mood to run the gauntlet of microphones and aggressive questioning as he dashed from the car to the front door. He hadn't phoned either, and she was mortified about how he was taking all of this. And would he be able to face his staff at the bank next morning, now that it was a certainty that most of them would have seen the news?

All in all, things weren't going very well. The curtains were all closed against the prying press outside, and she had no lights on. It was still very light outside, but the curtains were heavy and lined on all of the windows, throwing the interior of the house into a fitting gloom to suit Julie's mood.

She grabbed a plush scatter cushion and clutched it to her lap. The tears increased as she began to contemplate too, that her daughter was now home a few days from Crete and still hadn't rung. Nor was she likely to now. As for Jerome, did he get any UK news out there in Crete? She could only hope that he didn't, although if he'd talked with Amanda then he'd surely be up to speed with the events of the day.

Perhaps she should ring Jerome, she thought. But then, what would it accomplish? What could she say to anyone except, 'OK, I'll give a voluntary DNA sample,' which she was so frightened of doing. That's the only thing that everyone would tell her to do.

How vividly she was now coming to appreciate that deeds done in the past hardly ever remain hidden. Everything has its way of coming to light sooner or later. It may have been 'later,' in this case, but she had a tumultuous churning in her stomach that told her that soon now, things would have to come out, things that would wreck her life for sure as that iceberg had the Titanic.

And she was afraid.

Her phone buzzed on the coffee table in front of her. Through the blur of tears, she picked it up and tapped the screen. It was a text from Gavin.

"Staying over with Trevor and Daphne tonight. Not sure when I'll be home TBH."

29. Philip Trent, August 2018

The printworks in a nondescript commercial district of Swindon hadn't changed all that much in decades. The machines had changed from offset litho to mainly digital, but otherwise Printit Ltd. was much as it had been for a very long time.

The company logo was still the same as it always was, and there were still a few staff members there in 2018 who'd also been there twenty-two years earlier. One of the current directors, Philip Trent, looking every bit of his forty-nine years, was standing beside a Canon Océ ProStream 1000, which was humming nicely as it spat out A4 colour flyers at a furious rate.

Phil had started at the bottom as a teenager, worked hard, gone to classes, got some qualifications, re-trained when the digital revolution began in the nineties, and eventually saw the rewards for his labours. Now, just about 95% of everything they printed they did digitally. Back in his younger day, there had been dark rooms, typesetting companies and cumbersome off-set machines jostling for floorspace with a couple of old letterpress machines.

Phil was a man well-pleased with himself, although he'd freely admit over a pint in the local pub near to where he lived, that he'd gladly give his directorship to be twenty years younger again. Although, for 'pint', perhaps read 'double shot of malt whisky' nowadays. His girth was ample demonstration of the fact that he was no fan of exercise, neither did he take care to eat healthily. He took a rather fatalistic view of everything. When his time came, he'd go, that was about all the attention he'd pay when someone banged on about eating one's five-a-day, or cutting down on red meat, or power-walking (jogging had long been relegated to the realms of the no-longer-feasible for Phil).

Phil Trent was twice married, and twice divorced. Women weren't good at understanding him, that was how he'd put it. They'd have said that he always thought far too much of himself, never took responsibility (at least in the realms of fidelity) seriously, and treated women rather too chauvinistically. His hair had once been lush and wavy, but now his pate struggled to find protection when the weather was bad. He'd taken to wearing a baseball cap, or flat cap occasionally for variety's sake, most of the time when he was out of the house.

His house, now that was grand, surrounded by ample gardens and far too big for a lone divorcee. His fence was reinforced and he had security cameras everywhere. Even Jehovah's Witnesses didn't bother trying to penetrate its defences. The two Rottweilers that roamed the grounds freely, also might have been a factor. His friends, such as they were, all humoured him and none would have described him as one of their closest, even though he viewed one or two of them as such. He drove a late-model Jaguar and loved to 'plip' the automatic control on his huge gates when arriving home, watching them swing open, and then close again once the car was inside.

His needs at home were well cared for by the young couple whom he paid to live in and 'do' for him. They could hardly believe their luck, having such a 'gig,' as they called it. The young lad, Frazer, was the all-purpose DIY and gardening do-all, and his partner Daisy cooked, cleaned and tidied in the house. In exchange they received full board and could freely avail themselves of all the provisions in Phil's ample kitchen cupboards. As long as he had what he needed when he needed it, they were free to come and go as they pleased. He was frequently not home during the evenings anyway, and just as often ate out, so they considered themselves to be very happy, thank you very much. Daisy was not so comfortable with the dogs, but they'd made an uneasy peace of sorts.

So Phil, having inspected a few of the flyers spitting out of the machine and decided that they were looking acceptable, nodded to the machine's operator and retired to the little kitchen just off of his plush office, which was through a door in the print shop and up a flight of stairs to the floor above, where pallets stacked with publications awaiting shipping were replaced by extravagant potted plants and leather sofas for clients to relax in while waiting to be seen by someone. There were huge faux paintings adorning the walls, and, inside Phil's office, numerous framed photos of him with various local celebrities, gratefully shaking his hand at some charity event or other.

He flipped the switch on the kettle that sat on the worktop in the kitchen, popped the top of a coffee jar and threw some powder into his favourite mug, the bright red one with the Ferrari logo adorning the side. His fellow director, Colin, who'd worked his way up along with Philip himself, entered.

"I'll have one if you're making one." he said.

"I'm not, I'm just doing my exercises." replied Philip, grabbing another mug anyway.

"Seen the news?" asked Colin.

"I never watch the news. Why on earth would I want to be depressed?" That about summed up much of Philip Trent's philosophy. He shot some brown powder into his colleague's Manchester United mug.

"Well, if anyone knows that, I ought to. But I suspect that you do take a peek now and then, but you don't let on. Go on, you do don't you?"

"Perish the thought." replied Phil, opening the office fridge in search of some milk. "Bloody Norah, why is there never any milk in 'ere when you need it? I'll brain that Kylie. She doesn't have much to do with her time, so at least she could keep up with the office milk consumption."

"No worries. I'll have it black. Better for you, some would say."

"Yeah, then you go and get knocked down by a bus. So much for the whole keeping fit thing."

Once the coffee was made and both mugs filled with dark, steaming liquid, both men went round into Phil's office. They threw themselves into the deeply cushioned leather guest chairs on the other side of the huge desk from Phil's fancy swivel variety.

"So," said Phil, "why would you be asking me if I'd seen the news anyway? Has Theresa May been assassinated or something? One can live in hope." He said this as he stood again, and reached over his desk for a packet of chocolate digestives that he always kept in the top drawer.

"No, nothing as exciting as that. No, that story about the baby they found over near Bowden Hill. They got some woman apparently. Said she was implicated in that baby-snatch case from ages ago in Lyneham. They never found the culprit for that one. Anyway, this woman they arrested or something, they let her go. If you ask me they'll get her back in again before long.

"Now tell me if I'm wrong, but I could have sworn that girl you'd had a one-nighter with way back when, she was called Julie something-or-other, right? Well the woman they took in was called Julie, and she was about the right age. Didn't you say she'd been after you to try and trap you into marrying her or something? That Julie you knew I mean? Switch on the TV, let's see her photo, I think the police got hold of one somehow. They showed it and she looked very familiar to me."

Philip Trent's curiosity was piqued. He reached to his desk for a huge TV remote without half a million buttons on it, and pointed it at the flat-screen smart TV mounted on the wall across from where they were sitting. It burst into life and he then went about searching for the latest TV news bulletin. Both men watched with interest as the story unfolded. Then it reached the point where the photo of the woman under suspicion was shown. Phil paused the frame.

"Well, I'll be a..! It's HER! It may have been over twenty years ago, but I never forget a face. That's Julie Parfitt. Well, she was Parfitt back then, not Pillinger. Reckoned she was pregnant and I'd have to make an honest woman of her. Soon gave her the elbow." He stopped at this point and seemed to come over slightly nonplussed.

"'Sa matter Phil, seen a ghost?"

'Eh? What? Oh, no, no. It's just that... Well, I didn't believe her at the time. Not that it would have made that big a difference; but seems like, guilty or not, she was pregnant then. I might have a daughter after all. Or might have had one. It looks like that poor dodge they found in the wood may have been my flesh and blood."

Philip Trent, just for once in his life, was lost for any more words.

"When was it, then, all this with Julie Parfitt?" asked Colin. The question soon got him into gear again.

"Oh, I remember that all right. It would have been, hold on, let me think, yeah, May 1996. I can't get that wrong, because Man-U won the Premier League for the third time. Glen Hoddle had just taken over as

England manager. Can't forget pivotal dates like that. He'd managed Swindon Town a few years before, then went off to Chelsea. Swindon won Division Two in 1996. See, no doubts about the date.

"So, that would have meant, if she had been expecting, like she'd said she was, she'd have had the kid in..." Here he counts under his breath, using a few fingers to assist, "...Feb '97.

"Stone me, when was that baby stolen in Lyneham, then? They just said, didn't they?"

He jabbed at the remote and scrolled back through the report a way, then let it play for a few seconds. The BBC reporter was just saying: *"... the baby that was snatched from outside the Lyneham post office back in September 1997. There was a significant development today..."*

Here he paused the report again. Swallowing hard, he said, "If she'd had my daughter, then the baby would have been about six or seven months old. Oh my God."

"Well, there's nothing proven yet, by the looks of it. She's only suspected, it seems."

"Yeah, but if she was deranged enough to not report a dead child, go and bury it, then steal another, then I was well out of it. I mean, think Col, I could have been murdered in my bed or something."

30. Amanda, Bath, August 2018

After she'd been back at home for almost a week, Amanda became resolved to go and confront her mother; always, of course, assuming that Julie was actually her mother. Amanda had never felt so mixed up. She had really liked Christina and was genuinely thrilled that Jerome had accidentally stumbled on an entirely different life from the one he'd had planned before going off to Greece to live it up for the summer.

But, after the bombshell about the baby-snatch, and her mother having been nearby at the time, then this awful discovery of the buried baby and Julie's refusal to give a DNA sample, she was completely preoccupied with whom she was, where she'd come from. There was no way she could go on with her life until she was entirely sure for herself that she was the child of her mother. There'd never even been a question about it until now, no shred of doubt. Now, though, her head was exploding with all the implications of what had come out on the news. She pondered over whether to ring her mum first, but thought, no, she'd just drive over there and knock on the front door. She knew that right now her mother wouldn't be going out much, if at all.

She hadn't any appointments after 3.00pm on Friday August 24th, so she jumped in the car and headed off down the Warminster Road. It was just under forty miles and she knew that she'd be at the house in just over an hour, traffic permitting. She didn't know if there would still be any press hanging around outside the house, or if her dad had been home to support her mum. She only knew what she'd seen on the TV news.

Was she mad with her mother, or did she feel sorry for her? She couldn't even work that one out herself, although, on balance decided that she was more mad than sorry. After all, if Julie kept insisting on her innocence in this whole affair, why the resolute refusal to do the test? As Amanda drove on down through Monkton Combe, Limpley Stoke and on towards Woolverton, occasionally getting stuck behind a lorry and cursing the road for being so difficult to overtake, she found herself swinging first one way, then the other, but always coming back to that test.

Why wouldn't her mother do the test? It could only be because she had something to hide. What else could that be, but that she was guilty? But when Amanda pictured in her mind's eye a woman digging a hole in the cold, damp ground in an isolated wood, and then burying a dead child in it, she found she couldn't see her mother's face on that woman. This was not, though, because she didn't think her mother might have done it, but rather because she didn't want her mother to have been the one who had. If she were to accept that, then she also had to accept that she, Amanda Pillinger, was stolen goods. She was not, in fact Amanda Pillinger at all, but in all probability Rebecca Travers, and Chrissy was her half sister. She couldn't deal with the stress on her mind when she contemplated all of that.

An hour and ten minutes after starting the car up in Bathwick, she stopped on her mother's drive and switched off the engine of her Fiat 500. Then she sat there for a few moments. She needed to compose herself, to get a grip. It didn't look like that was going to work anyway, so she steeled herself, and opened the car door, just in time to see the curtains twitching next door, where that retired chap Mr. Anstee lived, he who'd had thirty seconds of fame on the TV news bulletin. She chose to ignore it and fixed her eyes on the front door of the house.

She'd barely set foot in the porch when the door opened, and her mother beckoned her inside. Amanda was shocked by Julie's appearance. She normally took pains to always look her best. Hairdressers and manicurists had made a very good living out of her over the years. Now, though, she looked like she hadn't slept for a week and her hair looked like she'd been dragged through a hedge backwards. She was wearing her dressing gown and she had slippers on her feet. To Amanda's eyes she also looked decidedly thinner than she usually did. The bags under her eyes were confirmation of the sleep-deprivation, and her pallor of lack of nourishment and daylight.

Her mother hastily closed the door, although there was no obvious evidence of photographers or reporters visible to the eye. 'That didn't mean that they weren't still hanging around though,' was how Julie thought of it. Once the door was closed she went to embrace Amanda, but Amanda was having none of it. She backed off, and walked on through to the kitchen and the conservatory, which appeared to be the only part of the house that had any light, as all the curtains downstairs were still drawn tight. She threw herself on to the sofa and waited for her mother to sit on the edge of an armchair, right on the very edge, hands between her knees, leaning forward.

"So, what the hell is this all about then Mum? You'd better tell me your side of it, agreed?"

"Yes, of course. Can I make you a tea, coffee, anything, before I start?"

"No, I'm fine. Where's dad by the way? Squash, golf, the pub maybe?"

"I don't know Amanda, I really don't know. He's only texted me a couple of times since the news on the television. He says he can't come home until he gets his head right. I think he's staying with Daphne and Trevor." Julie spoke in a monotone, as if she'd almost become an android. "Amanda, I have no one. Nobody's been near me since Wednesday, not Daphne, not any of the usual girls, none of Gavin's friends, no one. I can't go out and I can't eat anything. I don't know where this is all going to end."

"Surely it's down to you, mum. You give a DNA sample, it comes back negative, we're all happy, not to say very, very relieved. The way I see it, it's that simple."

"Except that it isn't, Amanda. It isn't at all."

"So, tell me, why? If you won't give that sample, then you obviously have something to hide. I mean, how in hell do you think I feel right now, Hmm? There I was, having a nice life, everything on track. Nice job, loving family, even a quick week in the sun with my baby brother, and now? Bloody hell mother, I don't even know if Jerry is my brother any more!

"I don't know who the hell I'm supposed to be. Can't you see that this is all your fault? You may well be wrecking your life, but you're doing a pretty good job of destroying mine too. Not to mention dad's and Jerry's. Come on mum, cut me some slack here. If you have something you're not telling any of us, I'd say it's time you started, and you can start with me, here and now."

Julie couldn't help herself. She burst into tears. It was all that Amanda could do not to get up, go over and put her arm around her, but Amanda's ire was up, and she was in no mood for reconciliation. Her mother tried to compose herself enough to speak.

"Oh, Amanda, sweetheart, it's not what you think. It's not what anyone thinks. And I'm not alone in carrying blame, you have to believe me."

Amanda wanted to press her advantage. So she replied, "I don't have to believe anything. Not until there is some pretty hard evidence supporting it."

'I never thought you could be so hard."

"Hard? Me, hard? Mum, I'm not getting through, am I? You don't seem to understand what this is doing to me, to all of us, but most of all me. I'm the one who now worries that I'm stolen goods, that I was somehow taken from my birth-mother and brought up by you, under a complete lie for all my life. It's not all about you, you know."

"I do know, Amanda, truly I do. It's just, well, I so want to tell all, I really do. But if I do then it'll wreck everything anyway. I don't suppose I can expect you to understand, who would? I can only say that, in regard to this whole baby-killing and baby-stealing thing, it wasn't me, it wasn't me."

"Well, you wouldn't be the first person guilty of a crime who protests their innocence. You have it in your hands to resolve matters. Once more I'll say, mother, if you don't do that test, don't expect to see me again. There's no other way I can handle this. What will become of you, of you and dad? I don't know. I care about dad, of course I do, but you're fast pushing me away by your actions, or lack of them.

"There. I'm done. If you have nothing else to say, I'll go." With that she stood and took a few steps towards the hallway door. Julie called out to her, desperation in her voice:

"AMANDA, PLEASE! I'm between a rock and hard place. I'm desperate, but don't go, PLEASE DON'T GO."

By the time the last word came out, the front door had slammed behind Amanda. She'd hesitated just a moment when her mother had shouted her appeal, but only for a moment. Once she realised that she wasn't going to hear a satisfactory explanation, she had no alternative, but to go.

That evening Julie summoned the courage to phone Gavin on his mobile, again. She just had to hope that he'd be inclined to answer it. He hadn't on the many other occasions when she'd called over the last couple of days. As it rang she found her hope fading more and more with every chime of that electronic ringing tone. Just as she was about to give up and sink ever deeper into despondency, she heard her husband's voice.

"Julie. Have you seen sense?"

"Oh Gav, please. Can we talk. Can't you come home, please? I'm so desperate. I love you Gavin. Don't you love me? I only want..."

"I love the woman I thought you were, of course I do. Trouble is, I'm not sure who you are any more."

He didn't seem inclined to expand.

"I'm still her Gavin, I'm still the same Julie. This whole thing's not what it seems, truly it isn't."

"Then what, precisely is it, Julie? Let me tell you something. Over the past two days my life has been hell. On Thursday morning I had to go into work and endure the stares of everyone in the whole bank, from the young clerk who opens the doors in the morning, to my own staff in the Department. Lots of talking behind the backs of hands, all that stuff.

'I was told by John Charles, who is, as you know, the only person in the whole region who's above me, that maybe it would be better if I took some time off, stayed away until this whole thing blew over. I mean, really – 'blew over?' How long's a piece of string? Only because he allowed me enough time to talk, and to explain that I was completely in the dark about all of this, did Trevor come around and agree for me to stay at his place. I couldn't have come home if I'd wanted to, there were that many gannets around the flaming house, cameras rolling, all the rest of it. You know that only too well. If you didn't do this, ...this thing, then it's about time you made it crystal clear. Because as long as anyone thinks you did, I can't be near you. I'd be implicated, I could lose my position here and I'd never get another post. Pretty soon we'd be bankrupt. Our whole damn lifestyle hangs on me holding down this job, and you know that only too well.

"So, just to make it clear, again, when the bloody police announce to all and sundry that they no longer suspect you, then we might have a chance. Until then? You can forget it. I'll have to come and collect a load of my things, clothes, books, toiletries, that kind of stuff. So I'll come at around 3.00 am. I can't think of any other way of doing it. I'd appreciate it if you kept out of my way while I'm there."

"But Gav..." He'd already hung up.

31. Jerome, Amanda and Christina

After Amanda had flown home, things had settled into the kind of routine that had been pursued prior to her arrival at Makrigialo. It wasn't the same, though. The elephant in the room was the situation back home regarding Jerome's mother and the cloud she was now under.

On Saturday morning, August 25th, Amanda called Jerry using WhatsApp and they talked face to face, with Christina sitting beside Jerome and contributing too now and then. Amanda was very upset, and still extremely unstable emotionally after the discovery of her possible identity, but she wanted to focus on what they could do next. The family still had no idea if the police were going to show up again and take Julie into custody. It seemed highly likely, but they had no real idea.

Slowly, Amanda was hatching one last-ditch idea to get Julie to cooperate about this DNA test. She said to Jerome,

"What about if we all gang up on her? You, me and dad together. It would mean you coming over for a few days, though. Do you think that would be possible, Jerry?"

"I reckon it would, yeah. I'll talk to Niko. See if he'll be OK to manage without me for a while. Incidentally, I should tell you, and you're the first in the family I've told about this, so keep schtum for a while longer yet, but Chrissy and I have decided to try and make a go of things here. Nikos' offer is too good for me to turn down. It's quite a major sea change in my whole plan for life, but I really can see myself making my home here. There are much worse places in this world. What do you think?"

"I think it's a great idea. After all, what a fab bolt-hole it would give me when I want a few days to chill and get away from it all."

"I hoped you'd say that. I'll talk to dad myself, and now it seems like I'll have the opportunity to do that face-to-face. I'll look at the flight situation, but I reckon the cheapest option will be to come for one week, Wednesday to Wednesday, so we'll have time to pressurise mum, I can talk to dad, and maybe we ought to go see Chrissy's mum Marsha too, what do you think?"

Amanda hesitated at this. It seemed like a no-going-back thing to do. It shouted acceptance that Marsha was her true birth-mother. She wasn't sure she could handle that right now. Jerome picked up on her wavering, and added, "It's no problem if you'd rather not. Maybe best to wait and see if we can finally get mum to give the sample. Then, after a few days everything would be much clearer.

"Mand, look, I know this is tough for you. And before you fire back about me not really being able to know how you're feeling, I accept that. Doesn't mean, though, that I can't sympathise. I've been torturing myself thinking about how you must be feeling right now. But let's see this through. Surely we'll know the facts before long, one way or the other, but, for what it's worth, with over twenty years of water gone under the bridge, whatever the outcome, you and I are still brother and sister under the law.

Dad's still your legal father, under the law. All those years of us being family, Mand, they count for a lot. I don't care what blood is in your veins, you're my big sister, and always will be."

Amanda couldn't help herself. She cried at this. "Now look what you've made me do," she replied, "turn into a quivering mess."

Christina was wet around the eyes too, both at the way Amanda was enduring, and at the thought that she may just be looking at the sister she thought she'd never live to see.

So they signed off with the assurance that Jerome would get back to England somehow, and they'd go, along with their father, to try and get Julie to reveal what it was that was stopping her from giving the DNA. If they failed this time, she'd be to blame for whatever befell her, possibly at the hands of the police.

Nikos was completely ecstatic about Jerome's decision and soon drew up a list of things they'd have to do. He'd help Jerome to get registered for a tax number, an AMKA number and a residency permit. He'd make sure that Jerome became a legal resident as soon as possible and then he could start earning a legitimate wage as a member of the team at the taverna. He felt a lot better about the situation, having been taking a bit of a risk with Jerome being there unofficially and working for him. Had the inspectors come calling and asking the wrong questions, the restaurant might well have been closed down, at the very least temporarily. Nikos also found a teacher to give Jerome one-on-one Greek lessons. Jerome was up for all of it. Strangely, the idea of cancelling his university plans felt like a weight had been lifted from his shoulders.

After all, what exactly was it that most people wanted out of life? To have been given this opportunity made Jerome feel like he had it now, while still only nineteen years of age. He was going to grab it with both hands.

It was amazing how in about seven weeks he'd been completely assimilated into Niko's family and business, and it felt good. It felt right. There would be no re-considering now. He was resolved, this was going to be his life from now on. If ever he met up with Lars again, he'd kiss him.

On the evening of Wednesday August 29th, over a month before he'd have returned had he been still going to uni, Jerome walked out of the terminal at Gatwick airport and boarded the National Express bus to Bath. He was going to stay with his sister, who was going to take him to Salisbury the very next day, where their father, Gavin, would also rendezvous with them, before going together in the early evening to the house in Britford, on the outskirts of the town.

This, then, would be their last attempt at getting Julie to cooperate, or at the very least reveal why it was she said she couldn't consent to the DNA test.

The thing was, the police beat them to it.

During the afternoon of Thursday August 30th, they again turned up at Julie's front door, this time in an unmarked car, and D.I. Stephens himself asked her to come back to the station for some further clarification.

By now Julie was almost out of it, mentally. So she simply slipped on a jacket, after hastily donning some jeans and a sweatshirt, slipped her feet into some pumps and allowed the detective to walk her to his car.

At least there was no sign of Mr. Anstee this time. Unbeknown to Julie, he was already on the phone to the local radio station, after which he'd be calling the local newspaper, and the BBC, whose reporter had given him a mobile number to ring if there were any further developments. He wasn't stupid. He knew an unmarked police car when he saw one. The fact that no one else had come within fifty metres of the house next door for a week or so also confirmed in his mind what was likely to be going on.

Julie found it difficult even to walk to the car. She'd hardly eaten anything, surviving for a week on what had been left in the fridge and the freezer anyway, but mainly on the odd bowl of breakfast cereal when she'd had no alternative but to eat something, and forcing it down. All she'd been drinking was water from the kitchen tap, or whatever spirits had been left in the drinks cabinet. There were now empty vodka bottles near the recycling bin, along with the same of whisky, gin, Campari and a couple of others as well. A little over a week ago she'd been a handsome woman still. Yes, she had a slightly wider waist than it had been twenty years earlier, but she'd always been immaculately turned out and would still have been described as looking younger than her forty-seven years.

As she walked with difficulty, and with the aid of a plain-clothed female officer, to the waiting car, she looked more like the kind of woman who'd be seen riffling through the bins under a London flyover.

Once at the police station, she was led into the same interview room as before. Her lawyer was called, and by five o'clock, about the same time that Amanda, Jerome and Gavin were meeting in the local pub near the house, the interview began.

"So, Mrs. Pillinger, have you had time to reconsider your decision about the DNA sample? Or do you recall sufficiently your movements on Thursday morning, 18th September 1997, to give you an alibi for the approximate time when the six-month-old was stolen from outside Lyneham post office?"

"Look, I want to say something, and it mustn't go any further. Can you confirm that what I might tell you now will not reach the ears of my husband?"

"Mrs. Pillinger, everything we now say will remain confidential, unless we end up in a court of law, when I'm afraid, as you'll probably know, it may be used against you. But as of this moment, you are not under arrest and we haven't read you your rights. So, if you have anything to say that might help us eliminate you from this enquiry, now would be the time."

D.I. Stephens sounded like he was actually feeling some sympathy for Julie. At least, that was how she was reading things.

"Well, I have a personal reason why I didn't want to give you a DNA sample." She began to wring her hands on her lap as she continued, "You see, I don't know how to put this, I haven't told anyone ever. I couldn't, because it would have wrecked my marriage and divided my family beyond repair."

Here she stopped, and was clearly fighting with herself. The D.I. was a patient man. After a couple of minutes, during which Julie dabbed at her eyes a great deal, he said:

"Go on."

Two hours later, the car returned Julie to her home, where she was surprised to see her husband's car parked on the drive. Her heart leapt at the thought that maybe he'd come home to support her. How would he deal with what she might have to tell him now, though?

Letting herself in, and not waiting to see the police drive away, she shuffled along the hallway and into the lounge, where she was shocked to see both of her children sitting there, along with Gavin. None of them looked too happy. Gavin spoke first:

"Let me guess, you've been for a nice cosy little visit with the police again, right?"

"I gave it to them." She may have been mentally exhausted, but she felt a thrill of 'let him put that in his pipe and smoke it!' To use an old expression that she remembered from her childhood.

"You gave it to them? You gave them what?" said Gavin, although he and the children could only imagine one answer to that question.

"You know what. After all, that's why you're all here now, isn't it? Let's gang up on mum, tell her to stop being so stupid, right?"

They all shifted slightly in their seats. Gavin got up and went to stand in front of the substantial log-burning stove in the hearth. It wasn't lit. This was, after all, still August.

"Well, you have to admit, it was probably the right thing to do mum." said Amanda.

"Well, then, I've done the right thing now, haven't I. Isn't anyone going to get me a drink?"

Jerome sprang up, and ran out of the door and along to the kitchen. Julie sat down on the arm of the sofa where Amanda was already sitting. Gavin said, an undisguised air of frustration in his voice:

"May I ask, if it won't upset you too much, quite why we had to go through all of this, then, if you were going to give them the ruddy DNA anyway? You could have saved us all a great deal of trouble. The bloody BBC and ITV and all the rest of them camping outside our door, that nosy old git next-door probably negotiating a lucrative deal with some shabby tabloid to blow the lid on the baby-killing woman he'd lived next to for a couple of decades. What about what you've put the kids through? Especially Mandy, who's in pieces over all of this. For God's sake, your son has forked out to fly back for just a week to lend his support to our 'campaign' to get you to see sense, and now you walk in and say, 'I gave it to them,' just like that.

"Don't think Julie, that we're impressed, because we flaming aren't."

Jerome came into the room carrying a glass of water.

"Sorry mum, there isn't anything else out there."

"Water's fine, son, it's what I wanted." Julie was hoping beyond hope to not have to tell her family what she'd told the police before she finally consented to the DNA sample being taken. It didn't look much like there would be much alternative now though.

32. Lily

Marsha was making her plans to move out to Crete again. Since Nikos had come, stayed a while and returned home, she missed him terribly. She knew now, too, that it was time to try and get on with the rest of her life. There wasn't much point any more, after twenty one years, in still expecting Rebecca to walk back into her life. She had a wonderful daughter in Christina, whom she thanked God for daily. She ought to be grateful. The police weren't likely to crack the case now, even though they'd reopened it.

She found herself feeling sorry for Jerome's mother, Julie Pillinger, after she saw what happened on the TV news. Yes, she'd told the police about her, but hadn't really expected it all to hit the fan like it had. What if that poor woman wasn't the one who'd done it? What had she gone and put her through?

Still, the latest news report said that, after some weeks of persuasion, Jerome's mother had finally consented to give a DNA sample. Half the press said it would prove her guilt, while the other half theorised that she'd be proven innocent. In a couple of days everyone would know anyway. The evening news on the TV said that it had been earlier that very day that the DNA sample had been taken, and that the police would be inviting her daughter to also provide one. Since Chrissy had told Marsha that Jerry had flown home to bolster the family's attempts to persuade the mother to cooperate, she could only imagine that their efforts had borne fruit.

It still troubled Marsha why Jerry's mum had held out so long against the test though.

While she was contemplating all of this, the front door knocker sounded. It was mid evening, and she wasn't expecting anybody. So she went to the door and opened it just a few inches, as the darkness was gathering quickly now.

An attractive young woman stood there, tall, about Marsha's height, quite tastefully dressed, and clutching a Burberry handbag. She had a crumpled piece of paper in her hand, but no clipboard, so she wasn't from yet another energy company trying to get Marsha to switch suppliers, again. Marsha couldn't help but think, 'She looks like me, twenty years ago. How odd.'

The young woman spoke.

"Um, I'm looking for a Marsha Pavlidis. I was told this house-number."

"Yes, that's me. What can I do for you?"

"Well, my name is Lily, Lily Wilson, but I believe I may have been born Rebecca Travers, your daughter. Do you think I could come in?"

Meanwhile, in the Pillinger home, in Britford, Salisbury, just forty miles away, the telephone rang. The police were phoning for contact details for Miss Amanda Pillinger, since Julie had told them that she lived in Bath now. Jerome had answered it and told them they could speak to her right away, since she was present at the house for a family discussion. Amanda came to the phone, and very quickly concluded an amicable conversation. When she put the phone down, the others looked to her inquisitively, although probably guessing what it was about.

"Yes, I've agreed to go and give a DNA sample too." Amanda said.

By the time Lily had said the words '...come in,' Marsha had fainted. Lily had no idea what to do, so she stepped into the hallway, managed to get the door closed and went looking for a kitchen to find some water, or perhaps something stronger to help revive the lifeless Marsha on the hallway carpet.

A quarter of an hour later, with Marsha having revived, both women were seated either side of her modest kitchen table, their hands intertwined across the table surface. Lily spoke:

"I want to give you my whole story, and then I think you'll agree with me that I am Rebecca, although, up until July last year I'd never even heard the name."

Marsha, still shaking from the shock, said, "I want to hear it all. Leave nothing out. I've had my hopes raised and dashed so many times, I may need some convincing, although, what excites me is not only your similarity to me, but I can see Becca's father in you too, my Richard, who died so tragically at far too young an age. So I'm not going anywhere until I've heard it all."

"Well, I was born, so I believed, on March seventh, 1997, and my mother was Nadia Wilson. I never knew my father. Mum raised me alone. Right up until my mother died, in July of last year, I'd never had any reason to doubt who I was. Mum scrimped and saved to bring me up well, and never married. Once I was old enough, she did get a job again, working as a check-out girl. It was humble work, but regular, and her shifts meant she could juggle things and still look after me pretty well.

"I'd been born when she lived in Pound Close, Lyneham, where I believe you also lived at the time. But when I was only about a year old, we relocated to Milton Keynes. I don't know how mum got her place there, but that's where I spent the rest of my childhood.

"When I left school, I got a job with an insurance company, and eventually re-located to Swindon. I always had a great relationship with mum, really I did. And I never had any reason to suspect that I wasn't her real daughter. I never knew my father, and so I had no idea what he looked like, which explained to me the reason why mum and I weren't very much alike. I must have had my dad's genes, or so I always thought. Had mum not died of a haemorrhage on the brain, without any warning, I'd never have known any different. It was tough when she died. I mean she was only forty-six. She still worked for Tesco. She collapsed in the staff room at work. By the time the medics arrived, she was already dead. I found it very hard to cope with, even though I wasn't living with her by then. We were close, always close."

At this point Lily seemed to drift away a little, then regathered herself to carry on.

"See, I'd never heard of the baby-snatch case in Lyneham. I suppose now, looking back on it and knowing what I do now, that mum would obviously have been careful about keeping any news of it away from me. But, to be honest, by the time I was old enough to know what was going on around me, the case hadn't been news for a couple of years.

"When mum died, I was totally lost. I've had a few relationships, but was single at the time. I have been since then too, because of what's happened since, I suppose.

"You see, I realise now that my mother must always have had a pang of conscience about what she'd done. It's why I can still love her, even though I know all the facts now. A week or two after she died, I was talking to her solicitor. She hadn't had much cause, or even the wherewithal, to use a solicitor all that often, but she had apparently left a will, plus an envelope for me, only to be given to me if she died before I did, and not otherwise.

"I was totally phased when the solicitor handed me this huge brown envelope, all bulging with paperwork inside and sealed with a few feet of sellotape wrapped around it to stop it coming open. The solicitor even told me that he didn't know what was in it, only that he'd been charged with keeping it, and of giving it to me if mum were to die unexpectedly, which, of course, she now had."

With this, Lily lifted her substantial handbag, which Marsha hadn't really noticed up until then, and placed it on her lap in front of her. Marsha found herself longing to take ahold of this girl's hands again, but withdrew her own and placed them on the table in front of her, fingers interlocked to help fight the shaking. Lily drew a huge brown envelope from the bag, bulging from the weight of paperwork inside. She placed it on the table, and then withdrew the contents, placing them on the table between the two women. On the outside of the envelope Marsha could see that there was only one word, written in black felt-tip, "Lily."

Marsha was amazed to see that much of the paper was comprised of newspaper cuttings, some huge and with photographs, some just small clippings. Lily began to spread the cuttings out, with the type placed so that Marsha could read them. They all concerned the stealing of her baby Rebecca, September 1997, and Marsha's eyes almost burst from their sockets. Just about anything that had been printed in the press seemed to be there. Amongst all of this there was also a deluxe envelope, which had evidently been prized open impatiently, judging from the way it was ripped along one of its longer edges. Lily pulled out a handwritten letter and offered it to Marsha. She said, as Marsha took it from her:

"Here it is, my mother's confession."

Marsha could hardly hold the paper for her shaking, but did her best. This is what she read:

My darling baby Lily,

If you're reading this, then I'm dead. I won't know what happened to me, only that Mr. Swithins would have given this to you, along with all the cuttings about the hurt I caused. First and foremost, know that I love you and I would have done, did do, anything and everything I could from the day I first held you, to keep you safe, secure and happy. I hope you can agree that I managed that, at least.

But now to my confession. You are not my natural daughter, Lily. Had I not died and left you, you'd probably never have learned this, and I'm not even going to ask for your forgiveness. Far more important to me is that you know the truth. And I'm such a coward that I could never have faced up to it while I lived. I couldn't bring myself to go to the police after it had gone so far as it had. I couldn't have gone on living either, if I'd told you and it had turned you against me. I did a very bad thing, and I know that. But, when I did it, I was out of my head.

I had a baby, yes, I had her on your birthday, well, what became your birthday. She was the sweetest little thing I'd ever seen. She was only six months old when I lost her. Cot death, you see. Or SIDS, as some call it. Whatever it's called, it's horrific, unjust, cruel. To have the small human you love beyond measure simply die on you, and in what ought to be the safest of environments, her own crib, is indescribable. I lived close to that woman Marsha Travers. I had nothing against her, please believe me. It was just, well, I knew that her baby should have been mine. Why hadn't hers died and my Lily stayed alive? It wasn't right. It wasn't fair.

So I took my little princess and I gave her a private burial, out there in the wood where there's a small lake, just outside the village of Sandy Lane, and on the way up to Bowden Hill. I buried my little angel there and went about replacing her. I liked the place. It was peaceful, with a lovely country view. I could do no more for her. Then I took you from her. I watched her for ages, got used to her movements. I know, it all sounds so callous, calculated, and I suppose on one level it must have been. But all I could see was that I needed that child. She was mine by rights, and so she became mine.

When a couple of weeks had gone by, the police had been around doing their house-to-house enquiries, and I was still scot-free, I knew I'd got away with it. I didn't think for a long time of how that Miss Travers must have been affected. All I thought was, I have you now, you're mine, and I'm going to be a good mother to you.

So, there's not a lot more to be said. Only that, I knew, even though I could never face the consequences for what I'd done, and even less so as the years passed, that I owed it to you to tell you the truth if ever I were to die.

So, if you are reading this, I don't ask forgiveness. Only that you do the right thing. If, in your mind, it means going to find your birth-mother, I'm happy. If it changes your feelings for me, then it's no more than I deserve.

With all my love forever,

Nadia.

Marsha held the letter, eyes fixed on the final few words, for a long time. So much was rushing through her mind. The years of pain, the raised and dashed hopes, the moments of sheer desperation. Now, here she was, almost twenty-one years after that horrible day when she came out from the post office to see that empty stroller, sitting across the table from her daughter.

And she felt anger. She felt rage. She'd love to have had just one chance to confront this Nadia woman. She had flashbacks of moments in the streets around Lyneham when she might well have walked right past her own daughter and not known. Had this Nadia been able to see her home, her front door? Which of those women who'd lived nearby was she?

But, as soon as the rage infused her, it dissipated again. Finally she lifted her eyes and gazed in wonder at the young woman sitting across from her. Without a word they both arose, came around the table and fell into each other's arms.

In Makrigialos it was approaching eleven pm, and Christina's phone lit up as a call was coming in. As it happened, she was sitting at the cash register, sifting through the customer bills for the evening. Picking up the phone, she saw that it was her mother making a video call.

Tapping the right icon on the screen, she saw her mother Marsha's face, looking more like a Cheshire cat than a Cheshire cat.

"Hi mum, news about when you'll be able to come, maybe?"

"No, not yet Chrissy, darling. But I've had a rather unexpected evening. There's someone here I want you to meet." With that Marsha angled her phone's camera so that Lily came into shot.

Lily waved and gazed in wonder at her little sister. She gave a very broad smile and said, "Hi Christina, nice to meet you. I'm Lily Wilson. I know your mother."

"That's the biggest understatement in the history of the world!" interjected Marsha, who couldn't contain herself any longer. Chrissy, meet your long, lost sister!"

33. Clarification, to a degree

At the breakfast table the next morning, apart from the fact that there wasn't much talking going on, an observer could have been forgiven for thinking that all was as it used to be in the Pillinger household.

Gavin wasn't best pleased with the fact that the breakfast TV news had carried a brief piece about Julie being a suspect yet again. The bulletin quickly informed the great British public that Mrs. Julie Pillinger had been taken into police custody yet again but that, according to their sources, she'd now agreed to give the police a DNA sample. Results were expected before the weekend. He dealt with this only because he now already knew about the DNA sample, and had begun to believe that his wife may finally be innocent of baby-killing and baby-snatching after all. He did, however, seethe at the thought that it was probably their next-door neighbour who'd informed the press about this latest development, and resolved never to be civil to the man again.

Jerome still had a few days before flying back to Crete and was fighting with himself about how to put his new career plans to his father. With all that was going on, he didn't feel too great about broaching the subject right there and then. While Julie tried to look busy in the kitchen, having finally tidied herself up a little, Gavin, who'd spent the night in the spare room, sat at the island biting into some toast and marmalade and sipping a filter coffee. He'd made an early trip down the road for some provisions. Jerome was in the conservatory watching breakfast TV while he scooped yogurt straight out of a large plastic pot, Greek-style as it happens.

Jerome's phone tinkled into life, playing something by the Kaiser Chiefs. Grabbing it, he was pleased to see that it was Chrissy from Crete, and it was a video call. As he was tapping its face to answer the call, he also shot out of the conservatory, through the kitchen, and up to his room, so as not to hear Chrissy talk about his plans in his father's hearing. Yogurt covered the arm of the chair he'd been sitting in, in white spots.

Slamming his bedroom door behind him, he threw himself on to his bed and his face lit up for seeing Chrissy's.

"Missing you soooo much!" she began. "How's it going over there?"

"Things are improving a little. Mum's given the DNA and so we think it'll all settle down now. I'm sure it'll come back negative and that will mean a huge amount to Amanda, not to mention all of us really, but her especially. She's been feeling like she doesn't belong in her own family this past few days. How about you and your dad?"

"It's all good, but I called you for a specific reason. There's been a massive development, and you won't believe what I'm going to tell you now. I can see you're not standing up, so, are you ready?"

"Stupid question, tell me, tell me."

"Mum called last evening, and she had someone with her, a young visitor." She paused here, just to build the suspense. She smiled at Jerome, waiting for him to beg her to carry on, which, of course he did.

"Well, first I must tell you that mum and I agreed that I would be the one best placed to tell you all this, since you haven't actually met her yet, but she hopes you will very soon now. Last night Rebecca came back to life, Jerry. She knocked mum's door, found her through the police and the local post office apparently, and came looking in the hope she'd..."

"Hold on, hold on, HOLD ON! I don't think I heard you right. You said Rebecca... Rebecca, right? The name of your sister who was snatched. You're having me on, surely?"

"No, Jerry. She's the real thing, and she could prove it. Seems that her mother died and left her a confession. All the proof was there, and it was given to her in an envelope by a lawyer after the death. Her mum died of a brain haemorrhage and, if she hadn't, Rebecca would still be none the wiser. Looks like the woman could never confess, due to fears about what would happen to her, but had drawn up a letter, which she'd put in an envelope with all the newspaper clippings from the time, and it had kept by the lawyer, only to be given to Rebecca after her death. If she hadn't died, Rebecca would still be Lily Wilson. Well, she still calls herself that, obviously. It's the only name she's ever known. So it's all a bit messy, but I saw her Jerry, they talked to me last night and she looks so much like mum, you won't believe it. What about that, eh?"

"You're telling me! It's a miracle. A ruddy miracle. So, what happens now? I mean I suppose that after all this ridiculous fiasco about the DNA test, it's all become unnecessary now. Mum's in the clear, and Mand's really my sister. Phew! She'll be ecstatic. Still not sure I can take this in, myself."

"It is rather huge, isn't it. I'm pretty knocked out myself, too. I mean, all my life this shadow of an absent older sister, who I never thought I'd ever live to see, has been in my life, and now, there she was, in real flesh and blood, and, well, you should have seen my mother! I've never seen her really happy ever, but I think that now, finally, I have."

"So, what happens now, do you think? I mean, this girl must already have a different life. It's gonna take some adjustments for all concerned, I'd imagine."

"Well, it's only last night that she turned up, so all the details haven't even been talked through yet. Boy, was mama happy that she'd stayed in the area, though. I mean, think about it, she was a hair's breadth from moving back out here. Not that that would have meant that Rebecca couldn't find her, but it would have made it a little more difficult, taken longer for a certainty."

"So, you want me and Mand to go and visit them? Is your sister staying with your mother, then?"

"She's agreed to stay a few nights for now, but she has a job in Swindon apparently, and a flat. But she's not married, or in a relationship or anything. I don't even know if she has any relatives through her false mother, so that'll all come out in time. But don't go for now. I think it'll be best for you to meet them for the first time when you and I are together, don't you think?"

"Whatever you say. Can I tell the family here, though?"

"Of course, especially Mandy. She has to know right away."

There was a slight pause. Then Jerome said:

"Just a slight oddity, though. Fly in the ointment, maybe. But, if this is all true, and sounds like it must be, why on earth did mum hold out against that test and cause all that fuss? She nearly went half crazy herself. I don't get that."

"While we're on the subject of oddities, something else crossed my mind too, Jerry. I don't think it's a big deal, or anything, but I still can't work out why your sister does seem to have a few features that make her look like my mother. How do we explain that, then?"

Julie was still standing in the kitchen. She turned and, leaning against the worktop, spoke to her husband.

"Gavin, I owe you an explanation, I know."

"Understatement of the century, I'd say," he replied, still staring at the breakfast TV show playing on his iPad, perched in front of his plate. "I still don't know if I want to stay around quite yet."

"Gavin, I understand, really I do. But I was frightened. I don't want to lose you. I love you. I've never stopped loving you."

"Really? Yet you wouldn't tell me what all this was about. All this frigging fuss about that stupid test. I don't get you, Julie, I really don't. You'd think after all these years I would, but I don't."

He shook his head, tapped the iPad screen to switch off the broadcast, and swallowed the final piece of his brown toast and marmalade. He closed the tablet's case and turned to look at his wife. He grabbed his coffee cup and drained it. Heaving a very large sigh, he continued, "I'm not going in today, as it's Friday, and 'his highness' told me to kick back a bit anyway, what with all that's going on and all. But I think I want to take a very long walk, see if I can clear my head. Then maybe we'll be able to talk."

"But Gavin, there's something, ...something I've needed to..."

"You are NOT going to believe what I've just heard!!" Jerome's voice boomed between them as he re-entered the kitchen, looking extremely pleased with himself.

His parents both turned to look at their son, the moment lost. Julie deciding that she'd have to await another time, yet again, to tell her husband what was on her mind for so long now. It struck her as ironic, the police knowing her deepest secret, and her husband still in the dark. In fact, she could still see the face of the Detective Inspector when she'd told him. He'd almost laughed, before telling her that it was now a virtual dead cert that she'd be in the clear from the point of view of their investigation, if not from the point of view of her family. Now there was a two-edged sword, if ever there was one.

Both parents just stared at their son. Neither said a word. He didn't seem to notice that he'd interrupted anything, but then, what son does in such circumstances?

"Chrissy's just called. Her long-lost sister has been found! Not only that, but she turned up on Marsha's doorstep last night, with the proof as to who she really was. So now, no way could you have been involved mum, see?"

Both parents now exhibited the same look of amazement. And still neither could think of anything to say. So Jerome went on:

"Well? Aren't you going to say anything, the pair of you?"

Now it was Julie's turn to be indignant. "You come in here now, telling me that you've decided to believe me only because that girls' finally turned up, but you couldn't believe your own mother when she told you she was innocent? You expect me to be pleased, Jerry, really? You didn't take my word for anything, but now you'll take someone else's? Well thanks for your vote of confidence."

"Give the boy a break, Julie." Gavin had found his voice, "You haven't exactly made it easy for us, have you? What were we expected to think from your holding out against that flaming test all that time? Putting us all through it? You'd better think for a moment."

"Dad's right, mum. When all this started to come out I was a hundred percent in your corner. It was your own actions that started me doubting. I'm sorry, but that's how it is. I thought you'd be pleased. Imagine how Mand feels right now, eh? She's been agonising over not knowing where she belongs. And why? Because of you and your attitude to a simple DNA sample. Sorry, mum, but you need to think it through before you get on your high horse." By this time he'd thrown himself back down on the chair in the conservatory and resumed where he'd left off with his yogurt pot, giving off the kind of body language that suggested he was happy to conclude the conversation right there. The TV was still showing the breakfast news, with the sound muted.

Jerome had gone from ecstatic to thoroughly miserable in a few seconds. Fortunately, Julie, still his mother despite everything, allowed her maternal instincts to come to the surface. She walked over and slid a hand around her son's shoulders.

"I'm sorry Jerry. You're right, of course. You're all of you right. I can't believe how Christina's mother must be feeling right now. Oh, for some of that."

The front door slamming made the two of them turn their heads. Gavin had just gone out.

That afternoon the police detective called, this time on his own, and politely requested if he could come in for a moment. Jerome was in the conservatory again, this time tapping away on his laptop, and Julie was sitting at the island, slowly rotating a glass of wine between her fingertips, when she heard the doorbell.

The officer had come to tell her that, as expected now, her DNA had shown up no evidence of her being related closely to the baby they'd found in the wood, or of Amanda's being the daughter of Marsha. He congratulated her on being in the clear, wished her the best with sorting out her 'other difficulty' and rose to make his way out. When he reached the front door, Julie was right behind him.

"Thank you inspector, and thank you again for your patience and understanding."

"There was one thing that the DNA showed up, Mrs. Pillinger. It's in no way going to implicate you further in the case of either the dead baby or the child that was stolen, who, of course, I know has by some miracle now turned up, but it is a little strange, let me put it that way.

"You see, the DNA matching suggests that in some way your daughter Amanda could easily be a more distant relative of Marsha Travers, and hence of her daughter Rebecca. I can't even begin to think how that might be, but I thought you ought to know. Of course, regarding the guilty party in both the case of the baby that was found in the wood and the snatch case, the evidence that Lily Wilson was able to supply us more than adequately proved her mother's guilt. There's little doubt, nay, no doubt, that Lily is Marsha Travers' lost child. Sometimes miracles do happen, eh?

"It seems that the single mother who'd died just over a year ago, one Ms. Nadia Wilson, was indeed the one who'd done the deed, as it were. If she hadn't died, whether we'd ever have caught up with her or not, that's a moot point now. Water under the bridge, eh?"

With that he tapped his brow, smiled and added, "All the best, Mrs. Pillinger. I hope you can work things out." And he turned and walked to his car.

Julie closed the front door slowly, and wondered when her husband might deem to come home.

Next day, on the lunchtime news, Saturday September 1st, the top story was the fact that Mrs. Julie Pillinger, who had been implicated in an old baby-snatching case that the police had re-opened after the chance discovery of a baby's body in the wood near Sandy Lane village, Wiltshire, had been exonerated of all suspicion, following the results of DNA testing. Her daughter Amanda was also definitely her real daughter. The piece went on to report the miraculous re-appearance of a daughter who'd been lost for over twenty years, the very one that had been the baby stolen from outside the post office in Lyneham, also in Wiltshire. It was now known beyond all doubt that the girl, who was named as Miss Lily Wilson, of Swindon, had been brought up by the woman who'd stolen her from Marsha Travers, back in September 1997.

Once that part of the news bulletin had been dealt with, and the newsreader passed on to yet more about the dreaded Brexit, Philip Trent turned the TV off. His feet were propped up on his desk in his office at the printworks. He mused for a moment or two, then said to himself,

"I think it's time I got to meet my daughter."

34. Complications

The story about Julie Pillinger and the fact that allegedly she buried her child to steal another had affected Philip Trent more than he realised. In front of Colin, he'd done the usual, put a brave face on it, acted like believed he was well out of it with Julie. After all, turns out she was probably unhinged.

Yet now, things were different. Instead of Trent feeling an unexpected sadness at the thought that he may have had a daughter that had died, probably even been murdered, so he theorised, he was suddenly excited that he most likely still had that daughter. She lived, and she was called Amanda.

And he was going to see her, however it could be organised.

His two failed marriages hadn't produced any children, much to his chagrin. He knew deep down that he'd love to have had a son, not that he'd ever admit to that in public. But to at least now have a daughter was some compensation. As he sat there at his desk, on a quiet Saturday when the presses weren't running and the print floor was in darkness, he contemplated what he might do now. He was in the habit of going into the office on a Saturday morning. There were times when the work was piling up, or when there was a big job with a tight schedule, when the place worked the weekend, but he liked to shut the place down, usually. He felt that the workers on the presses and in the finishing department were the happier for having weekends off most of the time.

On a Saturday he could go through paperwork, put quotes together, plan sponsorship events, that kind of thing. Anyway, he had no one at home to cuddle up to, so he was happier in his inner sanctum here at the office. He liked being in the building when it was quiet. He'd let himself in through the printshop doors, disable the alarm, fix himself a strong coffee and plant his ample rear in his leather-clad executive chair.

The TV on the wall of his office was usually on. He rarely met clients in here anyway, usually making use of the plush conference room they'd fitted out a few years before, not long after he'd become a director. That room had a large oval mahogany table and plush carpets and some posh architectural plants in huge pots standing against the full-length plate-glass windows. In his office the TV made him feel comfortable, perhaps a little less alone, plus he liked to keep abreast of what was happening in the world, especially the sporting world. He'd keep the sound muted most of the time, but this particular Saturday, as was his habit, he'd hit the mute button to switch the sound on when he saw the introductory titles to the lunchtime news.

"Things are looking up," he said to himself. Tapping his palm with the pen he held in the other hand, he continued, "Might turn out to be a lot of fun. I mean, let's face it, the kid probably knows that the bloke who her mother married isn't her real father. Maybe she'd like to find me, have some kind of relationship with me. I'd make it worth her while, all right."

He'd often contemplated the fact that, when he died, he'd have no one to leave his estate to. It would end up going to cousins, nieces and nephews, but not to his own kids because, up until now, he didn't have any. More importantly though, he loved the thought of having someone else to impress.

Which was why this young Amanda threw a whole new light on things. He couldn't begin to imagine what effect his turning up might have on the family concerned. All he could think about was the prospect of taking his daughter places, proudly introducing her at functions, perhaps, too, giving people the old sob story about how he'd fought for years to find her, that kind of thing; his great quest to discover what happened to his long-lost daughter, whose mother had so cruelly taken out of his life when she was too young to understand.

It would be dead easy to find where the family lived. After all, he'd seen the news report when that reporter had been standing outside the house, and he knew the house was in Britford. That was a tiny place on the edge of the city of Salisbury, it wouldn't take more than half an hour mooching around to find the house, he was sure of that.

Ought he, though, first to make contact by phone, maybe social media? Maybe not, after all, could be that Julie wouldn't take kindly to his reappearing after over two decades. And he knew that it was he who'd shut her out pretty unceremoniously when she'd told him she was expecting. He hadn't believed her at the time, since the whole idea of a young girl trapping him into a loveless relationship with a false premise was all too likely, to his way of thinking. He was never truly honest with himself though. The real reason was that he'd been running scared.

No, if he were to turn up at their doorstep, ring the front door bell, they'd have a harder job getting rid of him. The only problem was, that he thought he'd read somewhere, in one of the reports in a newspaper, that

Amanda now lived in Bath, that she was a masseuse and beauty therapist in a private spa. It shouldn't be too difficult to track her down there. Maybe it was a better idea. Circumvent the possible awkwardness with Julie's husband, just go meet his daughter face to face and tell her who he was. Yes, that was it. It shouldn't be too hard to trawl through a few web sites for private spas in Bath, check out their pages, lots of them have photos of their teams, along with their CVs and qualifications, their experience on the job, all that kind of stuff. A couple of hours on-line and he reckoned he'd find her.

He leaned forward, reached for the keyboard on his computer, and tapped a key.

Two days later, Monday September 3rd, Philip Trent was in Bath. He had a couple of clients to visit anyway, people who Printit Ltd. did regular work for. No harm in paying one or two of them a courtesy call. Plus he had the address of the spa where he was now sure his daughter worked as a therapist.

Having managed to get over his regular irritation at how difficult it was to park a car in the city, and having decided to park a long way up Bathwick Hill and walk into town, he planned to get to the spa at around 12.30pm, hopefully when Amanda may be thinking about a lunch break. He'd take a taxi back to his car later.

The spa was situated in a fashionable Georgian terrace, with a couple of terracotta pots out front, each of them with a well shaped miniature olive tree growing in it. 'Olives, symbol of their oil, one of those miracle substances that health freaks always bang on about,' he thought, as he walked into the foyer.

The pretty young girl in an immaculate white overall with a name badge pinned above her left breast smiled at him.

"Good morning, sir, can I help you?"

"Well, I hope so. You see I'm looking for Amanda Pillinger, I believe she works here, right?"

"She does, yes. I'm not sure if she has any appointments available today, sir. Usually one has to book a few days in advance, would you like me to look for you?"

He couldn't help but smart at the idea that men, too, availed themselves of this kind of place and what it has to offer. 'Soft in the head, the lot of them,' he thought, before replying:

"Well, no, I don't want a treatment. It's slightly delicate, but I'm a long lost relative, and I think she'd be thrilled to see me. So, I was hoping to surprise her, if I could."

"Let me see what her programme is for today." The girl threw her complete concentration into her keyboard and computer monitor, allowing Trent the opportunity to study her. He was enjoying the process when she stopped, looked at him again and said, "She'll be off for lunch in about twenty minutes. Then her next appointment will be at 2.15pm. Would you like to wait?"

He thought about this for a moment, and then decided that this foyer, in full view of the receptionist and anyone else who may be present at the time, would not be the best place for Amanda to see her real father for the first time in her life. What to do about it was a problem, one that he hadn't fully thought out. He had to think fast. Then an idea hit him, and he hoped it would work.

"Tell you what, if I give you my card, could you tell her that I'll be around the corner in that wine bar there as soon as she comes off duty. If you'd be so kind as to tell her it's a relative who's keen to meet up after many years. I'll wait for her there. Would that be OK?"

"Well, it wouldn't be for me to say, but we'll give that a try if you like."

With that she accepted the business card that Trent handed her and they bade each other goodbye, he taking pains to seem the perfect gentleman as he thanked for for her help.

Half an hour later, as Philip Trent sat in a window seat in a trendy Bath wine bar, he saw his daughter in the flesh for the first time in his life. He was forty-nine, and Amanda twenty-one.

Amanda walked in, wearing tight jeans and a light t-shirt of simple white, with a designer logo emblazoned across the front. Philip Trent did a double-take and drew a deep breath, a very deep breath. He hadn't been prepared for quite how his daughter was going to have turned out. She stood there, just inside the door, looking perplexed and beginning to scan the room.

Philip waited until her eyes reached him and he made a small signal with his hand, as if to say, it's me you're looking for. He stood up as she approached his table, pulled out a chair for her and waited until she sat down before asking,

'What can I get you? It'll all be on me. Look, let's order you a drink and then I'll explain all, is that OK?"

"Umm, yes, sure. I'm a little fazed right now." She told him what she'd like to drink.

Philip went over to the bar and returned a few moments later with a glass full of sparkling liquid and a slice of lemon, accompanied by a half-empty bottle of Perrier.

Placing it before her, he began.

"First, let me introduce myself, I'm Philip Trent. I don't know if that name means anything to you?"

Julie had never mentioned his name to her daughter. All she'd ever told Amanda was that he was a bastard and she'd be better off not knowing anything about him. So she thought for a moment, before answering,

"No, sorry, I don't think it does."

"Well, there's no easy way of saying this, Amanda, so I'll come right out with it, then perhaps you'll allow me to tell you my side of the story."

"OK, whatever you want. I'm completely flummoxed, to be honest."

"Your mother, Julie Parfitt as she was, well she and I were an item many years ago. It all fell apart before I knew that she'd fallen pregnant, ...with you. So you see, Amanda, I'm your father, and I've been hoping to find you for a very long time."

Amanda's jaw dropped. She stared at this man and, in a flash, saw in his features a few of her own. Of course, why had she not already seen it? But it still hit her like a lightning bolt. She didn't know how to react, which Philip seemed to understand.

"Look, I don't know what you heard from Julie about me, and it's all such a long time ago, so I was hoping to explain a little, and to see if there was any way I could be a part of your life now. Not a big part, I'll understand if you'd rather not, but, well, you see I have no other children and I... Well, if I were to be permitted, I'd be only too thrilled to shower a lot of love on you. I know there's no making up for twenty years of absence. I know that, to all intents and purposes, we're total strangers. Yet there is a connection there, don't you see? Blood is thicker than water, so they say, right?" He was running out of things to say, and was so hoping for a positive reaction from Amanda.

"You'll have to give me a moment," said Amanda, "because this takes some assimilating, I'm sure you understand."

"Can I ask, did you know that your father, the one who brought you up, wasn't your real father? I might be wrong in assuming that you did, in which case this will have been an even bigger shock for you, I get that."

"Yes, I knew. But I had no information whatsoever about my birth-father, and dad adopted me as his own when my parents married. I was only months old, so I know no different. He's been a brilliant dad. We're a close family, despite what you may have seen in the news..."

"Wait a minute! That's how you found me, right? You saw the news about mum being suspected."

He threw his hands up, "Yes, you're right. It was my breakthrough after wondering what had happened to my daughter for all those years." He was a good liar, it has to be said. "Once I'd seen where they lived, read about you in the paper, and where you were living, it was a simple job of checking the web sites for the private spas in Bath, and here I am.

"Look, maybe it's not a good idea to talk for hours now. I don't want to rush you. How about I give you my card, and you can take a few days to think about all this, 'cos I know it's a huge shock for you. Then perhaps I can ring you, maybe towards the end of this week, and we can talk again. Maybe I could take you out for a meal or something, how would that be?"

Amanda was still in a state of shock, but nodded an answer, "OK, OK, that would be fine."

With that her father gave her a card, and said, "Can I write down your number?" She told him her mobile number.

"Right, well, look, I'll go. Give you a chance to think on it. Maybe you call me when you're ready, yeah, would that be better? You will call though, won't you? I want to tell you all about myself. Hopefully you'll like what you hear. Look, I'm not one for shouting my mouth off or anything, but I am pretty well set up, if you know what I mean." Here he just couldn't help himself, so he went on, "You'd not regret coming to know your real dad, it would be well worth your while."

He smiled, somewhat awkwardly, bent as if to kiss her head, stopped part-way down and shoved a hand out to shake hers instead, and made for the door.

35. More Complications

It hadn't been a pleasant weekend in the Pillinger household, but at least Julie was grateful that Gavin had stayed at the house and not gone off back to Trevor and Daphne's place, even if he was still in the spare room. He had, though, gone out most of the daytime hours. Jerome was at home, spending most of the time on-line, and talking to Christina almost every hour of the day.

Both Julie and her son had things they needed to discuss with Gavin, but he'd given neither of them the opportunity over the weekend. Now, on Monday 3rd, Gavin had gone in to work as usual, and Julie was trying to occupy herself with the mundane household chores. She'd done a whole load of washing. Much of which had piled up while she'd been 'under siege' as it were. She did go out once, driving to the local supermarket and stocking up once again, in the hope that Gavin would be staying for good now. The only problem was how he'd react once she'd finally been able to unburden herself about why she hadn't wanted the DNA test.

At lunchtime Jerome sat at the kitchen island stuffing his face with beans on toast. He'd poured a generous dollop of HP sauce all over it and his mother had also cracked a can of beer and placed it in front of him. He couldn't help noticing, though, how his mother would cast odd looks at him when she thought he wouldn't notice. 'What was that all about then?' he thought to himself. 'She's been looking at me in funny ways for a couple of days now, so there must be something on her mind. Maybe she just thinks that give me a few weeks away and I've already changed a bit. I do have a tan, so that's something,' he thought.

Ought he to ask her? He thought not, at least for now. Maybe she was simply thinking – 'That's my son, and look how he's grown. Can it really be that all this time's gone by and he's no longer a child. Women, mothers, they're like that, aren't they?' he reasoned.

During the afternoon Jerome finally decided to go out. He'd been in touch with a couple of his mates and was going to hang out with them for a while. He so wanted the next couple of days to go by, so that he could fly back to Crete and be with Chrissy. Julie decided to fill the afternoon by cooking a sumptuous meal for the evening. Maybe she'd finally get the opportunity to talk to Gavin, and, if he'd eaten a really good casserole, a dish he loved, and imbibed of a glass or two of his favourite wine, maybe, just maybe, he'd not be too hard on her.

At around 5.30pm Gavin walked in, and, much to her delight and surprise, came into the kitchen and kissed the top of her head.

"How've you been today?" he asked her. She thought 'well, knock me down with a feather.' She answered, aware of the need to be cautious, not to gush, "Oh, so so. I've been busy."

"I can tell, smells like it. You've done a casserole, I'll bet." With that he went upstairs to shower and change, leaving her in two minds. She so wanted to get everything off her chest that evening, but his slight change of mood might make things even harder. She had no alternative, though, she had to go through with it. Until he understood, there would be no going back to the way they were before all this blew up.

There may well be no going back anyway, but she'd have to wait and see about that.

She was hoping that Jerome would stay out a while longer, giving her and Gavin the opportunity to finally talk without pressure.

Ten minutes later, as she was laying the dining table for their meal, he came into the kitchen in his robe and slippers. She decided to risk asking him a question.

"How were they at work today?"

"Decidedly nice to me. Everyone, to a man, or woman, fell over themselves to sympathise, giving me all that about how heavy-handed the police can be sometimes. Lots of them sent their love to you, 'Tell her we're on her side', stuff like that.

"They were hardly the same people that had looked at me sideways when the TV was banging on about how you were a suspect. Never ceases to amaze me how fickle people can be."

He went and sat at the table, in his usual seat. He still hadn't been as warm as usual, but she was genuinely relieved at his overall mood. She served up the casserole, along with chunks of fresh, wholemeal bread, and poured him his wine. She sat across from him and they began eating. She didn't know how to start, but felt it had to be after they'd eaten and had retired to the conservatory settee. After a few mouthfuls, though, Gavin spoke.

"Look, Jules, I may have been a bit too hard on you. I'm not saying I approve of the way you handled things, but I suppose I ought to try and see it from your angle. I can't imagine how you must have felt when they accused you of those things. You might just have to give a me a little time, but I'll be OK, I'll get over it. That's it really."

"It's not your fault, Gavin, really it isn't. I was stupid, and ought to have known better. But..." She knew that his comments had begun the conversation earlier than she'd intended, but maybe it was just as well.

"But..?"

"But, there was a reason I didn't want the test. And it has to do with something I should have told you about a long time ago."

"Oh dear, what might that be then?" from this she concluded that he didn't have the faintest idea about what she was about to confess to him.

"Oh, Gavin, you know how much I love you, don't you?"

"You're worrying me, now. You'd better come out with it."

She sighed, fleeting thoughts about how their marriage might just be about to go up in smoke. But she knew she had to go on.

"You were away, back in November 1998, one of your overseas trips that you used to do more often than you do these days. It was all a big mistake and it happened before I realised it."

Her husband's facial expression was changing fast. She knew that she couldn't stop now.

"Trevor and Daphne were having a bad patch, and she'd gone to spend the weekend at her sister's. I didn't know that when I knocked the door, really I didn't. I was lonely, what with you being away, Amanda was only two and my mother was babysitting. I'd been out shopping, getting my hair done, and I just thought I could spend a few hours with the two of them, to help me get through your absence.

"Trevor answered the door and invited me in. I didn't know until we got into the lounge that he was alone, that Daphne wasn't there. We talked. He poured his heart out about their problems. I could tell they'd get over them, but at the time he was really down. He broke out a bottle of sherry. Gavin, I..."

Gavin sighed, ran his hands through his hair. Then said, "Trevor, of all people. Trevor, who I've just gone to for support. The bastard. You mean you and he..."

"No, Gavin. I mean, yes, all right. The sherry talked. Next thing I knew I was waking up in his bedroom. He wasn't there, it was late. I didn't have a mobile phone back then. I called mum and she said everything was fine with Amanda, no worries. I told her I'd be home in half an hour. I left without even seeing him.

"Don't be too hard on him, Gavin, please. I don't think either of us meant anything to happen. Circumstances conspired... you know how it is..."

"Well, no, I don't actually. If you knew the chances I've had while away from you Julie, if you only knew. But I've never in my life, never in all our years together so much as looked at another woman." He buried his face in his hands wiping them down across his features as though cleansing his face from the agony.

"Gavin, the thing is, I'm certain, there is no doubt in my mind, because I calculated it so many times. Jerome, he..."

Gavin could listen to no more. He slammed his hands on the table, sending his wine glass toppling, rolling, spilling red wine as it rolled and then fell to the terracotta-tiled floor, smashing on the tiles. He stood up, threw back his chair and stormed out of the room. She sat at the table in a daze, listening to the sounds of her husband banging around in the bedroom upstairs.

Five minutes later she heard him stomp down the stairs and out through the front door, slamming it so hard that the house shook with the impact. Then, as she continued to sit stock still, she heard his car start up and drive away.

Had she ruined everything for good? Probably. Had she been an idiot about the DNA test, definitely. She'd explained to the detective back there in that interview room that she feared that the DNA test would in some way enable them to connect with Jerome's origins. She'd believed that they'd probably want to test the whole family and so at all costs wanted to avoid that. She'd mistakenly thought that, if she'd provided a DNA sample, it would somehow come out that Jerome wasn't Gavin's, but Trevor's.

Of course, once she'd confessed this to the D.I., he'd almost laughed at her naivety, but it didn't change the fact that it was how she'd been reasoning. It devastated her to think that, had she told the police at the outset about her worries, they'd have put her mind at rest. Gavin need never have known. D.I. Stephens had said that there was no way that Jerome would have entered the equation, but she'd feared that in some way he would.

And anyway, was it right that Gavin be kept in the dark? Despite her distress, she felt that it wasn't. But now, where were they? Her husband had to face the fact that neither of his children were actually his. What might that do to him? Oh, to be able to wind the clock back twenty years and exercise more judgment, more self control. But it was too late for that now.

After she'd sat there for another half an hour, doing nothing apart from sipping wine, she got up, ignored the mess of broken glass and wine on both the table and the floor, ignored both her's and her husband's half-eaten meals, and went into the lounge, where she curled up on the sofa, in the foetal position, and stuck a thumb into her mouth.

At around ten o'clock that evening, Jerome came in. As soon as he'd slammed the front door he shouted out,

"Mum, dad! You're not going to believe this! I spoke to Amanda. Her real father's been to see her!"

Not the soul of discretion was Jerome.

He didn't even look in the lounge, but went to the kitchen and saw the mess. "Oh, oh." he said, and decided to clear up the glass and the spilt wine. His mother didn't move from her position on the settee. Jerome concluded that they'd probably both gone out, but under quite what circumstances, he couldn't begin to fathom.

An hour passed during which he talked to Chrissy, excitedly telling her all about how Amanda had had the shock of her life, when her real dad had turned up out of the blue, having discovered her whereabouts through the TV and newspaper coverage of the story about the baby-snatch and the baby in the wood. He was totally unaware that his mother had heard all of this and it made her even more depressed. After all these years, the last thing she wanted was for Philip Trent to be back on the scene.

Some time after eleven, Jerome went up to bed, still unaware that his mother was in the house. He even thought that maybe they'd made it up and gone out to celebrate, although the scene in the kitchen did still perplex him somewhat.

About the same time, Gavin was driving home with a sore fist, although his attitude towards his wife was, by now, somewhat more positive than it had been when he'd left the house earlier.

Gavin came in to a quiet house, all in darkness, apart from the kitchen, where the lights were still on. The lounge, where his wife had now fallen into a fitful sleep, was in total darkness, so he didn't think to go in there. Julie was still curled up in a vain attempt at getting a feeling of security.

Next morning, Gavin came downstairs first, casually glancing into the lounge as he passed the door on his way to the kitchen for coffee. He was dumbfounded to see Julie's feet, now protruding over the arm of the sofa. Because he'd slept in the spare room, he hadn't realised that she hadn't gone to bed at all. He backtracked a little and went in to stand over her. She was still sleeping soundly, looking rather beautiful, he thought. He sat on the carpet, quietly, and reached a hand to tuck some hair back, away from her face.

When he'd got to Trevor and Daphne's place the previous evening, he'd socked Trevor on the nose the moment he'd opened the front door. Trevor had realised instantly that Julie must have told him about what had happened all those years before. He fell down in his own hallway, as his friend stepped over him and stormed into the house. Daphne appeared at the lounge door and shrieked at what she saw. Her husband was trying to get up from the floor, hand over his face and blood flowing between his fingers. Gavin was rubbing his right fist with his left palm, with steam almost visibly coming from his nostrils. He made his way through to their kitchen and threw himself on to a dining chair. There he sat while Trevor and Daphne tried to organise themselves. Daphne ran back into the lounge and returned with a fistful of tissues. Then the two of them joined Gavin in the kitchen, not quite knowing how to play this.

"Did YOU know, Daphne?" spat Gavin.

"Ever since the day it happened," was her terse reply. "You really are a prize fool Gavin Pillinger. Do you know that? Julie loves you beyond distraction. Trevor was terribly contrite when I got home after it had happened. I could hardly have been too self-righteous about it, now could I? After all, it was me storming off in a huff, which I used to do all too often back then, that had forced them into the situation in the first place. As soon as I got home, he told me everything and begged forgiveness. I told him it wasn't for me to forgive him, but the other way around. I phoned Julie that very night and asked her to come back round, but she couldn't because of Amanda, who was just a toddler then, as you'll know.

"But we soon talked it out and Julie was beside herself with shame over the whole thing. She told us both that she so deeply loved you and couldn't understand herself why she'd let herself go like that. Drink, that's the simple answer. People who drink too much soon lose their inhibitions, you know that Gavin. We all agreed there and then that it would be put behind us and never brought up again. When Jerome was born we had our suspicions, but because he looked totally like Julie and not like either you or Trevor, we thought it best to simply draw a line under the whole sorry business. Let's face it, the way your family's turned out, wasn't that the best decision, anyway? If this dratted affair about the babies hadn't reared its ugly head, you'd never have been any the wiser, and in my opinion, that would have been for the best.

"I suggest you count your blessings and go home to your wife. She's suffered enough lately, without you turning on her. Right now she needs emotional support, and she needs it from you, you stupid oaf.

"That's all I have to say on the matter. Now, if you don't mind, I have a husband with a bleeding nose to attend to."

And so Gavin, tail firmly between his legs, had left and driven back home.

Now, here he was looking at his wife in awe. What she'd been through recently, coupled with the way he'd been reacting, left him in wonder at her ability to survive. He gently rocked his wife's body this way and that, sliding his arms beneath her, and then carried her out of the room and up the stairs to their bedroom, where he laid her tenderly on the bed and climbed in beside her, drawing the duvet over the both of them.

36. Slight Relief

The following morning, Tuesday September 4th, the atmosphere couldn't have been more different from twenty-four hours earlier. Gavin had to go to work, so he and Julie were in the kitchen at around eight o'clock, but this time he wasn't watching the news on his iPad and she sat beside him while they both ate breakfast. This time, Julie had prepared a feast of baked beans, bacon, egg, mushrooms, lashings of toast and tomato sauce, plus a dessert of Greek-style yogurt with chopped fresh peaches on top.

"So we're agreed, then," said Gavin; words in response to which Julie nodded and smiled a smile of relief. "Jerome is not to hear of this, ever, right?"

"Right. And thank you darling, I'm ...well, just – thank you."

"I'm not to hear of what, then?" asked Jerome, who, unexpectedly, had risen early and was just coming into the kitchen.

"Nothing of any consequence," said Gavin, and, trying to move on to something else (and succeeding) he added, "So, your mother tells me that Amanda's birth-father has finally crawled out of the woodwork. How's she dealing with it? I wonder if she'll deign to call us today."

"Works both ways, dad. You can always call her."

"Yes, sure, but isn't it a child's responsibility to ring their parents first? I mean, when you take into consideration all they've done for you over the years."

"OK, OK, agreed. She probably will anyway. Wait a minute, how did mum know? When I came in the other night, there was no one home."

"I was in the lounge, Jerry, I'd fallen asleep on the sofa. You woke me up when you came in, but apart from hearing your rather subtle exclamation about the news, I drifted off again. I was very tired, after all that's been going on. I didn't wake up again until six o'clock next morning, when your father's alarm went off. It was the first thing I told him before we even got up.

"But we don't have any details. Fill us in, do, please."

"Well, first of all, I'm not even going to ask you why the kitchen looked like a bomb site when I got home. As long as you two look happy now, which, amazingly, you do - I can't quite believe it - but I'll not pursue that line of enquiry. Anyway, she rang and told me that her real dad had tracked her down to the spa after all the publicity about this two-baby story. Reckons he had no idea you were expecting her when he ditched you, only that he thinks you were trying to trap him. Says he'd been searching for years, so I pointed out to Mand that his story already has inconsistencies. I mean, if he'd been trying to track her down for years, then he would have known that you were pregnant, wouldn't he? So something about him doesn't check out."

"Comes as no surprise to me, Jerry," said his mother.

"Well, he met her during her lunch break and said he'd like to be a part of her life again. Not sure I think it's a good idea, but that's about the size of it."

"If he turns up around here, he'll get pretty short shrift," said Gavin.

"You're not planning to sock someone else, now darling?" said Julie, who instantly regretted saying that, because it related to Trevor and something they'd just agreed not to let Jerome know about.

"Sock someone else? Blimey, what's dad been up to now?" Jerome picked up on everything.

"Long story, son, but it's to do with someone at work, no sweat." Gavin was pleased with that one, since Trevor did work with him, too, after all.

"Oh dear, someone push you too far about that whole suspicion thing about mum?"

"Yeah, something like that. Anyway, we'll have to wait and see on this one, won't we. But, like I said, he'd better not come around here, that's all I'm saying. Anyway, I'd better get myself into gear."

"Dad, can I talk to you about something?"

"Not much time now, son. Can it wait 'til tonight?"

"What about if I come into town later, and we go for a drink at lunch time, how would that be for you?"

"OK, sounds good. I'll see you outside the bank at one, then."

Gavin kissed his wife on the cheek, which just hours before, Julie had lost hope of ever happening again, and he got up to go upstairs to clean his teeth, put his tie and jacket on and make his way to work.

When he walked out through the front doors of the bank at a couple of minutes after one, Jerome was there, waiting on the public bench a few metres from the building. They made their way along the road and around the corner to the Ox Row Inn, which has tables and chairs outside. It was a fine day, and so Gavin told Jerry to get seated while he went in to order a couple of drinks. He emerged a few minutes later carrying two pints of real ale and a couple of packets of crisps.

As he sat down, placing a pint in front of his son, he also threw one of the crisp packets down in front of Jerome. "Cheese and onion, that's what you like, right?"

"Bang on. Thanks dad."

Breaking open the crisp packet by tugging at both sides of the top seam, Jerome begins. "Dad, you know I'm spending the summer in Crete, and that I've kind of settled in one taverna, been there for weeks, right?"

"I do." Gavin crunched a couple of plain salted crisps and took a sip of his ale. "Must admit, it's a far cry from what you'd had planned, isn't it."

"Yes, well, that's just it. See, I've been presented with a business opportunity."

"And this would have nothing to do with the pretty young thing who's the taverna owner's daughter, of course."

"Oh, right, so mum has been keeping you abreast, then?"

"Oh yes. Go on Jerry."

"OK, yes, I'll admit, Chrissy was a factor, but only to begin with. I mean, let me re-phrase that. I had every intention of keeping in touch, because, for good or bad, I'm besotted with her. But that wouldn't have been what made me think hard about what I want to do. I mean, had it just been me and Chrissy, I'd definitely be coming back in October to start at uni. I'd have hoped that she and I could endure the time apart. But it's turned into a lot more than that, which is why I wanted to tell you the whole story."

Gavin crunched a few more crisps, sipped a little more ale, simply looked at Jerry and waited. He knew all about how to apply pressure without seeming to do so.

"Look, dad, Nikos, Chrissy's dad, he wants to have me take on the business. He's so delighted with the way I've fitted in, not to mention how his daughter's fallen for the old English charm too, that he told me that he'd so prefer me to stay. He'll educate me completely on the ins and outs of the place, even make sure I learn the language, and – assuming me and Chrissy get married – he wants me to be his heir. In short, I have the chance to be running my own restaurant just a few years down the line, when he decides to retire and take a back seat.

"I know it all sounds improbable, but those are the facts, it's all true. He's dead serious, as long as me and Chrissy are too, and we are, dad. OK, she's young, but we're talking about getting married in maybe another year or two, that won't matter if I'm there, slowly learning all there is to know about the place. It's a little gold mine, dad, honestly. You wouldn't believe how great the place is, and the location, right on the beach in a really beautiful little village, where tourism's more select that places like Malia, which would be awful, to be honest. I'd so love you to see it."

Here, Jerome stopped, feeling like he'd said all there was to say. He now awaited the fallout, the disapproval, the derision, all the stuff about him and Chrissy being still too young, the missed opportunity of university, and the rest.

Instead, Gavin sat a while, deliberately letting Jerome stew, before truly surprising him in a way he couldn't even have imagined.

"Jerry, it's your life, not mine. Yes, I had big ideas for you, but if this is what you really want, then I'd be a fool to make you miserable by forcing you to stick to the original plan.

"You see, son," [and here he felt a pang, yet also a deep-down satisfaction of sorts] "I've learned quite a bit in the last week or two. I think I've learned what's most important in life. What's happened to our family this summer, well, it's changed me, that's the only way I can describe it. Do you remember that movie, 'Dead Poet's Society?'"

Jerome's face gave him the answer, which was a 'no.'

"Doesn't matter, it's quite old now. Must have come out in the eighties, maybe the nineties, so you'd probably not even have been born."

Here, Gavin had to swallow hard, to keep himself in check as images flashed across his mind. Jerome gave a shake of the head. He picked up on his father's emotional struggle, but concluded it was for another reason than the actual one.

"The thing is, that movie showed the folly of trying to force your kids along a certain path, when it's really not what they want to do. If this Nikos is genuine, then it could well be a wonderful life you've chosen. I don't know. If it all goes wrong, then you'll have learnt something, at least. So, what I'm really saying, Jerry," and here he couldn't help it, he placed a hand on Jerome's shoulder and gave him a squeeze of assurance, "...is go chase your dream. I've gone down the safe path in my life. Nothing adventurous. Many would say my job's only marginally more interesting than an accountant's. If you want to do something extraordinary, I am not going to stop you. I only ask one thing."

Stunned though he was by this response, Jerome managed to summon up the reply,

"Yes, dad? What?"

"You come back to me, to us, your mother and I, when you need support, help, advice. Because we'll do our damnedest to be there for you."

Was that moisture Jerome saw in Gavin's eyes? Surely not. But there was nothing for it, he leaned across the table and hugged his father with all his might, and he didn't care what the passers-by thought one jot.

37. Marsha, Lily, Amanda, Philip

Lily (née Rebecca) and Marsha had enjoyed an unbelievable few days together, during which the blood connection evidently cemented a close relationship between them. They both concluded that there is something about one's genes that can do that, make people identify with each other, even if they've never met. Marsha struggled a little to use the name Lily, but insisted that she keep trying, even when Lily offered to think about changing her name to Rebecca. "No," she'd said, "You've been Lily all your life, so your national insurance number, your bank account, your passport, your details with your employer, you don't want to have to go changing all of that now." So she'd pressed Lily not to worry, she said she'd get used to it eventually. What was far more important was the fact that they were together, mother and daughter, for the first time since Lily had been a few months old.

They spoke a few more times with Christina and Niko in Makriyialo, both of whom were ever more ecstatic about this new extension to the family. They talked about Marsha and Lily coming over for a visit, and this was what the two women wanted to finalise before Lily went back to her flat in Swindon, and her job.

So, while Jerome and his dad were having a heart-to-heart at the Ox Row Inn in downtown Salisbury, here in Lyneham the women were surfing the net to find flights to go out to Crete together before the season ended. They still had a little under two months before then, and Marsha especially was desperate to get together with her husband and other daughter, so that, for the first time in her life she could have all of her natural family in one place. She hadn't known such happiness since she and Richard had got engaged, not all that long before the tragic accident that had claimed his life. She felt so buoyant that she couldn't quite believe it.

There would be little doubt that, once she and Lily went out to Crete, Marsha would stay this time. Lily would then have to decide what she was going to do. She had a life, of course, but it was not brimming with an excess of socialising, although she did go out occasionally with a couple of girls from her office. Marsha secretly harboured the desire for Lily to think about also moving to Crete. Who knows, maybe there would be a nice young Greek fella she could fall in love with. But what she desired more than anything else was to be able to see her daughter as often as was humanly possible. During the few days in which Lily had stayed, she'd perpetually touched her daughter, stroked her cheek, her arm, cuddled her. It was all simply miraculous after all the years of emptiness and heartache. She was never going to lose Rebecca, or rather Lily, again, oh no.

After an hour or so of trying various web sites, they found flights from Gatwick to Heraklion for 19th September, for a week. It was too brief for Marsha, but it was at least a start for both of her daughters to get to know each other. Marsha also knew that Jerome would still be there, so that would be nice, because it was looking increasingly like he was going to become her son-in-law at some future time.

Lily hugged her mother so vigorously that it hurt as they said goodbye later that afternoon, Lily having told her boss that she'd be able to come back to work the next day, September 5th. She'd told her mother that she worked for a very good company, and her department manager was very accommodating, especially after hearing her story. She didn't really have any leave due to her, but he'd agreed over the phone that she could have some codes that would enable her to get into the company's intranet system and hence be able to do some work while she was away, as long as she took a laptop with her. Lily had no problem agreeing to that whatsoever.

All in all, Marsha's life had taken a gargantuan turn for the better. They agreed to meet in Swindon on the day of the flight, and take the National Express coach to the airport.

Whilst Lily and Marsha were looking for flights, and Jerome had been nervously explaining to his father about what he now wanted to do with his life, Amanda had been fretting over what to do about her natural father having suddenly turned up from nowhere. She didn't know whether to speak to her mother about it or not. She hadn't even thought about the probability that Jerome would tell her parents anyway. She had a limited idea of what her mother thought about him from the things she'd told Amanda about the time she'd first fallen pregnant, and the way he'd locked her summarily out of his life. Could he have changed? People did change, didn't they? What harm could it do to meet him a few more times, then see how she felt after that?

But then, how would her father Gavin feel about it? He'd been everything a real father should be to her. She was more than happy to have him as her father and felt a pang of conscience about possible issues of loyalty, gratitude for the way he'd brought her up, cared for her, always been there for her. This kind of thing could crush him, and he didn't deserve it, especially after all that had gone on lately. Most importantly, she loved him deeply.

Amanda hadn't seen or spoken to her mother in about a week and a half. She'd needed some time to think everything through. Jerome, bless him, rang her all the time, though, and so on that Tuesday, September 4th, the day before Jerome was due to fly back to Crete, she decided it was time to join the family at home for a couple of hours, which would also enable her to see Jerome before he left. And anyway, she was pretty sure he'd be asking her if she might just be able to take him to the airport.

She didn't ring, she just drove over and let herself in at around 7.00pm. Hearing voices in the kitchen, because she knew it would probably be time for her parents and Jerome to eat their evening meal, she shouted "Only me!" and, swallowing hard, went down the hall and into the kitchen.

The scene that greeted her could hardly have been more different from what she'd expected. All three were in good spirits, smiling, talking animatedly. 'Blow me down,' thought Amanda, it's like things always were before this whole sorry saga took off. How long had it been? It was the middle of August when the police had first come to the house, and so it was only about three weeks that had passed. How their world had changed during that time. Yet, now, wonder of wonders, here she was looking at a nice, happy, cosy little family scene, and she was flummoxed.

"Well, I'll not say it's not amazing, but what's changed, if I may ask?"

"Nothing much my sweet," said Gavin, "We've all just realised how much we mean to each other. That's about it really. Come here and give your dad a hug."

She did as he requested, then repeated the procedure with her mother and brother. Did she want to raise the issue of Philip Trent? No, she decided, she didn't. For the time being she'd handle it alone. She'd see how things went. Maybe she'd send him packing after another chat or two anyway. There was no sense angering, or even worse depressing, her dad about this now, especially after this dramatic improvement in things in the family home.

Jerome was really keen for his parents to come out to Crete before the end of the season, so they talked about Gavin taking a week off work. It could be arranged, he told them. Amanda too could probably wangle it somehow, even if she lost a little pay. So, as the evening progressed, they fell to all gathering around a laptop as Jerome took charge of the flight search.

By the time they needed to think about going to bed, it was decided that Amanda was staying the night, and anyway, Jerome had asked if she'd run him back to Gatwick the next day.

As she drove back from the airport that Wednesday afternoon, September 5th, she called her birth-father using the hands-free in her car.

"OK," she said, when he'd answered the phone, seen it was her, as he'd already put her number into his phone, and said, "Amanda, my little girl! How are things?"

He'd been very nervous since Monday, when they'd first talked face-to-face, and almost convinced himself that she wouldn't call again. He could hardly conceal his excitement when he saw it was her calling, but he managed it somehow. He was ever the man to try and appear calm to others, always in control.

"So, are we going to meet up again? Let me take you out to lunch, it would be my treat."

"OK," she said for a second time, "that might be nice. Is Saturday all right?"

"Of course, it would be perfect. I'll do a few things in the office and drive over to Bath to meet you. Where would you like to go to eat? You say, and I'll fix us a table."

"OK," she said for a third time, while making a mental note to try and stop saying 'OK.' "I fancy the Ponte Vecchio, near the Weir and Pulteney Bridge, is that all right?"

"Perfect. You could have said the Royal Crescent Hotel for all I care, Amanda. I'll book us a table and ring you when I'm on my way over, to arrange where to meet. See you Saturday then."

Saturday September 8th came around and Amanda woke up wondering if she was doing the right thing. She talked with her brother, now back with Chrissy in Crete, the previous evening, and he'd told her she must do what her heart moved her to do. That had helped, a little.

Her mobile rang as she was window shopping in the city centre at around 12.30pm. It was a nice day of sunshine and clouds, with the temperature around 18 degrees Celsius, as good as one could hope for in September in the UK. She was feeling lighter of mood because of it. She answered it to Philip Trent, who told her he'd be at the bottom of Milsom Street, where it meets Old Bond Street, at 12.45pm, would that be OK?

She said it was, although it was very short notice, but she was only a block or two away, so it was no problem. They met and this time he lightly held her upper arms and kissed her on both cheeks, she didn't resist. He then pulled her hand through the crick of his elbow, so that they were arm-in-arm, and set off on foot towards Pulteney Bridge, and the restaurant just beyond.

As they walked, he glanced her way and smiled now and again, but didn't try to converse overmuch, apart from the odd 'this is nice' or 'fabulous day.' He admitted to himself that he had a damned fine, beautiful daughter, and he was going to do whatever it took to have her in his life. He'd have clients eating out his hand at charity functions when they saw her, he thought to himself.

Once they were seated, and had ordered their food, plus a bottle of Valpolicella, he attempted to get a proper conversation going. She was obviously slightly nervous about this whole thing, which was understandable enough, he thought.

"So, are things back to normal with your family, now this whole 'being a suspect' malarkey is behind your mum, then?"

"Yes, pretty much." She half smiled at him. She was studying his features, he could tell.

"Strange though, isn't it? I mean, I'd probably never had ever found your mum again, or known about you, if this hadn't all blown up the way it did. Do you ever think life does things like that for a reason?"

She remembered Jerome's words about things not quite adding up. The last time they'd met, he'd reckoned that he'd been looking for her for years. She decided to let it pass, but placed an invisible tick in the 'negatives' column.

'No, not really. Things just happen, don't they?"

"You might be right. But I do wonder. Did you know, or rather, did your mother know this other woman, then? The one whose baby was stolen?"

"Not to talk to. She saw her around, that was all. You know I met her second daughter, don't you? No, of course, why would you? It's a bit of a long story really, but my brother's spending the summer out in Greece, and he ended up staying at a taverna where the bloke who runs it, well, he was the husband of the woman whose baby was stolen in Lyneham."

"And you tell me things don't happen for a reason."

"Well, I can't go down that route right now. But I went out there for a while and met them. Seems that Marsha, that's her name, went out to Greece the summer after she had the baby stolen and eventually fell in love with, and married, this man Nikos, who runs a taverna on the beach. They had a baby, who grew up to be Christina, who's now almost certain to become my brother's fiancee, so it's a nice story anyway, don't you think?"

Philip Trent was now excited to hear his daughter beginning to warm to the conversation. She'd got something to talk about, which was a relief. He knew something that she didn't by now, too.

"What happened to her first husband, then? I presume she was married when she had the first baby, the one that was snatched?"

"No, it was really sad. She and the father were engaged when she fell for Rebecca, the baby that was snatched. Apparently, he was a long-distance lorry driver and he was killed only months before their planned wedding. Big motorway pile-up on the M4. Seems it got on to the front pages and was all over the news for a day or two."

"Wait a minute, when was this exactly, the pile-up I mean?"

"I think it was a while after Rebecca was born, so it must have been late 1997. It was horrific, so Chrissy told me. His lorry caught fire. He was the only fatality, although I might be wrong about that, but they couldn't get him out in time. I can't imagine how awful it must have been for Marsha to lose him like that, and just when they were planning to get married and raise the baby together.

"Are you all right? You've gone a bit peaky."

"I don't think I am. From what you've just told me, well, I can't quite get my head round it, but the guy that died in that pile-up, the lorry driver, I never knew he'd been the father of the baby that was stolen. See, that woman Marsha, the mother, she's a cousin of mine."

"She's what? Are you sure? I mean, ...why wouldn't you be? You must know your own cousins, I suppose. You didn't know, then, that the man who died in the pile-up had been her fiancé? If it's the same accident, then it must be him. Now you do have me wondering about all these coincidences!"

38. Amanda, Philip, Sept 2018

The remainder of the lunch went OK, but Amanda was to some degree preoccupied by what she had learned about the odd connection between Marsha Travers (as she'd been then) and Julie, in that it made Marsha's baby Rebecca the second cousin of Philip Trent, and thus it made Amanda and her distant cousins. Trent was intrigued to have learned that the lorry driver who'd died in the pile-up, which everyone still remembered around the area, had been Marsha's intended.

Amanda did ask Philip how come he didn't know about Marsha and Richard, in view of the fact that he and Marsha were cousins. And then, of course, the case of the baby-snatch itself.

"Oh, you know how it is. OK, maybe you don't. But our family, well we were awash with cousins when we were little. The family used to gather at the grandparents' house on Saturday evenings and, while our uncles and aunties did grown-up things, like playing cards for money, or going down the pub, we played together. But you get into your teens and you tend to see your cousins less and less often. You move house, put a bit more distance between you, that sort of thing. By the time we were in our twenties, I think I only saw Marsha rarely, probably not even once a year, if there was maybe a wedding. She wasn't one of the ones I stayed close to. We never fell out or anything, but we didn't move in the same circles and didn't live that close, so that we'd have seen each other regularly.

"By the time that guy was killed in that crash, I hadn't seen Marsha in a long time and I had no idea if she was married, engaged, or anything. It was only after he died that we heard on the news about him having had a girlfriend, and a child on the way. I never made the connection to my cousin Marsha, though. OK, so I knew about her baby having been the one that was stolen but, and I know it sounds cold, because we didn't see each other any more, I kind of left it, didn't get in touch. In situations like that the time soon passes and you give up on the idea anyway. Not knowing what to say to someone in such circumstances was probably a big factor too, if I'm honest.

"Can't say more than that, really." And he didn't. They'd talked on about his print company, how he'd worked his way up to the board, and was now virtually running the whole show, and Amanda slowly began to see the real Philip Trent. Her participation in the conversation grew less and less, and he rattled on more and more. She heard about the rugby tournament they sponsored, the golf events they organised for charity, some of the big-name clients his company handled the print for, and the fact that he was a bit of a Jaguar freak and wouldn't drive anything else.

She was struggling to maintain the will to live by the time three o'clock arrived and he asked for the bill. He made a bit of a show about paying with his Amex Gold Card, and they got up to leave. Once outside he offered to walk her somewhere, but she said she'd arranged to meet a friend, so suggested that they part company at the river side.

As he walked away, having insisted he ring her next week some time, she watched him and made a resolve.

No, she didn't really want him in her life. She'd deduced that the main reason he wanted her in his was to serve as some kind of trophy. He couldn't now have a trophy wife, so a trophy daughter was the next best thing.

And Amanda wasn't the type to be put on show when it suited someone else to do so. She resolved to change her phone number, and only let her friends and family know about it.

Eleven days later, Gavin, Julie and Amanda were checking in at Gatwick airport for the flight to Crete. They were all in a happy mood and looking forward to getting together not only with Jerome, but also with his intended and her father, Jerome's new business mentor. Gavin was secretly harbouring thoughts, too, of 'vetting' the man, in case he might have to revise his feeling about Jerome taking this on.

They weren't aware that, in the next queue over, for the very same flight, Marsha and Lily were also chatting excitedly about the prospect of being with Marsha's Greek family.

And none of them were aware of the connection that Amanda now knew of, between Marsha's family and hers.

39. All's Well...

In the departure lounge, with a couple of hours to kill, Gavin and Julie went browsing in the perfume and drinks stores. Amanda hit the clothing stores and, as she browsed, decided to call her brother, to tell him about the weird connection between her birth-father and Marsha, and hence of Rebecca. She'd mentioned it to her mother, but not to Gavin. Julie had told her how Gavin had reacted when Jerome had mentioned that Philip Trent had been sniffing around, trying to make it up with his estranged daughter. She decided not to broach the subject with Gavin, as it would only annoy him all the more. Julie had wanted to talk more about it, but couldn't because Gavin had come in.

"Jerry, it's soooo exciting. We'll be with you in a few hours."

"Can't wait sis. Boy are we gonna have a blow-out tonight."

"You know I've met my real dad again, don't you?"

"I knew it was happening, but not when. How did it go?"

"Well, for one thing, I've decided not to see him again. But he told me something that's really weird. We talked about that bloke who was killed in that motorway pile-up when Rebecca was only months from being born. Well he knew the story, but didn't realise that the man had been Marsha's partner. He sprang it on me that he knows Marsha. Jerry, it seems that me and Lily are distant cousins."

"Did I hear you right? You and Lily, or Rebecca as she was, distant cousins? That would mean that your natural father was related to Marsha in some way."

"He is, Jerry, seems like he and Marsha ...well, their parents were siblings, making them cousins. So Lily and I have a connection through my natural father and her mum Marsha. Curiouser and curiouser, eh?"

Before they hung up, Amanda made Jerome promise not to breathe a word of this to anyone until she was ready.

As it happened, too, both had forgotten all about finding out quite why their mother had held out so long against giving that DNA sample. The way things had improved in the past few days had completely thrust that little detail from their minds.

A number of hours later, the passengers on the Gatwick-Heraklion flight were exiting the terminal building and Gavin was heading to the car hire office. Jerome had told his family that a hire car would be the way forward, since Niko's pickup wouldn't be big enough. He, Chrissy, and Nikos had decided not to mention that Marsha and Lily were also coming the same day, and probably on the same flight. They thought it would be fun to see their faces when they realised what a big reunion it was going to be. Nikos had come to collect Marsha and Lily, so as to be fairly sure that the Pillinger family wouldn't recognise him. He was immediately captivated by Lily and gave her a warm embrace, before giving his wife a long, lingering kiss and hug and then leading the women to the pickup.

Nikos knew that he could be back in Makriyialo long before the others got there, for two reasons. One, he knew the road all too well and, two, he drove like a man possessed most of the time. Marsha had warned Lily about this, but it didn't seem to faze her at all. After all, she was young and she drove in much the same manner.

By early evening, he'd arrived with his two charges back at the taverna on the beach. Chrissy had run to meet both her mother and her long-lost sister. Both girls found it weird to begin with, yet something deep within them clicked, they both felt it, and they were very soon involved in a long exclusive conversation. Nikos didn't mind. He had Marsha to keep him company, plus the prospect of her now staying for good, which made him feel in ebullient mood. They had arranged for Lily to stay in Chrissy's bedroom with her, so that the half-siblings would be able to really spend as much time together as they wanted to. Marsha needed to have no worries about them getting along. From the way it started, she could see they were going to truly become sisters.

Both Nikos and Chrissy told their newly arrived guests that Jerome's family were on the way, and Jerome, of course, already knew too, but had chosen to go out for a while when the two women first arrived, so as to allow the family, the newly expanded family as it was, to bond a little before he and his clan also entered the scene. He'd done an *'autostop'* as the Greeks call hitch-hiking, to Ierapetra a little earlier in the day and had told Amanda where he'd be on the road when they passed around the back of the town. He'd then be able to jump in with the three of them and arrive along with them as a foursome back at the taverna.

Gavin, of course, had his sat-nav working on his phone as they approached Ierapetra, and Jerome had told them exactly where to stop for him to jump aboard the hire car. They all saw him as they approached, standing at the roadside beside the beach just east of the town, the blue Mediterranean sea lapping mere metres behind him as they pulled over. He looked very relaxed and at one with himself. Once in the back with his sister, who gave him a bear hug as he drew his door closed, Gavin pulled away and they were then only twenty minutes or so from Makriyialo, a fact that had all three of the visitors bursting with anticipation at seeing what would very probably be Jerome's new home, and thus somewhere they'd hopefully all come to know very well in the coming years.

Of course, Amanda was also itching to be back with her friend Christina, thinking about how they'd have so much to catch up on, especially the details about she and them being distant blood relatives. She very much looked forward to throwing that bombshell into the conversation later in the evening, preferably after a sufficient amount of alcohol had been consumed. The only worry she had was her dad and how he'd react, but she decided that, in the environment that she hoped they'd all be immersed in by then, he'd not be at all annoyed, or perturbed, especially since she was also going to tell them all that her relationship with her birth-father was going no further.

They pulled up outside the taverna about an hour after Nikos had brought Marsha and Lily home, and Chrissy was outside to meet them, since Jerome had already called her when they entered the village from the west, a couple of kilometres away. As Jerome got out of the car, his parents were quite moved by the warmth of the hug and kiss, or perhaps that would be best described as a snog, that Chrissy gave their son. She then broke free and enveloped Amanda in a bear-hug too, before allowing Jerome to introduce his parents, whom she then proceeded to kiss on both cheeks while also grabbing their arms in turn.

Gavin was well impressed by the Greek ways of welcoming visitors. He was even more impressed by the beauty of his likely young daughter-in-law to be. His business head began its calculations even before they entered the building, but he was already computing ways in which he might get involved in investing in the business and thus helping Jerome to further show Niko how much of an asset he was going to be.

Once all the introductions were over out front, Chrissy was anxious to tell the arrivals that they had to come through to the dining terrace to share a drink before they all went upstairs to get settled in. There were a couple more people they simply had to meet right away.

Nikos, Marsha and Lily stood up from the table at which they'd been sitting to welcome Jerome's family as they came through the building from the front door. The amazement on their faces was a picture as Chrissy excitedly said to them all,

"Gavin, Julie, Amanda, I want you to meet my mother and my sister, Marsha and Lily. Marsha and Lily, Jerry's family, dad Gavin, mum Julie, and sister Amanda. There followed probably at least ten minutes of hugs, kisses, expressions of amazement, congratulations at how Lily and her mother had finally been reunited, all that and more. Such joy had rarely been witnessed anywhere on the whole island as was evident at this little gathering. When the excitement finally began to dissipate, Ulrika appeared with a bottle of ouzo, some chopped peach and melon on a huge dish, plus a pile of plates, forks and serviettes for all to enjoy. Nikos poured ouzo so generously that another bottle needed to be called for. After all, they were now a party of eight, and a bottle doesn't go far in such circumstances.

After an hour or so, during which the conversation had flowed like Niagara after a spring rainstorm, it was suggested that the visitors all go and get showered and settled in, to meet back there on the dining terrace at around 9.00pm, for a family evening meal. The idea was acceptable to all.

In the warmth of a Cretan September evening, the moon peeking over the horizon, they all finally got settled around two tables that had been pushed together for the occasion, and the food began to arrive. Nikos declared that he was going to treat everyone to a sumptuous Cretan feast and no one was to worry about money. It wasn't even to be spoken of for this occasion. In fact, all the guests who were liable to be leaving after a week or so, who amounted to Gavin, Julie, Lily and Amanda, were to be under the understanding that any drink or meal they might want to take in the taverna would be on the house, and Nikos would hear no arguments.

Some hours later, once the table had been reduced to a complete bomb site, and a couple of bottles of spirits, one Metaxa, the other Scotch malt whiskey, were looking decidedly well used, Amanda decided it was time to hit them all with her little bombshell. Only Jerome was aware of what she was about to tell them. She tingled with excitement at having them all on tenterhooks, when she stood up and said,

"Now listen up everyone. There's one piece of this whole jigsaw that might have had some of us wondering. And I know what it is. I hope you're all ready for this.

"When we first heard about the 'baby in the wood' case, and the police were theorising, correctly as it eventually turned out, that the woman who stole Rebecca, now sitting amongst us as Lily, of course, had buried her own sadly dead child secretly, and stolen Rebecca to replace her, the finger – and you'll forgive me for just referring to this for a moment mum – started to point at our mum, Julie. We're all aware of that. At the time, owing to our overactive imaginations, Chrissy, and then Jerome, began to look at me to see if I might perhaps resemble Marsha at all. If I did, it would have strengthened their suspicions about poor Julie.

"The strange thing was, they did see a slight resemblance, didn't you guys?" She said this glancing from Christina to Jerome and back again. "Now, as we're all together here for the first time, it doesn't take a rocket scientist to see that there are definitely some features about me that are like Marsha's and Lily's, can you see it?" Here she gave all present the chance to peruse the evidence, turning her head first one way, then the other.

"How could this be? One might ask. A logical question, and one that might appear not to have a satisfactory answer. Well, I'm hereby able to reveal that answer. Pause for effect..." She actually said those words, "Owing to the publicity surrounding poor mum, when she was the centre of attention for the dratted media, the lowlife who'd abandoned her all those years ago, saying he didn't believe she was pregnant with me anyway, came out of the woodwork and tracked me down at my place of work in Bath. My birth father had the gall to try and suggest that I might like to let him into my life, after all these years."

Gasps of amazement from Marsha, Lily and Niko. Julie, of course, knew that bit, as did Gavin and Jerome. What they didn't know (except for Jerome) was what had come out in the conversations that Amanda had had with her birth-father, before deciding to wash her hands of him.

"The reason ...and we could do with a drum roll here..." at this, Jerome duly obliged with his hands, battering the table in front of him to try and create the desired effect, "...the reason is, the low-life who'd fathered little old me is a cousin of Marsha's." As she said this, she looked in Marsha's direction, to see what kind of reaction she'd elicit. The effect was just about as she'd expected, jaw-dropping amazement. "His name is Philip Trent, and he still thinks far too much of himself. Now, if I may say so, in an effort to move swiftly on," and, with this, Amanda walked around the table to stand behind Gavin, who wasn't looking as contented as he had a few minutes earlier, she slid both hands down around his neck from behind and clasped them together over his chest, then rested her head on the crown of his. She went on:

"The fact that Philip Trent cast my mother off like an old rag will forever be a blessing to me. Not just to me, but to our whole family. When mum met dad, ...this dad," and saying this she cast her eyes down at the head beneath her, "it was the best thing that ever happened to her. It was because Philip Trent abandoned her, that we ended up with the best dad on the planet, bar none. Present company excepted." Here she grinned and gave a sideways nod in the direction of Niko, who acknowledged the thought with a nod and a smile. "Gavin Pillinger, I hereby declare you my one hundred percent real dad in every way that truly counts. I only told all of you this so you could see that there were genuine reasons for seeing some likeness between me and Marsha, and, having now met the wonderful Lily, née Rebecca, I'm even a bit stunned myself at our common bone structure. Such is the wonder of the way our genes work, eh, folks?"

With that she kissed the top of Gavin's head, which caused a great flow of relief to run through him, and he relaxed into her embrace, full of relief and love in equal measure.

Marsha thought for a moment, while they all clapped Amanda's speech, and spoke up herself.

"You know something, everyone? Of course I never knew all of you existed until Jerome happened on this taverna and struck up his relationship with Chrissy, and Niko, of course. So this is the first I've ever heard of what my cousin did to you Julie. I can tell you all something though, about my cousin Phil, that is. Even when we were kids, he was always the wise-guy, always putting others down and always full of how no one would ever get the better of him. In fact, it was his character that led most of his cousins, myself included, to drift away from him during our early teenage years. I'm only amazed at how wonderful a daughter he produced with you Julie, and I can only conclude that you [and here she looked directly at Amanda] have inherited most of your genes from your mother, except maybe for a few that affect your bone structure. Because oddly enough, I can see some of my family reflected in your face.

Like you say though, from my limited experience of your family this evening, you all came out the winners, and I'm thoroughly happy for you all as a result."

With that she raised her glass, which, as it happened, was empty, so Nikos quickly poured more Metaxa into it, and she waved it at everyone before knocking it back, with the others quickly following suit.

Julie now spoke up too. "Something I didn't tell anyone, was that after the police detective told me that my DNA had tested negative regarding the dead baby in the wood, and that it had proven that Amanda was really my daughter, ...let me see if I can remember his words... yes, he said, just before he left the house, something like, 'The DNA matching suggests that in some way your daughter Amanda could easily be a more distant relative of Marsha Travers, and hence of her daughter Rebecca. I can't even begin to think how that might be.'

"Well, thanks to my wonderful daughter, I now know what that meant."

"Amanda, darling?" It was Gavin this time, inducing a slight pause in the hubbub around the table, owing to the slight level of anxiety detectable in his voice, "May I ask, if it's not too much of an intrusion, are you going to let this Trent fellow into your life?"

Amanda paused, just for a second or two, mainly because she was sure she wanted everyone to hear the next bit. "Dad, there's no way I'm ever going to see him again. You're my father as far as I'm concerned. That's almost my last word on the matter. The actual last word is, I've got a new SIM for my phone, because that man has my current number. I'm going to put it in tonight, and when I do, I'll message all of you and you'll know to edit my number in your phones. Job done, eh?"

Jerome now decided to put the fizz back into proceedings.

"Drink up everyone. What say we all run down the beach and plunge into that sea? When are we next going to get the chance to take a moonlight dip all together? Well, well?!" He was already on the move.

Seconds later, glasses all drained, eight rather inebriated people were running down the beach to the glassy-smooth sea, fifty metres down the gently sloping beach, articles of clothing flying in every direction, and loud whoops coming out of every one of their mouths.

40. Dissatisfaction

Philip Trent tapped the screen for a third time. A third time he got the same message, "This number is no longer available."

He was not a happy bunny. What could be going on, apart from the fact that Amanda had changed her phone number, and why would she do such a thing? Wasn't he going to make her his heir? Wasn't he going to introduce her to a life she may never have expected to live? How could she be so ungrateful?

But then, how could a man with entirely material values ever understand the answers to such questions?

He threw the phone down on to his plush office desk, thrust his hands into his jacket pockets, and marched to the huge glass window overlooking the car park outside the print works. Staring out, he fought to stop his eyes from moistening in the corners. Philip Trent was in control. Philip Trent was on top of things. He could handle everything.

Except abject loneliness, perhaps.

John Manuel, Crete, February 2020

Every time I've completed a novel, I've told myself, 'That's it. There won't be another, because the likelihood of me thinking up another plot that would be engaging to the reader is next to zero.'

Then, usually months, even a year or two later, a germ of an idea has entered my brain and I've run it past my best and most even-handed critic, my wife, and gauged her reaction to the basic idea.

Some time last summer (2019), about the time that we learned that we were to lose our rented home in Rhodes and we began to carefully consider what we were going to do, this scenario came into my mind, so I mentioned it, to see what she'd say. Like myself, she is an avid reader and, as a result, knows a good book when she reads one. Much to my delight, she liked the premise for this story, and encouraged me to set to and begin writing.

I wouldn't pretend to try and place myself alongside the likes of the illustrious Jodi Picoult but, in one sense, and one alone, I do believe I can lay claim to being just a tad similar. Ms. Picoult usually tries to build her novels a round a moral dilemma, or social issue, that is relevant to our times. She then builds her story in such a manner as to get the reader to reflect on how they might react to the stuations in which her characters find themselves. You read one of her books, and you feel for the characters, and not merely the victims, but often also the perpetrators, since you are party to the situation or situations that tend to drive them to act as they do, and you think, 'How would I react to that?' If you're anything like me, you find yourself sometimes thinking that, whilst you may not do quite what the 'villain' did, you do nevertheless understand to a degree what made them do it. You understand the pressures, the emotions, and you say, "Although that person did a bad thing, are they really and truly a wicked person, or merely a victim of circumstances, someone who could have gone either way?"

I've endeavoured in my own small way to do something similar with my works of fiction. The first, "The View From Kleoboulos" touched on an issue which I'd come across in my own social circle many years before. In "Sunshine" I explored a theme that had come up in a drama-documentary on Greek TV, about a couple who were going to adopt the baby of a single mum who had no hope of being able to cope with the child.

The novel "Eve of Deconstruction" came about after I'd read an on-line piece about a scandal that had gone on in Greece for decades during the 20th century involving the illegal sale of babies to couples from other countries, and in "Can't Tell" I explored a tragically common societal problem that goes on, often unchecked, in isolated Greek communities, wreaking long-term consequences on the young victims of the practise. The main 'culprit' in that story I imagined, not as some predatory monster, but as someone who'd simply allowed a close friend to arouse his curiosity, to begin with. Then, as the consequences began to catch up with him, events almost dictate what he must do to cover up his past misdemeanours.

"Two in the Bush" came about as a result of my musing over just how far ex-partners might go to get back at their 'perceived as guilty' ex's and in "Panayiota" I tried to demonstrate, much as did one of my favourite books, "The Book Thief" (by Markus Zusak), the human side of the Nazi overlords who occupied and generally abused and oppressed their subjugated underlings during the occupation of Greece in the Second World War. Much of that novel is drawn from the experience of my own mother-in-law, who lived in Athens through the war. It fascinated me to consider that there must have been many who wore the German uniform who weren't cruel by nature, and I wondered how many of these would have dealt with the situation in which they found themselves.

And thus we come to this one, 'The Crete Connection.' What lengths might a distraught mother go to if she were to lose her child to Sudden Infant Death Syndrome? How many crimes are committed by people who, but for a single tragic event in their lives, may never so much as had a parking ticket otherwise.

I hope you enjoyed the book. Thank you for spending some of your precious hard-earned cash on it.

There is just one more point I'd like to make, and hopefully you'll agree. I've read some rather sweeping comments on-line by some seriously judgmental people, to the effect that self-published authors must be rubbish because of the fact that they are exactly that - self-published. This is a naive and over-simplified view of the matter. I have read some books that were published by respected print houses, and I have found them to be awful. By the same token, I have read some self-published works that were astoundingly good. Getting published by a major publisher these days is a near-impossibility for a new author. Not only that, there are some, like myself, who, although would obviously like a larger audience, are actually quite content to self-publish, because it gives us complete control over our work, and maybe we just don't want the prolonged stress and hassle of endlessly submitting manuscripts, with all the expense that it involves too. At the end of the day, a work stands or falls on how good it is, not on how it got to be before the eyes of the reader. I would suggest that, if the majority of reviews on a book are positive, then it's probably well worth checking out. There will always be some who don't like a work for whatever reason (or reasons) but, in the case of reviews on on-line bookstores, or indeed sites like Goodreads, democracy, I would postulate, does tend to work.

Further details on all of my works, both non-fiction and fiction, can be found here:

https://johnphilipmanuel.wixsite.com/works

Printed in Dunstable, United Kingdom